A TASTE OF MAGIC

A TASTE OF MAGIC

J. ELLE

BLOOMSBURY
CHILDREN'S BOOKS
NEW YORK LONDON OXFORD NEW DELHI SYDNEY

BLOOMSBURY CHILDREN'S BOOKS
Bloomsbury Publishing Inc., part of Bloomsbury Publishing Plc
1385 Broadway, New York, NY 10018

BLOOMSBURY, BLOOMSBURY CHILDREN'S BOOKS,
and the Diana logo are trademarks of Bloomsbury Publishing Plc

First published in the United States of America in August 2022
by Bloomsbury Children's Books
www.bloomsbury.com

Bloomsbury books may be purchased for business or promotional use.
For information on bulk purchases please contact Macmillan Corporate
and Premium Sales Department at specialmarkets@macmillan.com

Library of Congress Cataloging-in-Publication Data
Names: Elle, J., author.
Title: A taste of magic / by J. Elle.
Description: New York : Bloomsbury Children's Books, 2022.
Summary: Twelve-year-old Kyana bakes up a plan to keep her inner-city magic
school open after redistricting and gentrification threaten to close it down.
Identifiers: LCCN 2021056248 (print) | LCCN 2021056249 (e-book) |
ISBN 978-1-5476-0671-9 (hardcover) • ISBN 978-1-5476-0672-6 (e-book)
Subjects: CYAC: Magic—Fiction. | Baking—Fiction. | Contests—
Fiction. | Middle schools—Fiction. | Schools—Fiction. | African
Americans—Fiction. | LCGFT: Novels.
Classification: LCC PZ7.1.E438 Tas 2022 (print) | LCC PZ7.1.E438 (e-book) |
DDC [FIc]—dc23
LC record available at https://lccn.loc.gov/2021056248
LC e-book record available at https://lccn.loc.gov/2021056249

Book design by Jeanette Levy
Typeset by Westchester Publishing Services
Printed and bound in the U.S.A.
2 4 6 8 10 9 7 5 3 1

To find out more about our authors and books visit
www.bloomsbury.com and sign up for our newsletters.

For Grandma Eaglin,
whose magic in the kitchen and whose sass
made me who I am

A
Taste
of Magic

CHAPTER 1

∗❋*∗*

Turning twelve should feel like a big deal.

Last night at dinner, over a wedge of pound cake (with a lemon glaze just the way I like it), Momma promised me this birthday would be better than the others. Not because this year she'd be able to buy me a gift (she can't). Not because this time she'd be off work to celebrate with me (she isn't). But because, according to Momma, sometime while I'm twelve I'll finally get to learn *the family secret*.

I choke down a laugh remembering it all and slide my tray sideways. But so far this morning, my birthday feels pretty normal. Thompson Middle School's lunch line is like any other lunch line: bumper-to-bumper people avoiding eye contact with hair-netted lunch ladies, hoping they won't put that obligatory scoop of green mush on their tray. I think it's a vegetable, but Memaw and I cook together all the time and I know how to tell mustards from collards from kale. They even smell different. Cooking is like music, finding the perfect harmony. And the green mush awaiting me is not a song I'm trying to hear.

I hold my breath and slide by. My best friend, Nae, is two heads behind me in line. I give her the it's-the-unrecognizable-green-stuff-day face and she pretends to retch. I chuckle and the lunch lady's gaze snaps my way.

"Kyana." Her face is stern, but she's nice. We talk food all the time.

I smile nervously.

"Your tray." The plop lands with a squish and I gag.

"What is it?" I ask.

"It's your vegetables, pureed. Put a few sardines in there too for flavor."

Oh god. Salty, fishy sardines in a puree of green mash. I slide down another step and a slice of sizzling-hot pepperoni pizza lands on my tray. I almost sigh in relief, until Lunch Lady shoves it a bit too far and it brushes up against my "vegetable medley." I'm gonna be sick. I'm actually gonna—

My finger twitches.

The kid in line next to me slides down and it's my turn at the register next.

I reach for my tray to shimmy it sideways and my fingers twitch again, this time vibrating uncontrollably. *Huh?*

I peer around, but everyone is immersed in their own conversations, including Nae, who's trying to smile her way out of her scoop. Not gonna work, girl.

White sparks fizz from my fingertips, crackling like electricity.

I blink.

It's gone. *What the—*

A tingling feeling climbs up from my toes and down my arms like a rush. I shove my hands in my pockets. They tremble and I feel sparks shoving through my skin like needles. The sparks snuff out against the cotton of my zip-up with a hiss. The kid next to me taps his foot and I realize my little freak-out is holding up the entire line.

"Next," the register lady says. The back of my neck is all sweat as I swipe my card and hurry to a table in the furthest corner of the cafeteria.

What's wrong with my hands? I flip them back and forth and there's no hint of sparks or needles or any of that stuff I just felt.

"Key!" Nae's tray slams the table. She shifts her rainbow twists over her shoulder and shoves a shiny, turquoise-paper-wrapped box tied with an orange satin ribbon in front of me.

I feign a smile, distracted by whatever just happened to my fingers.

"Well, you gonna stare at it or open it?"

"Oh! This is for me?" I thought it might be an example

3

of party favors or something for *her* birthday party, which we're planning. Our birthdays are a week apart, so we're basically twins. And for Nae's we're going all out. Her parents said she could do it up fancy this year.

"Duh! Happy birthday!" She pushes the box toward me. "Girl, where is your head today?"

"Thank you, Nae," I say, smiling for real this time and pulling the orange ribbon.

"Sorry I couldn't swing by for cake last night. My momma was bugging about homework."

"Nae, this is so sweet. You didn't have to get me anything!"

"Girl, hush." She rolls her eyes and I laugh because Nae always gets me something. I just feel bad because I don't usually have much to get *her* something.

I pull my hands out my pockets hesitantly, just to make sure whatever I felt or thought I felt is gone before ripping off the wrapping paper. I open the white box underneath a bit more urgently than I mean to. Nae's gift is sometimes the only one I get each year and I'd be lying if I said I didn't look forward to it more than anything.

Inside is half an orange heart, inscribed with *BFF* in gold letters and hanging from a thin gold chain.

"Aww!" I swoon, clipping it around my neck and tucking it in my shirt. She pulls a twin necklace out of her shirt and winks. "Thank you, Nae."

I ball up the paper and my hands warm again, but not in

4

a normal way. In like a *is-that-really-lightning-shooting-from-my-fingertips?* way. I drop the trash and shove my hands in my pockets.

"You gone' pick that up?" a kid tossing trash asks.

"Uhhh . . ." My fingers tingle and I dig deeper in my pockets. "Would you mind? Nasty paper cut." I wince and the lie feels icky.

"Yeah, sure. Whatever." He tosses my trash and I mouth "Sorry for lying" to the back of his head before plopping down again. My thoughts race, Momma's words about the family secret coming back to mind. I wonder if—

Fingers snap inches from my eyes. "Are you listening to me? I'm trying to tell you about the party favors I picked."

"Right, sorry." I keep my hands tucked away and chew my lip, trying to focus on what Nae's saying. "Yeah, lemme see."

She whips out her phone, looking around to be sure teachers aren't nearby, and shows me a pic of tiny little boxes with purple-and-turquoise bows.

"We're gonna stuff them with chocolates with my name on them. Cute, huh?"

The heat in my pockets fades and I flex my fingers. Normal again. But for good measure I keep them tucked away. "Really cute. When are we doing this?"

Nae and I have been planning her twelfth birthday party since she turned eleven. From multiple cakes, a DJ, and a caterer to holographic invitations, her parents promised to pull out all the stops. She wants it to be the talk of school. I have no doubt it will be.

"Saturday morning." She peels off a pepperoni and tosses it in her mouth. "I figured you could just spend the whole day. That way we can do our nails and stuff."

"I need to get my hair done. But maybe Ms. Moesha can move me to Friday. I'll talk to Momma. I'll tell her you're making me study math while I'm there too, so she'll want to go along with it."

"And that would be *true*."

Ugh. Nae rides me about my grades worse than Momma sometimes. She's a math genius. Numbers just make sense to her. Math's like a foreign language to me and Nae's my translator. The only reason I'm passing now—and I mean, *barely*—is because of our Sunday study dates at the library.

She goes on, explaining the mermaid theme and plans for decor, and I feel that funny feeling in my hands again. I immediately hop up.

"Sorry. Uhm, I gotta go to the bathroom. Can we finish this on the walk home from school?"

"Uhhhm, okay." She stands. "I'll come with."

"No, I—" What do I say? "It'll be a while. That green stuff isn't agreeing with my stomach."

I hurry off, hoping she doesn't notice I didn't even take a bite.

* * ✳ * *

I am fifteen minutes late to my next class because every time I tried to leave my stall, I got that fizzy feeling again. I gotta get this under control.

Ms. Jones is cool when I come in late. She's pacing the room, flipping images on her presentation. I usually love this class. African American History and Diaspora Studies is an optional substitute for American history at Thompson Middle and Momma says that's really unusual, which is wild to me because our history is so rich. Plus, I got tired of hearing about Columbus over and over like five years ago.

But today, no matter how interesting Ms. Jones makes it, I can't focus. We break into groups and I'm barely paying attention, my hands firmly rooted in my pockets.

Early release day means class is only forty-five minutes. And they *draaaaag* by.

After we do our discussion questions, someone from our group has to present. Normally I'd volunteer, but that requires use of my hands. So I sit back and zone out, wondering if Momma will still be home when I get there.

I have so many questions for her.

Does this have to do with the family secret? *It has to.*

Applause snaps me from my daydream and Brittany makes her way back to her seat, cheeks flushed.

Ms. Jones lays out the homework assignment and minutes later the bell rings and it's sweeter than pecan praline frosting.

Nae's waiting out front of school and despite my hands cramping from being wedged in my pockets so long, I'm actually breathing a little easier. *Please let Momma be home.* Memaw will be there, of course, but even if she knows something about what's going on with me, I doubt she'll remember any details.

Red-brick-and-white-siding apartments rise on either side of us, and a block away is the city bus stop, next to Glenda's Grocery and Ace Liquor. Avalon Street splits like a Y a few blocks up ahead, one road toward Nae's gated neighborhood and the other toward my complex.

We cross the main thoroughfare and leave Thompson Middle behind. Thompson's the school all the kids in Park Row, my neighborhood in southeast Rockford, go to. It's a mixed bag, since Park Row sort of has two sides to it. There's my side, with apartments and older homes. On the other side of the Row are blocks and blocks of gated townhomes. Lots of new houses have been going up in place of much older ones, too. Families moving in on that side—Upper Park Row—have fancier cars and usually more than one. With our uniforms at school, it's hard to tell who lives in Upper, but kids who live around each other tend to stick together. The ones from Upper tend to steer clear of us from the apartment side of the Row.

Nae is the exception. Her parents grew up here and bought one of those fancy houses to stay close by. We been stuck together like glue since first day of kinder, and that's never gonna change regardless of how big her house is.

"So I gave last-minute invitations to Shelby, Marceaus, and Tatiana," she says.

"Ugh, Shelby?"

"I know, but our dads work together so I sort of had to." Nae tucks her phone, in its frayed mermaid case, into her bag.

"So what are you wearing?"

"I don't know, something in my closet. May spring for something new, but not sure yet."

"Nae, you have *days* left and you don't know what you're wearing?"

"I *knowww*."

"Well, *I'm* wearing my purple dress with the rainbow back and my Keds."

She squeals, throwing her arm around my shoulder. "I love that dress! And it fits the mermaid theme and everything. You're the best, Key."

We pass Glenda's Grocery and then come to Scooter's Skewers, this creole kebab place. Hints of bay leaves and garlic swell in my nostrils and the door on Scooter's glows.

Like literally *glows*.

I gape at the door, which is still pulsing with light. "Huh?"

"I said, Saturday, do you think we should eat first, or party games first?"

"Uhm, games first." I try to concentrate on what Nae's saying, but there's a door pulsing with green light in the middle of Avalon Street. And judging by the crowd getting off a bus without a look that way, no one notices but me.

The restaurant door cracks open, still glowing, and an old man with a stained apron pokes his head out. Nae looks that way and I wait for her to flip out, too. I can't be the only one seeing this!

"Hey, Mr. Scooter." She waves.

Mr. Scooter waves back and Nae keeps rambling. "His food is *so* good. They're catering the party," she whispers to me.

She doesn't see it.

I blink hard. I'm hallucinating. I have to be.

Mr. Scooter's gaze falls on me and he winks. The door closes and the glow is gone.

"You better close your mouth before a fly ends up in there." Nae laughs. I snap my mouth shut and shake off what must be my overactive imagination.

What's wrong with me?

Before I can conjure up some explanation, I spot a familiar face ahead.

Nae is practically hyperventilating next to me. The boy's slim-fit jeans and tee are as clean and crisp as his tapered fade. It's Russ. He goes to Thompson, but he's never real chatty with me. I don't know if that means he isn't nice or if the attention everyone gives him has gone to his head. Either way, I couldn't care less. I look the other way, but a wave of something warm washes over me as he passes and for a moment his icy earrings and gold chain are all I see. I keep walking and with distance the feeling fades. But Nae's pinned to the spot, staring.

"Kyana, Naomi, sup?" he says, turning to walk backward. Kind enough to say hi, I guess, but too busy to stop and talk. That's Russ.

"Party Saturday, right?"

Naomi squeaks.

"Yes. Saturday," I say. *What's wrong with her?*

"See you there." He turns and keeps walking.

"Girl, you're a whole mess," I hiss at her. "You literally invited everyone."

"Russ *has* to be there. He's the coolest person at school."

Yeah, everyone would probably agree he looks really cool. But that flashy stuff just doesn't impress me.

"You think he'll really come?"

My street comes into view and I reshoulder my bag. "Nae, anyone not interested in being at your party isn't worth being friends with."

We pound fists goodbye, and my fingers feel funny. *Not again.*

I promise Nae to call later and rush to my complex just ahead. *Please, Momma, be home.*

CHAPTER 2

* ✳ ✳ ✳ * *

Mom's home, but the purse on her shoulder says not for long.

Memaw's in her recliner, but she starts easing up as soon as she sees me. I hurry to help. She lives with me and Momma—or we live with her, I should say. But Momma does all the working and bills now. Memaw's too old for all that. She says she's still a young forty-seven. We let her believe it. I'm not great at math but I can subtract just fine, and she's seventy-two this year.

"Hey, sugar," she says. "Let me go get dinner going. Kyana, meet me in there. Earlene, you better get going before you be late."

Momma makes a face at Memaw. The family's in its usual motion, like a well-oiled machine: Momma getting ready for work, and me doing homework before helping Memaw with the dinner and house chores.

"Hey, boo, how was school?" Momma plants a kiss on my cheek and pulls off her morning work shoes for the pair she has to wear to her night job.

What do I say? Do I just come out with it? "Mom, you got a minute?"

She presses an earring into her ear. "I'm listening, baby. What is it?"

"I wanted to talk to you about something that happened at school."

She stops and heaves a huge sigh. "What happened, Kyana?"

"It's not about grades or anything."

She exhales but checks her watch. Time with Momma is rare. She works. A lot.

"Baby, I have to get going. Out with it." She pulls on her coat.

"It's . . ." I can't believe I'm really saying this. "I had some sparks or something coming from my fingers—"

She gasps and grabs my shoulders, her eyes glistening like a glazed pastry. "The Impetus! It's happened? I mean, I read it could happen anytime before you turn thirteen, but two days in? That's a good sign, baby! Oh, Kyana—"

Bang. The sound comes from the kitchen and we rush in to see what it was. Memaw's hunched over the stove, gas flame lit with a plate on top.

"Memaw!" I dash over and turn off the flame while Momma removes the plate.

"Now don't go moving my pot. We making red beans and rice with the andouille sausage you like tonight."

"Momma." Momma exhales, clutching her chest. "That's not a pot, it's a plate."

Memaw looks half stunned and half skeptical. I hand her the big pot she thought she had and give her shoulder a squeeze. The hot cracked plate goes in the trash and the moment of panic dissolves.

"I have to go, Key," Momma says. "But we're gonna talk more about this soon. Real quick, a few things to remember: magic ain't no joke."

Wait—*magic*? *That's* the family secret? My mouth is on the floor.

She tucks a strand of hair behind my ear, smiling. "You're a witch, baby."

I . . . ?

Magic . . . ?

No way!

I'd ask if Momma's joking, but her knitted eyebrows and wagging finger make it clear: she ain't!

She steps to the door. "Now listen, ya hear?" Momma isn't known for beating around the bush, so I'm not surprised she's leveling with me. "I'm not a witch, but it runs in the family, popping up from time to time. I don't know much 'bout it because none of that was ever in our house growing up. But your great-aunt Pearl had her dose of it. Drove Big

14

Momma up the wall. You see, magic is finicky. I heard Aunt Pearl ended up with twelve fingers on one hand and tulips growing out her ears because she said one of them spells wrong. Get a handle on magic or magic'll get a handle on you."

She's for real. Witch? I'm a witch?!

Momma details the rules and I half wish I had a notepad, but my head is spinning too much to take notes. This is serious. "First, Kyana, no telling *anyone*. People knowing about magic would change our lives. And not in a good way."

Right, okay. No one but Nae.

"That *includes* Naomi."

"But, Momma—"

"But Momma nothing. You mind what I say, or so help me I'll take you downtown and have your magic sanitized."

I can't tell if she's bluffing or if that's a real thing, but I'm not trying to find out. "Yes, ma'am."

She steps to the door and I hand her her lunch sack. "Second," she says. "Magic isn't for messing around, okay? You learn what you're doing. Only use it when needed. Not just for fun."

What?! I glue my lips shut, hoping my disagreement doesn't show on my face. It must, though, because now she's wagging her finger. That's like saying we can only spend money on bills and never anything fun. And I mean, sure, we *don't*. But that's because Momma works so many different jobs there's never any *time* to do anything fun. (Or money. Which is ironic because she works *so* much.) When I get a job, I'm going to make *sure* it pays enough so I can have an *actual* weekend.

"And one more thing . . ." The phone rings and Momma answers, holding up a finger. "Hello?"

"It's Nae," she says. I reach for the phone, but she holds it back. "You better get your homework out first and help Memaw with dinner before y'all start and end up on that phone forever."

"Yes, ma'am. But it's probably about math." My go-to excuse. "Can I talk?"

She purses her lips and hands me the phone.

"Hello?"

Nae's going on about her parents landing DJ Klux for Saturday. He's the local radio disc jockey on 97.8.

"Wowwww, Nae, that's dope." I cover the mouthpiece. "Yeah, math stuff, Momma. Well, math and party stuff." I can't lie to Momma like that. She knows me better than I know myself, she always says.

"Fine, we'll pick this up later. Don't be long, and get in that kitchen with Memaw before she burn this house down."

"Yes, ma'am."

"And, Kyana, one more rule."

"Yeah?"

"Mandatory magic training, every Saturday for the next six months, with Ms. Moesha."

"Ms. Moesha, my beautician?! She's a witch?"

"Trust me, I know how wild that sounds. But it's true. She showed me how her hair irons don't actually plug in. They're magicked to self-heat."

"How'd I not notice that before?"

"Magic's all over this world, chyle. You'll be shocked what you see now that you know what's what."

I think of Scooter's Skewers but can't get a question out before Momma's waving goodbye and the door to the living room creaks shut. Nae's still talking my ear off and I insert a grunt here and there to let her know I'm listening.

Wow, *magic* school, every—

Uh-oh.

I can't go to Nae's party.

CHAPTER 3

*·**✳**·*

Being a witch isn't so exciting when you can't share it with your best friend.

Tuesday we had a volleyball game in PE. My fingers fizzed as I spiked the ball, and it shot all the way to the ceiling. So I spent Wednesday trying to make up some reason for Nae about how I'm suddenly super good at volleyball, while avoiding Nikki Camen, who's hounding me to join the school's team. Thursday Nae was busy with Math Club all day, which gave me time to actually stew on this witch thing. I still can't believe it. I've almost told her twice, but Momma's wagging finger haunts me like a ghost.

Finally, it's Friday, the day before my first day at magic school. And as if this week couldn't get any worse, it's fifteen minutes before the bell rings and instead of remembering the definition of "hypotenuse," I'm racking my brain to figure out how to lie to my best friend about why I suddenly can't go to her birthday party.

Everything that comes to mind sounds nonsensical. Or unbelievable. Or both. I might throw up.

"Miss Turner, those answers aren't going to write themselves." Ms. Sameer is standing right next to me, fiddling with the rims of her glasses.

Hunched over my scratch paper, I imagine my problems don't exist and try to focus on the Pythagorean theorem. The curser on the screen blinks again and again, taunting me as if to say, "I'm listening . . . Tell me the answer."

I don't know.

Math is my nemesis—an evil set out to destroy me. I dig a nail into my sweaty palm as Ms. Sameer moves on, the hem of her pale pink hijab fluttering. My breath comes a little easier at the sight of her back. Of the seven questions on my math quiz, two have answers, and I'm almost sure they're both wrong. I press my temple. *Think.*

Scraping sounds titter past as Nae, also known as Math Club President, files her nails. *How is she done already? How?* Ms. Sameer stops a second at her desk but then keeps walking.

Nae gets her math brains from her parents. Her dad has some sciencey job I can't remember the name of, and her mom's a researcher. They're smart as heck. And I mean, Nae and I have a *lot* in common, being connected at the hip and all—we can even finish each other's sentences and we usually coordinate our hairstyles. I wish some of her math genius would rub off on me.

Two minutes until bell and all I've managed are flower doodles drawn in pink eraser. Ms. Sameer is heading back my way. I dust off the eraser and shade my paper. Maybe if I *look* like I'm concentrating she won't say anything.

If I fail this math test . . . Okay, who am I kidding? *When* I fail this math test, Momma is going to take away my TV and phone for a year.

Rrrrrringgggggg.

Class done. Math quiz over. The computer screen goes black and Jude comes down the aisle collecting our scratch papers. I plop mine in the tray and my stomach sinks. Earned that F like it was a first-place prize. Nae's in my face before I can even get up.

"How'd you do?"

I give her the look.

She knows the one. "Key." She throws an arm around my shoulder. "We went through the equations before lunch. Are you doing practice problems like I told you?"

Nope.

"Ten minutes a day makes so much difference," she says.

"I keep forgetting, to be honest. I'mma start, I swear."

She folds her arms. "You promise?"

"I promise."

"Good, because girl, your momma is gonna flip if you keep bombing math. She might not even let you come to my birthday party tomorrow if you don't pass this quiz. You'll be locked down on punishment." Her hand rests on her hip.

"Uhhh . . . about that." This is the moment. I have to tell her.

We scoot into the hallway and voices swell like someone's turned up the volume dial at Thompson Middle. She narrows her eyes, now both hands on her hips.

"What do you mean, 'about that'?" She says the last part with air quotes.

This isn't going to go well.

"Nae, I know I promised, but I can't go to your party tomorrow." I brace for impact and she delivers.

Somehow her voice rises an octave above the noise. "Kyana Lacreshia Turner, you got me messed up if you think you are skipping out on my birthday party! We been planning this for an *entire* year!" Her voice cracks.

I feel awful. We don't keep secrets, and we *never* lie to each other. But what can I do? Momma said *no one* can find out I'm a witch.

"But maybe . . ." I pleaded with Momma after she got home last night.

"There's no buts, Kyana," Momma said. "You mind, or you won't be doing no magic school, period."

21

I can't skip it. Not the first day!

I mean, my grades are *okay*, even though I suck at math. But I'm not president of any social clubs, and I don't play on any sports teams because Momma works in the evenings so it's just me and Memaw. I don't know—I don't ever get to be the special one with the championship trophies or cool weekend club field trips.

Until this.

I'm not going to be some fancy engineer or scientist. This is my *one* special thing.

Who knows what I'll be able to do when I learn a few spells? Maybe there's a spell for helping with laundry. Between jobs, Momma folds laundry for *hours* watching her stories. Or maybe there's a spell for dishes. I *hate* doing dishes, but Momma's back hurts from standing all day and Memaw's been breaking one too many lately, so I make sure to do 'em. But if there was a spell to help with that, I'd die. Like in a good way. Or who knows? Maybe there's a spell for money or luck or . . . A million possibilities.

Excitement shoots through my insides like rockets and my fingers feel fizzy again in the gloves I wore today. It's not cold outside, so people spent half the morning staring, but I don't care. I'm prepared.

Magic could change my family's life, and that's not a chance I can pass up.

"I'm sorry, Nae, I really can't." Could I fake being sick?

Eh. She knows better. Nothing keeps me and Naomi apart. Momma even let Nae come over last time Memaw went to the hospital, and Momma gets super weird when Memaw's sick. She shuts everybody out. Even her sister, Aunt Irene. But Aunt Irene's wild, so maybe there's more to it. Nae is always at my side, no matter what.

How do I find a lie that she'll actually believe?

"I'm calling your momma." Nae pulls out her mermaid-covered cell phone.

"What? No!" I laugh nervously, snatching the phone. "Stop. Momma's working, and besides, she's the one who said I can't go."

"But why?" She has tears, *real* fat beads, running down her face. My stomach sinks. Nae and I planned every little detail together for her party. Words—truthful ones—hang on my lips. But I swallow them back down and smooth the tears from her cheeks.

"I—I . . ." Nae was there when I lost my first tooth. We went together the first time I got my nails done. And in second grade when I got in a fight and was sent to the principal's office, she punched someone too so she'd get sent with me. She's my girl, through and through. This may be the *one thing* she doesn't know about me.

Think of something. "Momma got some tickets to see *The Lioness* downtown at the fancy theater. She's been saving it up as a surprise and"—the lie stings my lips—"I *told*

23

her I didn't want to go if you couldn't and she had a fit. Said she paid big money for us to go to this show and I wasn't going to miss it."

"Yeah." Her voice is calmer now. "I begged my parents for tickets to that for my birthday, actually, but it's been sold out for months." She smiles and her eyes do, too. "I can't even be mad. Wish I could go with you."

Relieved, I squeeze her against me, but inside I'm almost sure there are rotten eggs doing cartwheels. "Me too, Nae. Me too."

"But you'll tell me *all* about it?" Her eyes light up. "And take *lots* of pictures so it's like I'm there! Right?"

"Yeah. Sure will." I gulp.

My pocket vibrates as hers chimes and I slip my phone out.

"Grades posted!"

My heart lodges in my throat as I swipe right. I much prefer pencil-paper tests. Gives me a good few days' buffer before having to talk to Momma about my grades. *Sigh.* But not at Thompson Middle. They're all about gadgets and devices. Some philanthropist donated a class set of iPads to the math department and we've been tap-tapping our test answers ever since. Speedy grades? *Not helpful, Ms. Sameer.*

I take another deep breath as the page loads.

Grade: F. Note: Parent-teacher meeting requested.

My stomach drops. At least I don't have to find ways to

lie to my best friend about Saturday magic school anymore. With this grade, I'll be grounded until I'm grown.

* ✳ ✳ ✳ ✳ * ✳

"You what?!" Momma's voice is so loud my ears are ringing.

I can't swallow, can't talk. I knew she'd be mad.

Memaw hovers in the background, arms folded. She's not mad, too, is she? Memaw's always in my corner. My ace.

"You know"—Momma's pacing—"I told myself you'd be able to handle this witch business. But you're completely unfocused."

That's not true. I always struggle with my grades in Ms. Sameer's class. But I ain't stupid enough to say so now. I'm frozen, still standing in the doorway.

"Get in here."

I obey quick.

"Get your homework out. I need to call and find some time to visit your school. I can't take off time from work like this, Kyana. Every hour I miss is an hour I'm not getting paid." She storms out the room in a tizzy, mumbling. "I don't know how much longer I can do this."

I didn't think about how my grades cause Momma stress. She works so hard all by herself. Keeping my grades up so there's one less thing she has to worry about is the least I can do. If a cog stops working, it can throw off the whole machine. I'm going to do better. Ten minutes of math a day it is.

Memaw's hand is warm on my shoulder, her eyes hugged in a million creases. "Help me candy some pecans and get a butter pecan cake in the oven before you get going on homework. That'll cheer you up."

She tugs me along to the kitchen and my mind is still whirring about Momma's disappointment. I pull out the cake pans and preheat the oven.

"Pecans, first," I say, my cooking instincts whispering to me. I combine water, sugar, and orange juice over the stove, then stir in the pecans. The orange gives candied pecans a fun twist.

Memaw peers over my shoulder. "Thatta girl."

The cake batter comes together next: softened butter, room-temperature eggs, and lots of sugar. I've baked this cake so many times, I could make it in my sleep.

"You better pick up that lip before it gets stepped on," Memaw says, and I can't help but chuckle. She tosses me a napkin and I wrap it around my hand and dig out a bunch of Crisco. Before I even realize it, I have three pans greased and full of batter, an oven preheated, and Memaw hip-bumping me trying to get me to dance.

We slide the cakes in the oven and I reach for the timer.

"Your nose'll know when it's done." She taps my nose. I nod and slink back to my seat to start my homework.

"Hey now." She rubs my shoulder, then gasps in delight. "Oh, I know what'll cheer you up." Memaw disappears for a few minutes, then returns and sets a giant book in my arms.

Spellcasting & Potions

Vol. III

Intermediate to Advanced

"Is this for me?" I lift the cover and it's much heavier than it looks, like it's made from wood or something. I slide my tingling fingertips delicately across thick pages, and sparks buzz at my fingertips. *I'll be glad when that goes away.* "How old is this?"

She smiles and gestures for me to keep looking.

"It's so . . . Wow." I turn the page and it crinkles. "Memaw, this is . . ." Cohesive sentences escape me and my cheeks burn from grinning. I can't believe this is real.

A witch? Me! I pinch myself for good measure. I can't let being down spoil this for me. I'm gonna do better with my math grade.

Memaw sits beside me. Tiny lines of handwriting cover the next page, so faded they're hardly legible. Whole patches are missing, but I can sort of make out the gist. A sketch of a plant that looks like a cross between a cactus and a rose-bush full of purple flowers is next to what appears to be a recipe.

"Memaw, are these recip—I mean, potions?"

She gazes over my shoulder. "Sure are."

"Where you'd get this?"

"Oh, just something my sister used to keep around. Dug it out for you. Your great-aunt Pearl had her nose in it all the time. You'll get a newer version, I bet," she says, peering closer. "This old thing is about worn out."

My fingers twitch for my phone to text Nae. She would think this is *so* cool. But I stop myself.

"Funny how magic skips around, huh?" Memaw tugs at her necklace. "My sister was something, all right. Not patient, though. She made all sorts of mayhem, drove our parents up the wall. And you know back then Black folks couldn't go drawing attention to themselves." She smirks, simmering on the memory. "All right now." Memaw winks, closing the book. Then she pulls out a chopping knife. "You got a peek. Gon get your math lesson out while I cook dinner and those cakes cook and cool. Afterwards we'll work on a potato pie for Miss Gladys next door. She's been having a hard time."

"Do you think I can make extra for Momma?" Momma *loves* sweet potato pie.

Memaw looks at the oven clock. "You think you can ice that cake *and* do a pie before bed?"

"I know I can."

"You young'uns and all that energy. If we could bottle and sell it, we'd be rich, I tell you." She grabs an armful of sweet potatoes, checks their firmness. "I think we can squeeze two out of these. Let's do it."

I plop down at the table, pulling out my homework. Only English today, which is the easiest. I *love* books. Momma said I fell in love with a book about a unicorn with natural hair at three years old and never looked back. We used to go together to the library across town each weekend, before she took up that extra job. But the pay is good, so I'm not complaining.

I flip to chapter 17 where I left off and read, keeping an eye on Memaw, who's waist deep in a lower cabinet.

"Okay now, che." "Che" is Creole for "girl," "child"— really anyone. Memaw's from Louisiana. She says that's why her cooking is so good. *Nobody* throws down in the kitchen like Memaw. Momma loves it, too. Means keeping food prepared isn't one more thing on her plate.

"Tell me the first one."

I glance up from my book. I help her with cooking every day after school while I do homework. She slays dinner and *I* get to make dessert (with her supervising, of course). Tonight, it's jambalaya, my favorite. I know the recipe like

29

the back of my hand. At first, Memaw'd let me fetch her things. Then she started letting me mix stuff, quick to smack my hand if I didn't do it *exactly* like she said. And eventually, when her memory got fuzzy, she let me tell her what to do.

"Diced onion." How much again? Oh! "One cup." My phone dings.

Nae: 😕 I'll miss you tomorrow.
Me: 😟 Take lots of pics! And wear the purple dress.
That blue one makes your booty look flat.
Nae: 😐 Purple it is. LOL!

"All right, baby," Memaw says, sliding a heaping handful of onion into the pot. "And next? How much of that seasoning?"

I tuck my phone away. This is where things get interesting in Memaw's recipes. She doesn't measure; she has me memorize arbitrary amounts. But I mean, food's always on point.

"Uhm, a *good* amount," I recite.

She nods as if that makes sense and a bursting aroma of onion and garlic fills the air.

"Next is the butter. Two tablespoons."

She drops three tablespoons in the pot. "You always need a bit more butter than you think. That and sugar when you baking. Don't ever measure those two *too* exact, ya hear?" She winks and I go warm all over.

We finish up and my favorite rice-sausage-and-shrimp dish is steaming on the plate next to the reading-comp questions I just finished. I gobble it down between vocabulary questions.

"Thanks, Memaw. I'm done—what can I do?"

"Get them dishes clean and we'll start baking."

"Yes, ma'am." Work's never finished, I swear. I'm crossing my fingers that chore spells are a thing. Momma could use help. I do what I can, but she always says taking care of a house is a lot of work. And she said if we take care of it good enough, some banker might pay us money for it one day. As the only witch in the house, I hope my magic is gonna help ease Momma's load. Heck, maybe magic can help me be better at math. I don't know. Butterflies flutter in my tummy.

I have a feeling magic is going to fix everything.

CHAPTER 4

*·**✳**·*

Today's the first day of magic school and I got almost no sleep last night. I double-checked every page of my homework, dusted the furniture twice, and even put my own laundry in the wash to be *sure* there was no way Momma could say I couldn't go.

Since I could hardly sleep, I channeled my nervous energy into perfecting a couple dozen apple cinnamon scones as a thank-you gift for Ms. Moesha.

Nae's been messaging me all morning, asking what I'm wearing to the theater. I'm skating so easy on the lie at this point, I text her two different shirts, playing along. It feels icky, but she's my best friend and this tiny white lie won't change that. I'd never keep anything else from her. *Just this.* What other choice do I have?

As we step into Ms. Moesha's hair salon, smokiness and the scent of burnt grease assault me. I hold the door open for Momma and she sets down my plate of treats. I blow out a deep breath. The crowd's light for a Saturday. Usually, haze makes the burgundy plastered walls lined with dryer chairs hard to see. But today their dryer hoods are glowing bright green like Scooter's restaurant entrance. I nudge Momma. "Can you see that?"

Her brows wrinkle and she gestures for me to get out the doorway so she can close the door. *Guess not.* In the center of the salon, two tattered leather couches sit back to back, with low tables covered in old *Essence* and *JET* magazines. Voices talk from a TV across the room; a glowing cord snakes behind it. I skip to my usual spot, a corner seat, and scour the scene for any hint of where our magic lessons will take place, for what I missed every other Saturday morning I've been here. *How did I miss that she is magical?* And now of course I see it—the washbowls and drying chairs aren't plugged in, but the chairs' domes are glowing. Ms. Moesha's walls are lined with cabinets, several with glowing handles. She pulls out towels and aprons from the same two or three. The other ones must be full of magic supplies.

She tugs on a drawer and whips out a hairbrush with glowing bristles. She passes it one time through freshly blow-dried Ole Lady Wanda's hair, which morphs into big barrel curls like . . . like . . . *magic.*

"*Wow.*" The excitement spills out before I realize it and I have to remind myself to close my gaping mouth.

"Hey, girl!"

"Morning, Ms. Moesha." I stare real hard at her, half expecting her to be in a robe. But she's in a sundress with a strappy top and matching nails. Her shoes are tennis, per usual. She's on her feet from the time her shop opens at seven-thirty until it closes at two. So I know her feet hurt. I always wondered why she closed so early . . . now I understand. *Magic school.* I uncover my scones and frown at one that isn't quite the golden brown I wanted.

"Whoa!" She pulls off a corner of one and plops it into her mouth. "This is as delicious as it is gorgeous. Your momma said you could bake, but, girl, you can *bake.* That could come in handy."

My cheeks warm. "Just a little thank-you."

"I was so excited when I heard you'll be staying after today." She winks real exaggerated-like, her bangs swinging in her face as she rolls a glowing marcel iron through Wanda's hair.

Smoke coils toward the ceiling. Ole Lady Wanda's here every Saturday. The rest of the usual Saturday crew are the twins, Neesha and ZaZa, plus Ms. Bridget and her granddaughter, Trina. But I see only Trina under a glowing dryer, head covered in a rainbow of rollers. I set the rest of the treats at her station.

"Where's everybody at?" I pluck a takeout menu from a basket. To my disappointment, it doesn't glow. I'm *dying* to know if there's such a thing as magic food and what it tastes like.

"The twins canceled. So I should get through y'all quick today."

Momma gives me a look, widening her eyes.

I snort. Ms. Moesha is the best beautician in Park Row. We been going here as long as I can remember. Memaw says loyalty is a big deal for beauticians, but Momma hates how many heads Ms. Moesha stacks on her schedule.

"She could do it like other folks and schedule one client at one time," Momma said once when she was real upset. "But *noooo*, she stacking appointments to stack more money. Got us in that shop all doggone day."

Ms. Moesha could have twelve heads to juggle on a Saturday. You don't have a real appointment time. Show up early and you'll still be there until afternoon. That's how it goes. She "works you in," as she calls it. It annoys Momma. It tickles me.

"Early, you say?" Momma winks at me.

"Don't start with me today, Earlene," Ms. Moesha titters. She and Momma go way back. They went to high school together or something. "You know I'mma get you outta here as fast as I can."

"I been here since dawn." Ole Lady Wanda—the

notorious instigator—winks, a piece of her hair in pins and the rest in perfectly bumped curls. She looks like a floating head above the pink cape wrapped around her neck.

"Don't you start stirring mess," says Ms. Moesha. "You ain't been here that long either and you know it."

Trina, still under the dryer, is laughing at their banter. It's not a normal day in the shop unless someone's gossiping or arguing. I stuff a giggle down my throat, trying to choose between the six different lo meins on the menu.

Momma slips the menu from my fingers. "You don't need none of that high-dollar delivery food. Nothing wrong with the usual."

I bite back an eye roll. Momma says it's important to support Black businesses. That if we don't support us, who will? So when the fish man comes through every Saturday with stacks of Styrofoam plates, it's not even a question. It's good, I just get sick of eating catfish. Every. Single. Saturday.

Regardless, I clamp my mouth shut. Today there isn't *anything* I'm going to say to risk getting in trouble.

My turn is up before I know it and I'm neck-crooked backward in the bowl and Ms. Moesha is squeezing a glowing bottle of Magnificent Majeque shampoo. "Majeque . . . Magic," I mouth, grinning at the hints of magic everywhere. Honey and jasmine scents waft, and warm circles dig into my scalp. I let my eyes roll back. The head massage is the best part, I swear.

Ms. Moesha leans over for a whisper. "You excited about today?"

"I am!" I grin. "I can't wait to see what sort of spells—"

She looks around, a soapy finger at her lips. "Shhhh."

Oops! I drop my voice to a whisper. "I didn't bring anything. Is that okay? I don't even know what I'm supposed to bring. Momma doesn't do any of this."

"I have everything you need. I'm just so glad you made the cutoff. Those who didn't have their Impetus by this week have to wait to enroll *next* year."

"Wow, lucky me!" *There are others?* I didn't really think about other kids being like me, but of course there are, if it's a whole school. I wonder if I know any of them from Thompson Middle. That'd be kinda cool.

"Once I finish up your hair, you can head to the back. Next to the bathroom there's a hollow piece of wall. Press your palm on it, say 'Ooweppe d'yo,' and it'll let you step through."

Wait, what? "As in, talk to the wall?" *She can't be serious.*

She nods and her eyes smile.

"Uhm, okay."

Damp terrycloth is heavy on my shoulders as I plop into her chair. Ms. Moesha has Trina out from under the dryer, rollers gone, and curls fingered out before she gets back to me. Seconds pass like minutes as she blow-dries my hair and starts up her irons. I'm about ready to tell her I'll finish my flat iron at home, when the door chimes open.

Fishman Stan.

Momma hands off a twenty to Stan and returns with a stack of to-go plates from waist to chin. Stan slips something into Ms. Moesha's waist apron, but I can't make out what it is. She winks in thanks and the shop door closes behind him. Momma offers me a foam container, but my stomach's doing flips—I'm too excited to eat. I wave Momma off and she gives me that look. That you-think-you're-uppity look. *Not uppity, Momma. Just processing the fact that I'm a witch and my first lesson starts in, what? Minutes?* My hands shake, but I force them still.

My excitement swells like a balloon, then pops when I spot Ms. Moesha's calendar on the wall. My insides squirm and I whip out my phone.

Me: Happy Birthday!! Wish I was there with you. Take
   lots of pictures.

My phone buzzes instantly.

Nae: TY! I MISS YOU! 🙁 How's it going, btw?
Me: Me too! 😭 Good! Wish you were here. GTR.
   Huggies!:)
Nae: Kissies! Send me pics later!

I put my phone away without responding. The sound of ripping Velcro makes my heart flutter as Ms. Moesha removes the apron from my neck. *Finally.*

"All done," she says.

"Thank you, it's getting so long." I slick my hands over my hair, ends looking healthy and refreshed.

"It's a growing-serum treatment." She shows me a glowing tube of gold liquid. "Best quality on the market. And made by one of the most talented Magicks to ever exist, Madame CJ herself." She winks again. "Now go ahead. It's about time." With the shop empty now, just Momma and me left, she points toward the hall. "Go on down there while I finish your momma. I'll be down in a minute and we'll get started."

"Be on your best behavior, little miss." Momma winks. "I'll be back around four." She's proud. I know she is.

I kiss Momma goodbye and try to take a step, but my feet hesitate.

"Go on," Ms. Moesha says. "Don't be scared now. Ooweppe d'yo—'open this wall'—and she should let you walk right on through."

She? Mom cranes backward for a glimpse of Ms. Moesha's face to see if she's serious, apparently as confused as I am.

"The others back there should be settling down by now." Ms. Moesha beckons for me to go. And I do.

Next to the bathroom door, the plaster's scratchy on my palm. I knock where Ms. Moesha said I should and the sound answers like a high note on a piano. *Definitely hollow.* I press my hand to it, feeling like an idiot.

"Ooweppe d'yo."

Nothing happens.

"Ooweppe d'yo."

Nothing, still.

"A little louder and speak real clear, baby," Ms. Moesha yells. "These walls old, they don't hear good!"

This is wild. I gulp. "OOH-WEPPE-DEE-YO!"

A fizz of light sparks and dances up the wall from floor to ceiling. The light zips across and back down the other side and a chunk of wall juts out at me. Where plaster was, engraved panels of wood appear. *A door!* The patterns on the door twist into a smile and I gasp.

"Another new face," it says in a fruity voice with a deep southern drawl.

The door? The door is talking?

"I'm Lucille. But my friends call me Lucy." A door handle appears, sticking out toward me like I'm supposed to shake it.

I do and remind myself, yet again, to shut my gaping mouth.

"All-righty, sugar. Let me just . . ." She grunts, and the door hinges whine. "These hinges are . . . a . . . bit . . ."

The door puckers open. "There we are. You have a good ole first day, sugar."

My mouth is still wide open. "Uhm, thank you, you have a nice day, too." That sounds so strange. Can doors have nice days? She's nailed to a doorframe, so was that rude? I duck through into a corridor and try not to think about the hundreds of other ways I'm going to embarrass myself in this new place.

Lucy closes at my back and my eyes adjust to the darkness in the long corridor. A faint light dusts the floor up ahead, and barely audible chattering voices set my nerves on edge.

Someone's there. Several someones.

Who are they? Are they back here all the time? Are they new to magic too? Are—

A hand rests on my shoulder and I yelp.

"Oh, sorry." A boy about my height with swooped hair throws up his hands in apology. "I didn't mean to scare you. I'm keeping eyes out for students. I'm Eric." He offers his hand.

I take it reluctantly. "Kyana. What is this place?"

"Oh, this?" He grins. "Only the coolest spot in Park Row. Welcome to Park Row Magick Academy." He gestures for me to follow him down the dim hall. Dusty shelves piled with boxes and jars tower on either side of us. Funny smells like pickled sunflowers tickle my nose and I gaze all around, gaping. I bump into a shelf and glasses *tingle*.

"Oh, watch out."

We step over a cluster of supplies and the hallway empties into what looks like a large storage room.

"Academy? Like a prep school?"

"Sort of. It may not be much, but it's ours." He pops his collar, a silly grin on his face. "P-R-M-A proud!"

The bling around his neck flashes and a happy feeling settles over me. "Wow, nice necklace!" An urge to gush pries at me like vomit determined to come out. And I can't. Stop. Staring. At his jewelry. "It's so, so cool! And the studs to match." *Wow, Kyana, stop talking!* My head is a cloud and words claw at my lips. "You're so stylish and put together. I bet all—" *OMG, SHUT UP, KYANA!* I clamp my hands over my mouth—at least now the words are muffled, even though my lips won't stop moving. *What's wrong with me?*

"Sorry." He chuckles, stepping back a bit. "If you fan your hand in front of your face, the effect will wear off. Otherwise you'll keep tripping over my watch and stuff, ha-ha."

I try it and the urge to shout Eric's praises dissolves with the white spots on my vision. "What in the world was that?"

"Used my last BlingEnhancer this morning." He clears his throat and brushes off his shoulder. "Like to keep it extra clean for Saturday school. Keep folks checkin' for me, you know." He does a cheesy grin.

"Huh?" I'm just grateful I can see clearly again.

He laughs, harder this time, and points at his shoes. "Got

my InstaClean working, too." Eric's white-and-blue high-top Jordans with neon laces are like fresh-out-the-box clean. Next to my white-so-dingy-they're-basically-gray Keds, his look extra dope.

"BlingEnhancer. InstaClean. You know, charms?"

There are spells for stuff like that?

"Come on, don't worry. I'll show you around. You'll be hip to the game in no time."

I try to pick my jaw up off the floor. If they have spells to keep your Js looking brand-new, I bet they have spells to help with all sorts of things around the house.

Let's just hope doing magic is nothing like math. Then I'll be golden.

Park Row Magick Academy is full of way more kids than I thought there'd be. Thirty, maybe more.

Who knew there was this entire spot for magical folks tucked away in Park Row? For that matter, who knew there was magic, period?

Specks of dust tickle my nose. A row of gray lockers hangs above black-top tables on one wall. Piles of dusty books are stacked in a corner. There are doors at the far end of the room, though none of them have handles. Which, now that I've met Lucy, makes sense.

The rest of the walls are hidden behind storage shelves

buried beneath boxes and bins. Inside one is what appears to be a bunch of snapbacks and wigs.

Kids, laughing among themselves, are sprawled around on cushy pillows on fuchsia-and-purple rugs across the floor. A few of them offer hellos and my nerves settle some. There's a sign above a doorway at the back of the room that reads, New Students Here. That must be where I'm headed next.

"So you all just hang out here?" I ask Eric.

"Yeah. After finishing your training, the rest is optional. So a lot of us stick around. Help Ms. Mo out."

"Mo?"

"Oh, that's what the students call her. We keep it real chill around here." He points at a guy with a tapered fade, designs on the side, sitting with a basketball and a pair of Beats in his lap. "That's Isaac. He's a senior this year." Behind him is a group of folks cheering on what looks like a game, but the weird thing is, no one's sitting in front of the console. The chair's empty. *I don't get it.*

"Uhh, who's playing?"

"They're inside."

"Inside?"

"Yeah, like *in* the game."

What?! No way.

"Their turn is almost up . . . Watch."

The crowd roots and hollers for Invisible Player to miss a booby trap. Apparently they don't, because half the room gasps and sure enough, someone with hair curly on top, faded on the side, shoots from the game and lands hard in the chair, like the Switch gave them an actual kick in the pants.

"Almost had it," they say, kicking the floor. People jostle their shoulders and they slap a few hands. "I'll get it next time, watch."

"That's Russ's Switch. He brings it and lets us play. He's got it bewitched to transport the player into the actual game."

"That's dope!" *Wait, did he say Russ? As in . . .* "Russell?"

"That guy." Eric points.

I'd know that cocky mug anywhere. Russ from Thompson. He's a wizard, too?! He's wearing a long tee, slim-fit jeans sagging off his waist, and his kicks practically sparkle (not surprised). A crowd lingers around him as he stuffs a wad of more money than I've ever seen into his pocket. Mr. Popular here, too.

Ugh. He told Nae he'd be at her party, got her hopes up, *knowing* he had to be here? Not that lying is much better, but purposely disappointing her is . . . I stomp a foot in his direction.

Eric taps my shoulder. "You already have your supplies?"

"Wh— I mean, uhm—"

"It's okay, Mo keeps spares in here." Eric leads me toward a closet but before we step inside, I stop him to ask, "What's he selling, anyway?"

"Who, Russ?" Eric gestures to his own kicks and bling. "I got mine from him. And for the right price, Russ has a whole catalog of charms he'll sell you. Stuff that's not in the spell book. He *creates* his own charms, like engineers them using his own magic . . . recipe or something. Dude's a friggin' genius."

Wow. What if I could create charms, too?

"It's his hustle and no one knows how he does it. Ms. Mo can't even create charms."

I make out a bag of tiny boxes next to Russ, tied with blue ribbons that read Russell's Creations in bright yellow. He hands one to a girl with big hoop earrings and she hands him a folded-up piece of money, but I miss how much it is.

The girl opens the box, grinning. There's a burst of light, and a shower of confetti pops over her head. Lavender color creeps up her braids from ends to root and they twist upward into a fancy hairdo. Pops of sparkle flash for a second and harden into rhinestones, glittering on the high bun on her head.

Uhm, wow. Turning charms into a hustle? I'm not a member of the Russell Fan Club, but even I'm impressed.

"With Thompson's Homecoming game last night, he's probably raking in the dough." Eric rubs his chin. "Russ technically started training a while ago. But he didn't complete the mandatory training last time, so he's back."

Oh great, not only is he here, but he's in *my* class. I resist the urge to roll my eyes as Eric runs a finger down the closet doorframe and cackling laughter floats through the air. The supply closet door creaks open. This one's named Meryl, apparently, and she likes to be tickled before opening up. Wooden shelves, lined with books thicker even than the book Memaw showed me the other day, tower to the ceiling.

"You'll need one of these books for sure." A wand appears in his hand and he flicks his wrist.

Oo! I get one of those? A book floats from the top, loosing a cloud of dust, then settles in my grasp. *Oof.* It's called *A Safe Start to Spellcasting.* It's heavy, and my fingers tingle just touching it.

"Thanks. Wait, can I do magic at home? Like, not here?"

"Oh yeah. You can wand-carry as long as you're enrolled somewhere and once you complete your training. And no using magic in front of non-Magick folks, of course."

"Of course." My arms ache under the weight of the chunky tome, but he floats another one toward me: *The History of Magicks.* "How much is all this stuff?"

"Oh, it doesn't cost us anything. Mo covers the cost and tries to keep out-of-pocket fees low. You'll also need a cauldron."

"No way! Like a real wizard's cauldron? Something out of *Charmed*?"

"Relax." He grins. "It's just an enlarged pot. Real cauldrons are heavy and outdated. I think some kids in Europe

47

still use them, but . . . Here. This"—banging ricochets off the wall as he slaps the bottom of what I'm almost sure is a gumbo pot—"does fine."

"That's a pot, like a *pot* pot." I've cooked enough gumbo with Memaw to know a two-foot-deep gumbo pot when I see it.

He shrugs. "I dunno. I've never seen anyone cook in something that big."

Your family isn't from Louisiana. That's why. "Will any old one do? I don't want to take one unnecessarily. I have one of these at home."

"Oh, that's wassup! Got your supplies already. Cool, cool."

"No, I— Never mind."

"You're all set." He takes hold of a piece of my hair, pursing his lips like he's deep in thought.

What the—? I jerk away. I mean, I *just* got it done. Random people touching your hair is the strangest and most annoying thing.

"Be sure to ask Ms. Mo to get your wand."

"Ooo!" My lips pull back in an embarrassingly large smile. "Do I get a cloak?"

He laughs. "You got a lot to learn. You don't need a cloak to be a witch, Kyana. Regular clothes are fine."

I chuckle, too, pretending I knew that as we leave the closet.

"But to protect your clothes, you can throw on one of those snapbacks or wigs."

To protect my clothes? My eyebrows kiss. We scoot out of the closet and into the room for new students. The classroom is smaller than the rec area, but ten or so desks are spaced in neat rows in front of a large board. In the corner is a teacher's desk, with a blanketed mystery object sitting on its top. Squeaks coming from it make me hopeful and nervous to see what's underneath. A few other students huddle in groups, chattering, as Eric points out the box of hats and wigs.

One girl sits at a desk in the front row, muttering to a cactus in her lap.

"How does a snapback or wig protect my clothes again?" Maybe I missed it.

"Into the classroom and at your seats, everyone!" Ms. Moesha's voice booms like someone handed her a microphone before Eric can get an answer out. I grab a snapback from a box on the floor (just in case), hurry to the front row, and slide into an empty desk beside the girl with the cactus. My first magic class is under way.

CHAPTER 5

*·**✳·*·*

A single slip of paper sits on each desk; next to it, a pen. In a line at the front of the classroom are three pillars, and behind them Ms. Mo writes her nickname on the whiteboard.

"For the newbies. Now, we ready?" She tugs on a honey-blond wig from the same box where I grabbed the hat. The hair hugs her face—then it *literally* hugs her face, and I gasp. Each strand grows longer, wrapping her up like a cocoon. A scream claws at my throat—this feels like a scene from a horror movie—then suddenly the strands are gone and what's left is Ms. Mo in a honey-blond robe, fitted at the waist and sheer at the bottom, with pants underneath, and honey-blond curls bouncing around her head to match. She looks more like a goddess than a witch and excitement bubbles up inside me.

I get to be a part of *this. Me!*

"Protective robes for your clothes, plus a bonus matching hairdo—always optional, always recommended"—she winks—"and always stylish." She tosses wigs and snapbacks around the room. The quiet girl next to me sets her cactus aside and catches a green wig midair. Ribbons of color stretch as all the newbies cocoon and turn out in robes, the class now a rainbow of colors and a cloud of excited whispers.

"Gotta watch those knockoffs, though," Mo says. "They'll have you looking a whole mess. Wicked Edges." She primps. "The only wig brand I trust."

Wicked Edges. I wonder if they have normal outfits, too. Momma keeps her hair in a wig most days because it saves her time. She'd *love* a wig that's basically a free change of clothes, too! Ms. Mo offers me a purple one. I do love purple, so I take it and shove the snapback under my chair.

Russ is on my left, feet up, chair tipped backward. He plops a snapback on his head and in seconds he's robed in cobalt blue. I ease the hair over my new do. My insides buzz and my hands jitter. The wig stretches and twists until lavender fabric with a mermaid tint swishes at my feet. I catch a glimpse of myself in the reflection: my flat-ironed hair is streaked purple.

OMG, Nae would flip! I reach for my phone in my pocket. Missed messages from Nae light up on the screen.

Nae: Russ isn't even here. 😟 miss you . . .

I feel so bad. So, so bad.

Me: Miss you, too. Excited for library tomorrow!

My finger hovers over the keyboard, so much I want to tell her. She loves mermaid everything. But I close my hand in a fist. I can't. I'll find out all about the party later and I'll make it up to her somehow.

I tuck my phone away when Ms. Mo begins.

"Magic training is"—she whips her wand in a circle and a spark of fireworks pops—"exciting, fun, and even"—she swipes left and the firework sparks branch into stemmed flowers and roses shower the ground—"*full* of surprises." She tugs on her wand as if it's attached to an invisible rope. And the roses turn to flames.

The room erupts with gasps.

"But it's also incredibly dangerous if you're not careful. The simplest motion or misspoken spell can change every-thing, and not necessarily for the better." She zigzags her wand in the air with quick flicks of her wrist and rain falls from the ceiling, putting out the fire and evaporating with a hiss.

"*Wow.*" Collective wonder echoes through the room. I swallow and sit up straighter.

"Which is why the Magick Board ordained that any wizards or witches who show signs of magic"—she taps her wand in her hand as she paces—"*must* enroll in six months of weekly magic training at their zoned school." She stops, mutters a spell, and a giant scroll appears high above my head and unrolls onto my desk. "By entering our training, you agree to abide by the rules of magical practice outlined in Section 53." The words inches from my nose are highlighted in bright yellow and I read as fast as I can.

SECTION 53. MAGIC PRACTICE IS ONLY APPROVED UNDER THE GUIDANCE OF A BOARD-CERTIFIED MAGICK INSTRUCTOR. WAND CARRYING WITHOUT COMPLETING TRAINING IS STRICTLY PROHIBITED.

"Which means, while you're enrolled here, you may practice at home, but keep your activities aboveboard." She looks down her nose at us. "No experimenting." Her eyes dart to Russ, who glances around and sneers at me when he sees me looking. She raises her voice above the chatter. "I'm required to report any funny business."

The scroll unrolls further, revealing a signature line at the bottom. A pen appears in my hand. and I look around at the others, who are wide-eyed like me. Eric is against a far wall, arms folded, smiling.

"Signatures, please."

I glance at the girl next to me, who can't scribble her name fast enough. I sign as well, wondering if I should read at least some of the long scroll. I squint to read the fine handwriting, but Ms. Moesha claps and it rolls up with a snap and disappears.

"Now, with the formalities done, I have the distinct pleasure of welcoming you to Park Row Magick Academy, the heart of magic on this side of Rockford and my labor of love for the past ten years."

I tingle all over.

"For those of you who were at orientation last week, this might sound a bit familiar, but we have some new faces today." She winks at me. "So I'll go over it again." She taps her wand on her whiteboard. Bold letters appear like an ink spill.

GENERAL SPELLS
SPECIALTIES

CHARMS   LINKS   POTIONS

"All magic requires a foundational proficiency in General Spells. There are also three approved areas of specialty: Charms, which is more of an umbrella category for deeply advanced niches such as Summoning and Hexes; Links; and Potions."

I gulp.

"Now, not everyone needs a specialty. Magic works best when it suits your natural abilities, and that can vary person to person. All magic has a role and function, and each type is equally valuable and important."

My eyes glaze over at her words as the mystery object on her desk starts squeaking louder.

"Today we're going to take a look at specialties so you can think about what might suit you. Next time we're in class, you'll have the option to take the official specialty exam *and* present a community project idea if you'd like to help influence my decision." She paces, reciting the rundown like she has done this so many times she has it memorized. "Once I assign areas of focus, they are permanent and will require an appeal to the Rockford Magick Board to be changed." She lowers her voice and stops pacing. "So choose wisely. Over the next several days, practice, practice. I do try to take your preferences into account, so you can write yours here." She holds up a slip of paper like the one on my desk.

Whispering sprinkles through the class.

She shoots a stern look at someone in the back and the chattering stops. "As I was saying, today you'll be exploring different types of magic. You'll complete a series of quick . . . we'll call them exploratory assignments."

She aims at the first pillar. The cloth on top of it flies off to reveal a pan of coal. "General Spells are your bread and butter—they form the base for all other forms of magic.

Spells can do almost anything, including transformations. Have a car? Wish it was a horse? General Spells can do that." She mutters something, swishes, and the coal erupts in flames.

I shove backward in my seat, heat licking my face. This is what I get for sitting in the front.

Ms. Mo extinguishes the flames with puffs of air from the tip of her wand. "Everyone is required to have at least a basic understanding of how to execute a General Spell," she says. "Casting a spell requires clear enunciation and sharp focus. An aptitude for problem solving and planning is good as well."

I swallow. *Problem solving?* Like math problems? My knees shake. I had no idea this would be so much like school. She said "planning," too. I'm sort of good at planning . . . I think? *I hope.* Deep breaths.

The fire is an ember as Ms. Mo shuffles to the second pillar . . . which is empty.

"Charms, as you—"

Hoots and hollers ring out as Russ clasps his hands and shakes them victoriously over his shoulder. I roll my eyes deep in my head.

"Ahem," Ms. Mo continues. "Charms are spells that give an object a temporary emotional aura or cause a temporary change to an object. These spells can clean your shoes, protect your clothes from spills, and turn an overgrown flower bed into a rose garden in minutes. No need for an example here, since we're all familiar with Russell's Creations. But I will say this: Charms is a *hard-won* specialty." She narrows her eyes at Russ. "So don't expect to just skate into it."

The quiet girl with the cactus is half out of her chair, listening so intently I think she's going to topple over her desk.

"The Board only allows two students per academy per year to be assigned to Charms. So I have to weigh that decision with great seriousness. I look for clear enunciation and the like, but the biggest skill I look for in a Charms student is clever and quick decision-making. My deep analytical thinkers often struggle with this specialty. You need strong intuition, a gut feeling that you know how to listen to and trust."

I chew my lip. Is that like the feeling I get when I sit down to do math? Because its message is clear: RUN. The girl next to me is taking notes and Russ's cemented smile doesn't crack.

"Charms is a specialty that usually lends itself to a sweet job with the Magick Board. The Deputy Advisor, Hex Vestiges Examiner, MagickNet Regulator, Director of Enchanted Enterprises, which is the company that oversees all exchange of magical goods, and even Embezzlement Detectives—they're all former Charms students."

The room explodes in chatter.

A job? I sit up in my seat.

"Russell, CEO of Russell's Creations. Former Charms student," Russ says, and he and another boy slap hands.

Everyone at Thompson wants to be a doctor, lawyer, game developer, or baller. I mean, that's all fine and well, but math makes me want to barf.

But magic? Magic could be an everyday job?

I wanna do this!

And what if it could help Momma, too? Maybe her feet wouldn't hurt so much if she had one job instead of three.

"Now," Mo adds, "most of y'all will likely be assigned General Spells—"

The crowd moans in disappointment.

"Because"—she raises her voice—"it, by far, has the widest need in the community. So no pouting, those of you who don't end up with a specialty. General Spells are the most broadly used incantations." The disappointment settles and the quiet girl raises her hand.

"Yes, Ashley, is it?"

She's beet red. "Y-yes, ma'am."

"You had a question?"

She somehow turns redder, gazing at everyone staring at her. She shakes her head *never mind* and her gaze hits the ground, her curtain of shiny hair shielding her face.

"Oh, okay, honey. If you want to ask me after, that's fine, too."

I have a mind to ask her what her question was. I can ask it for her if she doesn't want to. But another hand shoots up and the moment has passed. A girl a few rows back wearing fuchsia robes asks, "What did *you* specialize in, Ms. Mo?"

"Funny you should ask." She pulls the cover off the mystery item on her desk, revealing what looks like a hamster cage.

We had a gerbil, Frank the G, in my kindergarten class, but Momma's funny about bringing animals into the house. We have a stray cat problem in Park Row and she has a designated spray bottle for keeping 'em away. She just doesn't do animals, period. So Frank never came home with me. But I don't think this is a gerbil. Frank was more round and fat, less long and . . . A musky smell curls my lips. *Ew.* Less stinky. Much less stinky.

"This is Eddie," Ms. Mo says. "My Link."

She holds up Eddie and I chortle at my ridiculousness. That's a ferret. No wonder it's so stinky. Eddie curls in a ball, his eyes blinking. He's so cute.

"Links hold a piece of their partner inside them. They can be gerbils, hamsters . . . I've even seen a Chihuahua linked to a wizard once. But ferrets are the most common Link. They have a tender disposition that makes them more willing to pair. It's a rare type of magic, but my family all had Links, so it was fitting for me."

Wow, imagine growing up in a family where everyone has magic. How much more I'd probably know.

She puts Eddie away in his cage and tucks her lip. He looks sad, too, between those bars. "But we won't be offering any Links specialty spots this class." She takes a deep breath, and for a moment it's like the weight of the world is on her shoulders. "Link training takes quite a bit of resources that we just don't have right now."

Mo paints on a bright smile as she uncovers the third pillar. "On to the last specialty we will discuss today—Potions. Only one spot available for this one." Ms. Mo goes on talking about Potions, but I'm fixed on Eddie. He follows Mo's every move. They really are bonded. It's sweet. But his eyes droop, and even his posture seems to slump. What's got Ms. Mo so down?

By the time my attention returns to the lesson, pink smoke curls from a silver pot and notes of ginger and vanilla dance through the air. Memories of baking buttery biscotti—with their toasted, nutty aroma and that creamy white chocolate Memaw and I would dip them in—swirl in my mind. Whatever Ms. Mo is brewing sings to me and I can hear every note of its flavor. A box of ingredients sits next to her cauldron.

"The leafy one with the tough branches," I whisper.

"You say something, Kyana?"

Oops, did I say that out loud? "I was just thinking the

60

leafy one looked like a good choice to add to that potion you're making."

"Oh?" She runs her finger down the spell book floating beside her. "That looks right." She tosses in the crushed leaves and the pink substance thickens, splashing over the edge like bubbles. Ms. Mo scoops out a dollop of coconut oil and adds it to the brew. She winds her wand around the pot and the sweet smells in the air pop with tangy lemon. *It's done.*

"Annnnd done!"

I knew that. How'd I know that?

"SureShrinker." Mauve liquid sloshes in a vial she holds up. She squeezes a single drop of the potion on a leaf, and the leaf disappears. I peer closer and realize it's still there, just tiny, sitting in the palm of her hand. "One drop on most things is all you need, and it'll shrink anything to half its size at least." Ms. Mo portions out the rest of the shrinking potion and calls on Russ to pass out the stoppered jars. "Take a bit home, experiment with it. Be sure to grab some Potion Base, too."

Can't wait to try it. When she's not cooking, Memaw lives in her garden and is always pulling weeds. She's gonna love this.

"Now you've seen a taste of the specialties, write down your preference," Mo yells over the cloud of conversations brimming with anticipation. "And drop them on my desk."

My pen hovers over my little piece of paper as I survey

the choices on the board. I kinda *got* Potions—but I think the best stuff, what I need to help Momma, is in Charms.

"Hey, Ash," Russ says. "Here's yours." He snickers, setting down her potion at the front of the classroom as if he can't tell she's really shy. He sets mine on my desk and I refuse to dignify him with even a look. That boy needs to be taken down a peg. I go grab Ashley's potion, and as I pass it to her we bump hands.

"Sorry. Uh-oh, oops!" we say at the same time.

She smiles, her long black hair shielding half her face. Her robes are lime, matching chunky lime streaks in her hair.

"I'm sorry Russ is being rude. Your hair is pretty, by the way."

"Thanks." She looks down, then forces her head up again. "And no worries. I'm used to it."

"Your question earlier . . . I could ask it for you."

"Oh, it's nothing. I—"

"I don't mind."

She meets my eyes, barely. "Okay, if you really don't mind. I was wondering if Ms. Mo will be allowing Summons as a co-study option this time for Charms students."

"Oh, you want Charms?"

She nods and her lips crack a smile despite her trying not to. Her hair ripples backward and I can see her honey skin and tiny craters in her cheeks.

"I want Charms, too." I cut a glance at Russ. "That is, if *he* doesn't get the spot."

"He's pretty into himself, from what I've seen."

"Oh, he is, trust me. I go to school with him. Where do you go?"

"I'm homeschooled."

"Oh, cool. I'm Kyana, by the way." I stick out my hand and she barely takes it.

"Nice to meet you. I'm Ashley."

"What do you say we make a pact that we both get Charms to take Russ down a peg?"

There's that smile again. "Deal."

This time she shakes hands for real. I return to my desk, rolling the pen between my fingers. I give Ashley a reassuring nod and she nods back, beaming.

"Pass your papers up, and in your seats, everyone," Ms. Mo says. "It's time to explore these areas on your own."

It sounds like a test. Ugh. I hate that word.

Please don't be like math.

I scribble "Charms" on the paper and set it on Ms. Mo's desk. This is for Momma, for Nae, for Ash. I gotta get this Charms spot.

CHAPTER 6

∗∗✳∗∗

The first assignment is Potions. Humid steam rising from my cauldron blows back my curls. All the straightness left a long time ago. I clip them back, out of my face, and check the instructions again.

InstaFlav is scrawled on the board in loopy handwriting. "One drop of this and it'll auto-season your entire dish," Mo said. "You can't keep this stuff on shelves in those fancy suburb areas. No one around here really buys it. But it's an easy one, perfect for trying out potions."

It's supposed to be a creamy yellow, but brown sludge bubbles in the bottom of my pot, a rotten egg smell pricking my nose. I swallow the gag and work my large metal spoon around the pot, making sure to scrape the edges, like I would mixing anything else. Everyone else has a wand in hand that they received at orientation last week. But when I asked

Ms. Mo for one, she said her supply was low on those. She disappeared into a closet and has been banging around in there ever since.

Don't be like math. Please *don't be like math.*

I stir the potion again and pretend it's pineapple upside-down cake, or triple chocolate fudge brownies, or *something* I know like the back of my hand.

The instructions on the board are clear:

To a base of toad water, add a cup of Bertha's Basic Potion Base (careful to level it off with a straight edge), a vial of wolf spider extract, three oleander leaves, and a drop of blueberry extract. After 43½ clockwise stirs, carefully do one counterclockwise stir.
Finally, fold in crushed moth wings.

And written underneath in small letters is

Substitute powdered sugar for wolf spider extract.

Hmm. I did that. I can follow a recipe any day, but this potion is stumping me.

Ashley drips a drop of blueberry extract into her cauldron and gurgling liquid spits back at her. She sighs but bites her lip in determination and keeps winding her wand.

I study the ingredients on the supply table at the front again and a jar of oily eyeball–looking things catches my attention. They're not on the list. I don't even know what they are, but the jar hums to me as I look at it. I scoop one out and add it to my brew. The brown sludge pales to yellow and my insides twinge with glee. I keep stirring. It might be the right color now, but it's far from creamy or anything like the example up front. Maybe I need to improvise, add something else?

Bang!

An explosion next to me makes me duck. Russ's pot flies into the air, smashing the lights bobbing over us and barreling into a supply shelf. The chaos clears and Russ looks bashful for probably the first time in his life. The class cackles. Guess he's not an expert at everything.

"All right, all right, show's over." He winds his wand, mutters a few words, and the room is tidy and orderly again. *Man, it feels like everyone's way ahead of me. Maybe Russ comes from a wizarding family?* Seconds later, a lemony scent billows in fragrant clouds around us. Ashley is done, smells like. She's pouring a silky substance into a glass bottle like one of the beakers we use in science class. She looks up, pressing her glasses to her face, and blushes. I offer her a fist pound, but she just smiles bashfully.

"Found one!" Ms. Mo pops up out of nowhere, takes my metal spoon, and tosses it over her shoulder. She hands me a purple stick. It's oddly shaped, rounded like an uncooked breadstick. "They're useless until we activate them."

It's pliable in my hand like a rubber spatula. Everyone's staring like something big is about to happen. I wait for a tingle or fizz or something. "What now?"

Ms. Moesha rolls up her sleeves and puffs her chest out. "Kyana, take your hair down."

My hair? This is getting weirder.

"Sit." She gestures to a seat. "Okay, honey. I'm going to touch your hair."

This is real odd. "All right, go ahead," I squeak. "I'm ready." I don't know why I'm so nervous, if it's everyone staring at me or the fact that I'm the only one here who hasn't done this before. Some people smile, others whisper to each other. Eric looks amused. What's Ms. Mo about to do?

"Your wand is a shell," she says. "A useless piece of chemical compounds. A stick, really." She rakes her hands through my roots with a gentle tug. Thankfully, I'm not tender-headed. Nae'd be squealing.

"But when you bond with it—give it a piece of yourself— then it becomes *yours*. I'd say you're about a 4C."

I must be losing my mind. Is she talking about my curl pattern? "Yeah. 4B, I think. Or maybe it's C. But, I'm sorry, how's that relev—"

Ow! My scalp stings as she plucks a tuft of hair from it, muttering a few words.

"Ms. Mo?!" I hop up.

"*Relaaaax.*" She touches my shoulders and my legs go

limp like noodles. "Sorry I didn't warn you. When I do, people usually tense up. Now hold your wand up nice and straight." I rub the still-stinging spot on my scalp and point what I'm almost sure is a silicone spatula handle at her.

She slips out her own wand and swirls it around my strand of hair. It wiggles a second, then stretches, bouncing like a spring. With a dramatic swish of her hand, the hair straightens. Like perm straight. Then retracts.

"Ugh," she mutters. Deep lines crease her brow. Her lips move fast as she mutters spells I can't make out. And wouldn't understand if I could. "Sometimes it's a little stubborn. Don't worry. I'll make this one work."

I hope so, because my hair's no longer up for grabs, pun intended. The hair wriggles like a worm. She thrusts at it once more and the tip of my purple breadstick splits open, glowing with golden light.

Whoa.

"Hurry," she says. "Make sure it's in your wand hand."

Which one is that? I switch hands, just to do something.

Mo wraps her hand around mine and I go warm all over. The light at the end of my wand pulses like I have only so much time to stick the hair in there.

"Now repeat after me," she says. "Makya'olla."

"MAH-KEE-YA OH-LA." I say each syllable very carefully. The hair moves closer to the light and my heart skips a beat.

"Again," she says. "Makya'olla. Yala Yala."

"MAH-KEE-YA OH-LA. YAH-LA. YAH-LA." The hair twists like a summoned snake and slips inside the tip of the wand like lead into a pencil.

"Now don't let go on this last one. Nice and loud. Makya'olla Yala No'wesse," she whispers.

I can't screw this up. Who knows what happens if you're half-bonded with a wand? And this is her last one. I lock my knees and stand tall.

Say it right. Say it right. Say it right.

"MAH-KEE-YA OH-LA. YAH-LA. NO WES-SEE."

The wand shifts, growing pointier as the hair disappears inside. The silicone hardens, narrowing into a sleek, supple wand. It sparkles like it's coated in purple glitter. Nae would die if she could see this! She bedazzles everything.

"That, baby girl, is your wand." Ms. Mo pats my shoulder. "Forged with your own curl pattern. It's uniquely bonded to you. Keep it safe. Never let it out of your sight." A crowd of applause picks up around me with shouts of congrats.

I don't have words. This is unbelievable.

"Any questions?" she asks.

Only one and it's kind of silly.

"What? Ask."

I lean into Mo for a whisper. "What if the hair don't have no curl to it?"

She cackles. "Chyle, you a mess. There *is* such a thing as a 1, a 2A, basically straight hair, you know? Works the same way." She gives me side-eyes.

"I'm not throwing shade, I swear. I just wondered."

"Mm-hmm." Ms. Moesha turns her attention to the rest of the students, most of whom are done with their potions. She claps. "Let's finish up those potions, best you can." Her voice is a high chime. "Stopper it and tidy your desk for the next assignment."

I swish the wand over my pot and start turning again. The mixture folds over on itself much easier than with a spoon. Everyone's cleaning up around me, so I swish faster. *Twenty-three . . . twenty-four . . . twenty-five . . . no, wait, thirty-four . . . thirty-five . . . Ugh. Where was I?* The batter is less chunky and there are pockets of smoothness. *Forty-three . . .* I wind my hand halfway around the pot, then backward one time, really slow. *Done.*

It's not as perfect as Ashley's or Ms. Mo's, but it's a vast improvement over the sewer sludge I managed at first. I stopper it and add it to the others just as Ms. Mo claps the class to attention again.

"Now, try Charms next."

I stand straight as a board.

"You'll use this simple cleaning charm to clean your cauldrons." She taps the board and the instructions change. "Pay attention to accuracy *and* technique."

Charm: Skuritszhi le plu

"You have twenty seconds. Go!"

Twenty?

Seconds!

Two pops split the air and Russ stands over a sparkly pot, Ash, too. My heart patters faster and I try to remember what Ms. Mo said earlier about Charms.

Speed, clear enunciation, and a gut feeling.

I clear my throat and aim at the pot with my wand. "SKUH-REET-SHE-UL-PLUH!" I will that pot to clean itself but it just looks at me, coated in residue like dried-up pizza dough.

"Zee. Lah. Ploo." Ms. Mo taps each syllable with her wand. More pops. "Nine seconds, everyone."

Hurry! "*Zee*, not *she*," I say. "La-plooooo," I enunciate, pursing my lips. I grip the pot more firmly, ready. "SKUH-REET-SHE-LA-PLOO!"

It rattles, but sets back down.

"Command it," Mo says. "Magic can sense indecision. Tell it what you want and *mean* it."

Ashley's watching and she gives an encouraging nod.

"SKY-REET-ZEE-LA-PLOOP," I say.

Someone laughs, but my pot pops up like a firecracker. It shoots in the air and clangs, hitting the ground clear across the room. I rush over, my heart in my throat.

Did I do it? Did it work?

It's dented and has a few crumbs, but the rest of it glistens. "It's clean!"

Ashley and a few others burst into cheers.

This is so cool! Imagine all Momma could get done with magic in the house. Clothes folded and ironed. Dishes doing themselves. We might get a real weekend and be able to do something as a family for once. This is the dopest thing in the entire world.

I'm a witch. A real witch!

Cleanup from the charm assignment takes no more than a winding swoosh from Ms. Mo—all the cauldrons snap like magnets to a rack on the far side of the room. In front of the class appears a tall, draped something.

"The last assignment for today is an extension of Charms with a mix of General Spellcasting, called Summoning. You'll need a *strong* affinity for charms to be able to summon. So let's give it a try, shall we?"

Oh, this is what Ash was talking about. I shoot her a grin and she grins back, her eyebrows jumping. Ms. Mo whips off the cloth and a tall chest of drawers with curved legs and antique fixtures towers over us. I'm glad for another shot at practicing Charms. I'll try to be faster this time, but something about the idea of a spirit summons sends a chill down my spine.

"Gus?" Ms. Mo smooths her hand across the dresser and

a drawer opens with a hacking cough, its top arching like eyebrows.

"Moeshur!" Gus pronounces Mo's name like it has an *ur* on the end but she doesn't correct him. "It's been quite some time. How you faring?"

"You always ask how *they* are doing, first," she says under her breath to the class.

"Oh good, Gus." She speaks in a raised volume. "And how are things with you?"

"Uhm, is that thing haunted?" I whisper to Ash. "Is Gus a ghost?"

"You could call him that. More of a free spirit from the Between Realms tethered to that dresser. They're called Availables."

The dresser's bottom drawer opens and closes, opens and closes. "Oh, you know, the same ole drama with Mags and her lot. That's a messy group of gals if I've ever seen one. Always stirring up trouble at the Committee meetings. And Rudy's no better. Got a nasty mean streak, that one. Winzhobble just ain't that kind of place, I tried to tell 'em. But enough of me. What can I do for you today, Moeshur?"

"You always wait until *they* offer their service," she whispers to us.

Ash's pen scratches her paper.

"Could you say hello to our newest class?"

"Why, of course!" Gus pushes out all his drawers and

props up taller on his wooden legs. "Helloooo there. You got the finest teacher in the land right here. The finest witch, I tell you, with a real talent for Links. I knew her great-great-great . . . oh, how long ago was it, Moeshur?"

"Gus knew some of my ancestors who migrated here from Winzhobble in the 1600s."

"That's it," Gus belts out. "Well, I bes' be going before Rudy gets his head stuck through those fine people's mirror again. Frightened them half to death. I don't think anyone's slept in that house since." The drawers of the chest rumble shut and it's just a plain piece of furniture again. Ash is practically salivating.

"Your turn," Mo says. "But first, coconut oil on." She tosses a jar to Russ, who takes some and passes the jar. When it gets to me, I scoop out the oil and smell it. Smells like regular coconut oil but with a tangy, pickle-like odor to it. The label's half peeled away but I can still make out what it says.

COUSANN'S CREOLE COCONUT OIL
Keep your loved ones close, but the dead ones closer.

"Coconut oil isn't just for moisturizing, it wards off bad spirits," Mo says. "Cousann's is the best brand out there. Straight out of the New Orleans French Quarter."

I rub the oil behind my ears like everyone else and rub a

good amount into my hands. I give it to Ash, but she holds up a jar she's pulled out of her backpack.

"Summoning an Available and tethering it to an object like Gus or Ms. Lucy—"

"Helloooo," Ms. Lucy sings from faraway.

"Is simple. And Availables are quite useful to have around. But mastering this skill is by far the most difficult form of approved magic." She aims at a clock above the whiteboard and its numbers turn into a timer. "To grab an Available, you have to hold their attention for eleven or so minutes. Technically it's ten, but there's disagreement about whether time starts when you start summoning or when you hook into an Available. So aim for eleven minutes to be safe. Now, if we were tethering today, you'd need to simultaneously use a tethering charm while holding the Available's attention. Very tricky! They don't take kindly to being bamboozled into tethering."

I don't know if tethering spirits to objects is the kind of magic that would be most helpful to Momma, but I can't help but crane my neck in curiosity. Ash is still jotting notes, her glasses slipping down her nose.

"Strong mechanical, analytical, and persuasion skills are going to be your best bet here. And charisma is critical."

Ash turns pink.

"You can do this," I whisper to her.

Mo taps the board. "When I say 'go,' you'll chant this

general spell over and over until you enter a hypnosis-type state." She levels her gaze at us. "*If*, and I mean, on the *small chance*, you're able to cast it correctly, you'll then be connected with whatever spirit happens to be in the Between Realms. You may try to keep them in conversation with you for as long as you can, but be sure to release them after that."

The whole thing creeps me out. I mean, Lucy and Gus are really nice, but I don't know, maybe I've watched too many scary movies. If it helps prove my Charms skill to Ms. Mo, though, I have to give it my best shot.

"And go," she says.

The words on the board are simple enough. I brandish my wand, chanting them, and my vision does something weird. Everything's fuzzy. *Again.*

"YA-YA-LEXZAH-ECH-ECH-COO. YA-YA-LEXZAH-ECH-ECH-COO." Dizzy on my feet, I grip my desk. Is it working? I try several more times, until my butt slams in the chair, the world spinning.

Ms. Mo sets a glass of tea on my desk. "Drink up, it'll help."

Its sugared peachiness is chilly going down my throat. Blinking the room back into focus, I see that most everyone is sipping tea. I'm relieved I'm not the only one.

Russ is still standing, his eyes closed. Ash, too. I dig my nails into the desk. *Come on, Ash. Don't let Russ win.* Ashley mutters under her breath, smiling and blushing. She chews her lip and her eyes dart back and forth behind her eyelids. *You can do it, Ash.*

The timer buzzes.

"Wands down," Ms. Mo says.

"You did great," I whisper to Ash.

"That's a wrap for us today, students," Mo adds. "Be thinking if you'd like to sit the optional specialty exam next time we're in class. In the meantime, keep up the practice!" She hands envelopes marked **PARENTS** to each student and I hold mine up to the light, curious what it says. No luck. I pile it and my stuff into my backpack.

Ash leans in. "I could see one, an Available, you know? I talked to him, but . . . what was I supposed to say?" She shoves her wand in her green backpack. "I got tongue-tied and lost his attention. He disappeared and I couldn't get him back. This sucks. I really wanted this."

"Ash, today was just practice. You'll have another try. And besides, you did the charm. Are you hearing yourself? You got a gazillion steps further than anyone else. No one else even tapped into the hypnosis state. Not even Russ."

"Really?" Her cheeks push up under her eyes.

"Really."

We high-five. No way Russ is going to get a Charms spot. We've got it in the bag.

CHAPTER 7

⁎⁎✳⁎⁎

Scooter's Skewers' door glows just like it did when I was walking home the other day.

So odd. I grip the door handle, half expecting it to be hot. But it's not.

"Thanks, Momma. I love Scooter's."

"Of course, baby. You deserve a little celebration after your big first day."

I step inside and a wave of something washes over me and I'm . . . lighter on my feet. Elated, maybe? I look around. Framed portraits, license plates, and other odds and ends are collaged on the wall. Booths line the walls, and there's a retro-style counter near the kitchen so you can watch the chef, Scooter, cook. He's known for fusing skewer-style foods with Cajun flavors. Momma likes his gumbo kebab, a mix of sausage, shrimp, and these breaded rice-patty things he does. So when she has a little extra cash, we grab takeout from here.

"Hey there now, Earlene!" Scooter himself comes out the kitchen. He turns to me. "Kyana, how's school?"

"Good." I grab a menu even though I know what I want. Then I realize Scooter's staring at me.

He folds his arms over his chest. "So?"

"So?"

"Well?"

"Uhh, well?"

He leans in, whispering, "The glowing. Figured you'd at least mention it."

"Wait, you see it, too?"

"Course I do." He gets even closer and mouths, "I'mma wizard."

I gasp and glance at Momma. Her expression says she's as shocked as me.

Scooter chuckles a big-bellied laugh and motions for us to follow him through his kitchen into a back office. He takes our orders and puts them in. "And put a rush on that for me, Tony," he says.

"Sure thing, boss," Tony replies before Scooter closes us inside his office.

"Now, where were we? Oh yes. Magicks are all over Rockford. A lot of us settled right here in Park Row.

Winzhobble, where magic originated, is where our ancestors are from. It's full of Magicks," he says.

I have to blink a few times to convince myself what's happening is actually happening. My favorite takeout chef is a *wizard*!

"Well, things got tense there for the ancestors. Disagreements about how magic should be used and by whom. The king in Winzhobble ruled with an iron fist but magic was always free—free to use, to express, to explore. But in his later years, King Frolacou started trying to redefine free magic."

I wrinkle my nose at that. "That doesn't make any sense."

"Right. So Magicks began leaving in droves. Most migrated to major cities in the Americas, which meant no using magic in public but at least they were free to use it how they saw fit. Our kind had to stick together then. We set up covens, community group events, called 'em family reunions, and elected Magick Boards in each place to oversee us. We enchanted the places we held meetings to give off a signal only a witch or wizard could see. Eventually we started enchanting any place safe for our kind with the Glow, as we call it. I saw the way you looked at the door when you were walking home the other day. And I knew you must be coming into your magic."

I didn't even think about how far back this magical thing could go in my family. I chew my lip, wondering what the magic in my family was like . . . I wish I could ask Memaw more about Great-Aunt Pearl, but whether she'd remember is a toss-up. "Wow. I had no idea about any of that. I mean, a glowing door did have me scratching my head."

"Anyplace touched by magic will glow. Now you'll see the Row in a whole new light. There's magic all up and through here."

That's *so* cool. I have so much to learn.

Momma is grinning big. "Kyana, this is special, baby. I'm just . . ." She presses her palm to her chest, eyes glazed.

I don't think I've ever seen Momma *this* proud of me. I squeeze her hand. I'm going to make her proud with this magic thing. I really am.

She turns to Scooter. "Well, you know today was Kyana's *first* day of magic school?"

"Oh yeah?"

I nod. It's so exciting to be able to talk to *someone* about it.

"You trying out for any specialty?" he asks. "It was Potions for me."

"I am. I'm going out for Charms."

"Oh, you fancy, huh?"

"Trying to be." We laugh.

"You over at Ms. Moesha's Beauty Shop?"

"Yep!"

Momma nudges me. "Yes, sir."

"Yes, sir."

"Dedicated witch, that woman is. Works so hard. You tell her I know what's going on and I'm keeping her and all of you in my thoughts. If there's anything Scooter's Skewers can do, let me know."

"Wait . . . what's going on?" *Mo didn't mention anything.*

"Oops." He presses his lips closed. "Forget I said anything. I'm sure it's all fine. I better finish wiping everything down and prep for tomorrow. You need anything, you come by anytime, you hear?"

"Yes, sir."

Tony pops his head in and hands us our order. We say goodbye to Mr. Scooter, hop in the car, and I kiss Momma on the cheek, thanking her again.

"No problem, baby. Wish I didn't have to work tonight. I wanna hear all about your day." Her expression shifts: haggard, heavy with exhaustion.

"I got the dishes tonight, Momma. I don't have any homework."

"Oh, thank you, baby." She sighs, backing out the parking lot. She takes my hand in hers. "What would I do without you?"

I grin.

"You still need to pop into the party store?"

I finger the wad of cash I've saved up to surprise Nae tomorrow at the library. "Yes, if you have time."

She sighs again, checking her watch. "It's fine, I got time. But in and out."

"Deal."

The Row sweeps by, a blur of streetlamps, boarded buildings, and houses—tiny replica homes knitted together on one side of the street, and gates, wide lawns, and half-circle drives on the other. The storefront window of Queen's Beauty Supply glows bright green and I press my nose to the car window. *There's a witch there. Magic. More people like me. In a store I've been to a hundred times!*

Noel's Mini Mart and a car wash a few blocks up are neon-green specks in the distance, too. I wonder what a magical car wash is like. That sounds so cool. Momma's hands are fixed at ten and two. I wish she could see it.

Scooter's Skewers' glowing door is a dot in the rearview. What was he talking about, though? Something is going on with Mo? And he offered help, so it must be serious. A sinking feeling settles in the pit of my stomach. I just hope Mo's okay, and that whatever it is, it has nothing to do with Park Row Magick Academy.

* * * ✳ * *

Memaw is already in bed when we get home, but she's left me a few homemade pecan pralines on the counter. After I do the dishes, I tiptoe into her room, plant a smooch on her forehead, hoping to catch her awake. But her TV is watching her instead of the other way around. I shut it off, force myself to do ten minutes of math problems since I promised Nae, climb into my own bed, and pull open my spell book.

The first page sparkles, but I'm pretty sure that's not magic, and just in my head. I'm so excited.

This Guide to Spellcasting Is Presented To

Kyana Lacreshia Turner

I write my name in my best handwriting on the line beneath, curving the *y* with a heart. I flip and flip the pages until I find the Charms section. I devour every line on the page, savoring the richness like in a plum pudding that's aged for weeks, until my eyes are heavy with sleepiness. There's so much in here. Spells for growing unicorn hair, turning tree bark into chocolate—even a spell that slows down motion for everyone besides yourself. *Man, that'd be useful for a test.*

I sit up, not ready to quit, and pull over the ancient book Memaw gave me. Its pages are much more brittle, crackling with each turn. Just like my new book, though, the Charms section is in the middle.

Illumino consectium makes footprints light up.
Vobritzio can make a mattress work like an actual trampoline.

I turn the page.

Audeacitro liquis disguises earwax as lemonade.

Ew. I turn again but the next few pages have been ripped out. Past the torn pages is a note in the margin in scrawny handwriting.

This one first.

As in *practice* this one first?

BINDING: MATTER TO MATTER
Say: Lugicible debrum
Do: Flick up, flick up, wind counterclockwise, tap & drag.

Seems simple enough. I whip out my wand and aim at something Momma won't lose it over if I break it. Just in case. A bobblehead that I won in a giveaway looks like a worthy candidate. I set it at the center of my dresser and clear my throat.

"Lou-goo-sybil duh-brum," I say, while flicking and winding and tapping.

The bobblehead doesn't move. *Shouldn't it puff sparks or something?*

"Lou-goo-sybil duh-brum," I say, flicking and winding and tapping, harder this time.

Still nothing.

One more time.

But this time I do it so hard I bite my lip and taste copper.

Ugh. I toss my wand by my backpack and shove the spell book off my bed. This is stupid. I suck at Charms just like I suck at math. I hop up to switch off the light and grab my bobblehead to put it away, but it doesn't move.

Oh my goodness!

I tug harder, but sure enough it's stuck like glue to my dresser. It worked! Maybe I won't suck at this witch thing after all.

I fall asleep praying, wishing, hoping it's true.

CHAPTER 8

* ** ✳ ** *

The next morning flies by like Sundays always do. Momma used to say we are supposed to take it easy on Sunday but she always works at least one of her jobs on Sunday, so it makes no kind of sense to me.

Memaw was wigged, church-hatted, and out the door to church with one of her Senior Club friends and back before I was out of pajamas. Then we cooked a quick lunch together, fried chicken and dirty rice, and Momma popped back by to scoop me up for my standing library date with Nae.

Nae tutors me in math every weekend. It's mainly her drilling me on math and asking twenty questions that I don't have answers to. So I didn't expect today to be any different. But Nae is already at a table wearing sunglasses when I slide in across from her. Her grin is as bright as Christmas morning when she spots me. "Key!"

We hug. "So tell me everything! How was the party?"

"Oh my god, Key, awful. Momma brought out my baby pictures. Had 'em blown up and taped all over the living room. Like I want everybody seeing me in the bathtub with Mr. Bubble when I was two."

"*What?* Momma Zoe did not."

"She sure did. And it gets worse."

"How could it possibly?"

"She paraded the few people who stayed at the party around the room to tell them about each picture. I was mortified."

"What do you mean, *stayed*?"

"A lot of people showed up but saw Russ wasn't there and left."

Wowwww.

"I mean, I knew Homecoming being Friday night some people wouldn't show, but I expected more than the ten that did. Shelby stayed, but when it came time for cake, she convinced her clique of mean girls to push my face into my cake."

"*Nooo.*" This is literally the nightmare of birthday parties.

"Knew I shouldn't have invited them."

"Nae, I am so, so sorry." Nae smooths her cheek under

her lens. "I should have been there." I pout, sticking out my bottom lip, and wrap my bestie's hands in mine. "And I'm sorry this party wasn't all you hoped, but we're gonna make up for that now."

I move to her side of the table and pull out the party hat, horn, and jumbo glasses I got from the party store. I plop the hat on Nae's head sideways, real cool-like, and put on the glasses myself since she's already wearing sunglasses. She pulls out her phone and we snap a few pics with silly filters until she's cracking up.

"You're the best," Nae says.

"No, you are. So what's with the sunglasses? I figured you'd take them off eventually but . . ."

She groans. "Shelby's aim was impeccable. My eye slammed right into the fondant mermaid tail Mom had all done up on top."

I gasp.

"It's so bad, Key."

She angles away from the rest of the people in the library and slips her glasses down. There it is, as big as day: a purpling swollen eye with glitter pressed into it.

"Oh, Nae." I let her talk more, making sympathetic noises and hugging her.

Apparently, after the cake smash, Shelby had a run-in with a piñata and ended up falling on her butt. She was so embarrassed, she left the party immediately. I'm mad I wasn't there to have Nae's back, but at least karma was looking out for her.

I cringe, thinking about the embarrassment to continue at school next week. She can't wear those glasses at school. It's against dress code. I wonder if that SureShrinker potion Ms. Mo gave us would shrink the swelling? *Hmmm.*

I slip out the jar from my backpack while Nae goes on about the rest of the decorations and how Tee Tee was there dancing her tail off. I unstopper the potion under the table. Ms. Moesha said one drop, so less than that can't hurt. The liquid is icy on my fingertip.

"Let me see your eye again."

She slips down her glasses.

"Oh, you have a little something . . . right . . ." I smooth my moist finger over her eyelid. "Here."

Please, for the love of all things witchy, work.

"Probably glitter. Thanks."

I stare, gaping.

"Key? Why are you . . . oh . . . ow . . . was something . . ."

Her eye's twitching. Blinking. *Please work.*

Her eye doubles in size and the purple spots deepen. *OH NO!*

"It's stinging." She whips her glasses around, stares at the reflection, and yelps. "My face! Kyana, was something on your hands?"

"I—I—"

"Oh my goodness, is it looking even bigger?" She puts her sunglasses back on. "Great. Just friggin' great."

"I'm so sorry!"

She lets out a huge breath. "Ugh, it's all right. I mean, what could you touching it have done? It's probably just gonna be a goose egg."

"I'm really sorry."

"It's not your fault. And honestly, I feel better just seeing you. This is always the best part of my weekend."

I lay my head on Nae's shoulder, savoring this moment, our friendship, and how badly I wish I could just tell her everything. About magic school, the potion, Russ.

"We should get started."

Oh, boo. I hoped she wasn't gonna make me work. She pulls her bag onto the table and unzips it and I follow suit.

"So, Shelby didn't even call me to apologize. Buuuuut . . . Russ actually reached out."

"Russell-too-cool-for-anyone-but-himself?"

"Yeah, it was weird," she says, stacking index cards and Post-it Notes in neat rows and fidgeting with the same one over and over again. "He called and when I said hello he just hung up."

I set my hand on hers. "Nae, I'm sorry the party was a bust, but worrying about getting in with the cool kids is a waste of brainpower. You are brilliant. You don't need their approval."

She purses her lips. "Well, I might not need it but . . . it sure would make a girl look fly, you feel me?" She snorts.

"Russ is gonna get his for being such a jerk. Don't you worry."

"What are you planning?"

"Nae, it's me. Come on . . . I'm just saying when people are nasty like that, the universe makes sure they get theirs. You just keep being the star you are. Russ is gold-plated and that stuff wears off. You're eighteen karat, solid gold, boo."

She grins real big at that and flips her hair. I wish I could tell her that Russ's cockiness is gonna hold him back from getting the one thing he wants—Charms. But I bottle up that part of myself and listen to Nae go on about her mom's response to Shelby's parents talking about suing her over the incident. Utter ridiculousness.

All I can hope is that Russ losing out on what he wants teaches him something.

"Key, you listening?" Nae's shades are off again, and her eye actually looks a little better.

I blink. I didn't realize I zoned out. "Barely. I was up so late." I'm so tired.

"Doing what?"

I can't do this lying thing no more, geez. "Reading. Studying." That's at least true.

"Well, I'm proud of you."

She assumes I meant math and I let her. I pass her the worksheets I've been working on and she looks them over.

"You got a lot of these right on the first try." She slides them back to me and where there are usually a million red circles, I see only like ten.

"Oh well, wow. Look at me."

"You still need to hit those formulas a little harder. It's just memorization, that's all . . . Flash cards can—"

"OMG, Nae. You're killing me with all this math talk."

"This *is* our math tutoring date, you know."

"Uh, yeah, but since when do we actually spend the whole time studying? Give me all the gossip. That's what I want. You really think Shelby's gonna sue over busting her butt?"

She makes a face and wraps a rubber band around a wad of flash cards. "At least take these. Ten minutes a day."

I roll my eyes and tuck them away. "You spoil me."

"Oh, how was the theater, by the way? I am *dying* to see those pics. It was your first time going, right?"

Oh crap. "Uhh, yeah. Never been. I see why y'all like it so much. It was really . . ." *What, Kyana? What was the theater performance that you never went to like?* "Artsy? Artsy, yeah, artsy."

"Pics? Show me!" She gestures for me to pull out my phone.

"Oh." I pat my pockets. "I . . . uhhh . . . left my phone . . ."

Her phone dings. "Well, shoot. My momma's here."

Thank heavens.

"Text 'em to me." She hugs me tight. "Thanks so much for redeeming my birthday weekend. If this was all I did, it was everything I needed. You better keep doing your ten minutes a day. I'mma be able to tell if you ain't." We laugh, hug again, and the door closes behind her. I exhale. That was close. Lying is the worst. I don't see how some people do this all the time.

CHAPTER 9

*·**✳**·*

The week flies by.

I took a math quiz at some point. Those are always imprinted in my memory because hashtag traumatic. But the rest? A blur. All I could think about was getting back to magic school. Going a whole week without even talking spells with someone was torture.

When Saturday rolls around, I'm in the car before Momma. The parent notice sent home last weekend announced we'd be meeting somewhere other than the beauty shop this time for a field trip.

"You get out all your homework, right? This magic school stuff isn't eclipsing everything else, now, is it?"

"Yes, ma'am. I mean, yes on my homework. No to the eclipse."

She doesn't laugh. Momma's always serious when it comes to school talk. Matter of fact, she's always serious, period. Reason 3,423,847 why we need a real weekend.

"Your regular studies come first, Kyana. You can't put your stock in that magic stuff in case . . . you gotta be practical."

"I understand." I haven't told Momma about all the things I could do with magic one day. She didn't grow up with magic or anyone around her using magic, so she has no idea how big the possibilities are. I'm going to show her. She's gonna see how great of a witch I can be.

Park Row disappears and interstate stretches out in front of us. No idea why we're meeting clear on the other side of town today. I should have peeked at that notice before Momma threw it away. Bigger homes and taller buildings with windows that kiss the clouds surround us as we exit the freeway. I press a hand to the glass, taking it all in. The streets are wider and the wide lawns are sculpted and tidy. It's like I'm in a whole new city.

We park in front of a courtyard with an artsy-type structure in the center, and I hear birds chirping as I step out the car. People with little furry dogs on little furry leashes walk to and fro, coffee cups in hand. I squint in the high sun, reading the building's names.

ROCKFORD CITY HALL
4TH DISTRICT COURT

And behind us another building, this one with glowing green letters:

DEPARTMENT OF LABOR, SECTION X

Oo!

I spot my class, hug Momma goodbye, and rush to catch up to Ash, who's standing off by herself picking at her kiwi-colored nails. Everyone else is standing around, and I give Russ a wide berth. Ms. Mo's looking every which way, shouting directions into her phone.

"Ash, hey!" She wears her hair partly pulled back today and I can see her face a bit more. "I should have asked for your number. I been wondering all week how you been."

"Oh, yeah. Good thinking. I've been practicing all weekend."

"Me too!"

I tell her about the potion snafu with Nae's eye and her eyes bug out her head.

"No, you can't use potions like that on injuries. Certain ingredients will react with the first layer of the epidermis."

"Epi-what-is?"

"The skin. It probably swelled bigger."

"It did. How do you know all this?"

"I've been reading spell books since I could read."

How, though? She must sense my confusion.

"My mom's a witch, too. My whole family is, actually. That's why I'm homeschooled. My mom wanted to be able to teach me about what makes our family special."

"So, you just have magic around all the time?"

"Yeah."

Wow, what's that even like? Before I can fawn over her being miles ahead of me magically, Ms. Mo calls the group to attention.

"I mentioned a community project last class."

Heads nod.

"To complete your mandatory magical training," she says, "in addition to performing well at each lesson, you also must prepare a community project. These projects are the glue that binds our worlds." She points to the glowing green Section X sign, glances around, and flicks her wrist. The Section X letters shift, spelling MAGICK BOARD.

I gasp.

"The building behind me houses our Magick officials, including the committee that brings many students' community projects to life. So when you come up with ideas, think big. If you can dream it up, there's probably a magical way to make it be. I can show you better than I can tell you, so gather 'round." She motions for us to surround her.

"Restreso," she whispers, her wand pointed at an intersection nearby. There in the middle of the street, a person appears out of thin air. "Now watch."

Cars honk, windows roll down, and not so nice things are shouted at the person in the intersection, but there she still stands, unmoving. The whole thing makes me nervous. She's in the *middle* of the street!

"Shouldn't she maybe move? I—"

"Ssh!" Ms. Mo waves a hand at me. "It's not a real person. Just the image, a magical hallucination, if you will."

A car approaches the intersection and the driver's eyes are on his phone instead of the road. *Oh no!* I blink, and despite what Ms. Mo says, it looks all too real for my brain to be convinced this is safe. He's approaching at full speed and it takes everything in me not to scream. He's going to run right into her. The car slams into where she's standing with a *crunch* and I shield my eyes. Gasps bloom around me and, peeking between my fingers, I see the mannequin girl still standing there, and the car stopped inches from her, its front crumpled like it has slammed right into a brick wall.

An . . . *invisible* wall?

I blink again. The mannequin girl vanishes when Mo flicks her wand, and I exhale. The car is another story. At least the driver's okay. Ash's mouth is hanging wide open.

"That's wild," she mouths, and I agree.

"INVISO is run by one of the smartest whips in the magic business—Max Wriggly," Ms. Mo explains. "He has developed all sorts of invisible, safety-oriented products, but this is my favorite one. The bewitched barrier can sense when a person, or in this case the form of a person, is in harm's way. It solidifies, invisibly, stopping the vehicle. They're all over the city of Rockford, most near schools and in suburban areas. Wriggly was a General Spells student in my class. Really good friend of mine." She tucks some hair behind her ear. "His community project won accolades from every award body of witches and wizards that exists, including an offer to sit on the Grand Council of Magicians."

"Wow," Ash and I say at the same time. There's so much more to this magic stuff than I knew. I've got some more studying to do.

Even Russ is staring, eyes glazed like lemon pound cake. Ms. Mo's expression is suddenly very serious. "Listen here, innovation is our currency. It allows Magicks to live in harmony with everyone else. Now don't misunderstand me, we aren't able to brandish our gifts wherever we like. Magical Order Number 572, Section K, is clear: Magicks are not permitted to reveal their abilities as Magicks to any non-Magick folk. It's expressly forbidden. But we live off the radar, doing our part to make a better community for all of us."

Wind tugs at my hair. I gape at the spot the mannequin just was, then pull out my wand and roll it back and forth in my fingers.

I'm a part of something . . . Something *really* special.

Mo claps. "Should we see another?"

The collective "yes" is so loud a flock of birds nearby takes flight.

"Follow me—this one's a bit more fun."

We walk what feels like a hundred blocks. (It's actually only like three.) Ash drags me half the way and I help drag Eric.

"Finally," she says when we reach our destination: Areala's Aviary. Thin glass windows wrap every side of the larger-than-life birdhouse. Clusters of trees with colorful feathers ducking in and out peek at us from the inside.

"What is this place?" someone asks.

"A birdhouse," Ms. Mo explains. The archway entrance glows green and anticipation simmers through me.

"Wands in your pockets at all times," Ms. Mo says. Inside, the aviary isn't too crowded, but there are groups of kids with their parents, an older couple on a bench, and some randoms sipping drinks and swiping phones.

Ms. Mo peers around, then sets a determined foot in a direction. "Ah, there she is."

The person she was looking for is hard to make out. She's folded over a book on a bench, cloaked in the shadow of so much foliage you'd have to know she was there to spot her. She wears sunglasses and a heavy coat to her ankles, even though it's not nearly cold enough for all that. Her face is shaded in a wide-brim hat, and tendrils of coiled hair lie across her shoulders and fall down to her waist. We stick close to Ms. Mo's heels.

"Areala?"

The woman looks up, perplexed.

"Areala, it's me, Moesha."

Areala pulls off her glasses and the creases on her fore-head disappear. "Oh, Moesha, my goodness, girl. It's been so long."

"I hoped to catch you. Got a group of trainees here brainstorming their community projects. Hoped you could show them the . . ." Her eyebrows jump a few times.

"Anything for you, Mo." She grabs her hand. "You're doing such a good thing by these kids." She tucks her lip. "I heard . . . and if there's anything you—"

"OKAY!" Mo clears her throat. "My good friend Ms. Areala is going to show you a little trick she has up her sleeve. Come over here."

We gather up as a long-winged bird swoops by, its feathers a smear of rainbow pastels, and that's when it starts.

Chirping fills the air like a song of all different notes and tunes. Where there were a few birds a moment ago, the ceiling of the birdhouse is a cloud of colorful wings. The melody of humming rings like bells at different pitches, all somehow singing in beautiful harmony. A chorus of birds. Ms. Areala's eyes are closed as she says something too softly for me to hear.

"Links," Ash whispers in my ear. "These birds are part of her."

"She's making them sing?"

She nods.

Crowds gather, kids squeal, and cameras flash at the magnificent display. This is a dream. It has to be. More people crowd into the aviary to watch the show. I catch a glimpse of Ms. Mo just as she smooths something wet from her cheek.

Several more moments pass and Ms. Mo gathers us back up. "I hope what you've seen today gives you some ideas of the ways you can use your magic to make the world a little better. Your community project ideas are due next class. Be ready to present. That's it for today. Use the rest of this time to practice. Optional Specialties exams are next week, too."

I check my watch. I told Momma I'd be another hour at least. She's not gonna be excited about wasting gas to come all the way back. If she'd known it was gonna be a short class, she'd have waited. I want to get home to start practicing so I can do well with Charms next week. I pull out my phone to text her and a bazillion messages pop up on my screen.

Nae: Yo, where you at today? Meet up?

Nae: Helllloooooo?

Nae: OMG, Shelby is calling. Should I answer? 😳

Nae: KYANA????

Me: Hey sorry! Yeah. I can ask Momma to drop me off there. Unless you can come get me? I'm downtown.

"Kyana?" It's Ashley.

I tuck my phone away. "Hey."

"I was thinking, since we have extra time to practice today, if you want to come to my house, I can show you some charms and stuff? Maybe teach you some things."

"You'd do that?" *Oh, I need this.*

"Yeah. I'd love to have a frien—I mean, hang out with some . . . *you.* I would love to hang out with *you.*" Her gaze hits the floor. "But if you don't wanna hang out like that, that's fine. I—I mean . . . we don't have to like call us friends or anything. I was just . . ."

She is seriously so nice. "Well, too bad because that's exactly what I'm going to call you—friend."

She beams.

"Let's do it. I mean, I have to ask my mom, but it's probably okay."

If Ash can teach me a thing or two, my hopes to get Charms may not be a complete bust. We head toward her mom's car and I pull out my phone to call Momma, grateful I now have good news to share: that she doesn't have to drive right back. But Nae's message pops up on the screen.

Nae: Yay! What time?

My finger hovers over the keyboard . . .

Me: Actually, today's no good. Library tomorrow
 though, right?

Nothing for several moments.

Nae: Sure.

CHAPTER 10

* ** ✳ ** *

Momma said I could go to Ashley's but I wasn't gonna ride with somebody's momma she hadn't met. She actually wasn't too far away since she'd had an errand nearby. Relieved I missed that smoke.

So she came to get me and we looped by our house, popped into the store for a few things because she "isn't sending me to anybody's house hungry," and then she dropped me off. Ash's house is not too far from Nae's neighborhood on the far side of the Row, with deep driveways and brick fronts. The manicured lawns are replicas of one another like the houses, but for a different door color here and there.

Except for Ash's. Her lawn is shaded by a wide, winding tree, bushes wrestling one another for sunlight, and clusters of purple plants I've never seen before, next to a sign that reads, Don't Step on the Splaukens. They Bite.

Baubles hang from eaves, chiming in the wind. And yard signs fill the lawn, so close you can hardly read any of them.

FURRY & FREE – WE ALL DESERVE TO BE

I scratch my head, following a tapestry of cobblestone and glassy blue pavers to the door, and ring the doorbell.

Nothing happens.

I ring it again. Still nothing. I step through the army of signs to reach a window.

Tap. Tap. Tap. "Hello, Ash? I'm outside." *Tap.*

"I hear ya all right." The window rises and falls with each word, talking to me. "Jus' a minute now with all that ruckus."

"Oh, I'm sorry. I didn't mean—"

"Sure you di'nt." The window clatters. "The rubbin' 'n' scrubbin', it's a downright nightmare. Hind's sore for a week a'leas."

"Kyana!" A door creaks open and Ash pokes her head out.

"Sorry!" I say to the window before scooting inside.

"Sorry, ignore Beverly. Window-cleaning days always make her grumpy."

Inside Ash's house is a dream. The furniture's normal

enough, but where the TV would be on the wall is a trophy case of fancy wigs, with rows of bookshelves on either side. I pluck a wizard figurine from it and turn it in my hands. The figure holds a purple-striped flag with a *WZ* wound into tree branches embroidered in its center.

"Winzhobble," she says, tapping its hat.

Where all magic originated, I remember Scooter explaining.

"A mog pie a day keeps the frog flies away," the figurine says, its eyes glowing. I yelp and almost drop it. Didn't expect that.

"Sorry." Ash takes it up and sets it back on the shelf.

"Did it say *frog* fly?"

"Yeah. Be glad frogs here only hop."

Winzhobble. A whole place full of magic? "Cool," I say under my breath. Ash leads me into what I think is a living room, but behind a big ole mustard sofa is a stove. And next to it is a funny-looking . . . toilet?

"Uhhh—"

She hides a chortle behind her hand. "That's not what you think." She tugs its lever and it gurgles. "It's for shoe cleaning." She puts her foot inside the toilet, pulls it out, and it sparkles. "Mom's *real* particular about the carpet."

"Shoe cleaning," I repeat. *Wow.*

"Benji Charles here," a staticky voice bellows from a TV in the corner of the room. The man on-screen waves a wand

and the papers on his desk float through the air and double in size, hovering over his shoulder. He smooths his pink feather vest and clears his throat. "More developments in the Magical Artifact investigation coming to you first, from WNZ, Channel Seven, this evening. With social unrest in Winzhobble at an all-time high, could a second migration be on the horizon? And are tensions coming to a boil between Rockford mayor Alfred Applegate and Magick Board chair Dr. Cromwell Dixon? Benji Charles here with these stories and more after this."

"Oh, sorry, I can turn that off." Ash swishes her wand and a cord plugged into the back of the TV twitches.

"How'd you get that channel?"

"Oh, Wizard News? It comes on three times a day, just need one of these." She tugs on the cord and, with a bit of fancy work with her wand, hands me a replica of it. "Plug that in the back. Might have to wiggle it, but it should work. And it'll open up a bunch of channels, not just the news."

"Wow." I tuck the cord in my pocket. "Thanks."

She leads me to what I think is the kitchen, but there's no fridge or doors on the cabinets. Canisters, potion jars, cereal boxes, fuzzy contraptions, and a whole wall of honey line floor-to-ceiling shelves.

"You want a snack or something?" She offers me a square, fudge-looking treat and I bite into it.

An explosion of citrus flavor is fireworks on my tongue. "Man, that's good."

"Have more. Mom gets tons of these."

I scoop as many as my hands can hold and fill my cheeks. "WHUH OS IS?" I swallow. "Sorry, what is this? It's chocolaty with a bit of orange, I think? So yummy."

"Kietchy Squares."

"Never heard of it."

She hands me the package. "Certified made by the UCW, United Covens of Winzhobble. Mom's big on buying stuff made by us."

"Yeah, my mom, too. I mean, not the witch thing, but like buying stuff made by Black folks. I don't even know where to find treats like this." I grab a few more and move a box of springy doodads and colorful streamers out of a chair to take a seat.

"Glenda's Grocery," she says, scooting in a chair beside me.

"Glenda's a witch?"

"*Yep.*" She purses her lips knowingly. "Back behind where she sells fresh tortillas is a whole section of magic supply stuff. Go check it out." Ash is so much more comfortable at home.

"I'm gonna tell Momma."

"Fifteen percent discount on everything else for student-witch families, too."

"Oh then, she's definitely gonna be about it." We laugh.

"You're really nice for doing this." I pull out my spell book and flip it open to a charm I found the other night: CushyKicks. "And I brought these." I pull out a pair of Momma's work shoes. "This charm is supposed to make it feel like she's walking on clouds."

Ash drags a finger down the page. "Yeah, that looks like an easy one. Up from the table and wand out." She stands, knees locked, back straight, and I mimic her. "You want good posture, helps your diaphragm and larynx position right." She lifts my elbow, presses my shoulders down, and lifts my chin. "Confident, but not too much."

Who knew all this went into proper spellcasting?

"And speed is king with charms. Magic can sense indecision. When you call on your magic, command it quickly and with certainty." She hands me one of Momma's shoes. "You can do it. Try."

I glance at the spell one more time, take a deep breath, and ready my posture.

"C-Casorti clototum."

The shoe flies from my grip and crashes into a window.

"*Oowwww*," Beverly howls. "That's 'bout it. I done had it with you lot!"

"Shoot. Sorry, Beverly!"

Ash casts her wand and pulls back. The shoe careens through the air toward me and I catch it just as it pummels into my stomach.

"Oops," I say.

"It's okay."

"It's not okay! I'm so bad at all this."

"You are not. It just takes pr—"

"Gurty? *Gurrrty?*" Ash's mom must be home.

"Mom, don't call me that, please. I have a friend over."

" 'Gurty'?" I say under my breath.

"Gertrude. It's my middle name. After my great-great-fifteenth-great grandmother. *Please* don't tell anyone."

I zip my lips as Ash's mother gives me a once-over. "Well, hello there." She squeezes my shoulders, pursing her bright pink–painted lips. She sucks in a breath with award-deserving theatrical dramatics. "A *friend*, you say?" She twirls me around. "Is she a witchy one?"

"Yes, Mom." Ash stares at her feet.

"Oh, even better! I'm Janice." She shakes my hand and throws an arm around my shoulder, leading me deeper into the house. A seat nudges the back of my knees and I plop into it. "How familiar are you with the groit population and its exploitation in this country?"

"I, uhm . . . What's a groit?"

She pulls a wand from her hair, taps her hand, and a plate of chocolate cookies appears in one of my hands, a glass of warm milk in the other. And I can't even resist. I mean, they're good.

"Might I have the opportunity to earn your and your mother's support?"

"Uhm, yes?"

"Did you know a groit is whisked away to captivity every 4.7 seconds?"

"No, I—"

"And did you know, of the seventy species of magical creatures, groits are the most ancient? More of them die from being caged than from starvation. And that's saying something, considering the streets are full of strays."

"No, actually, I—"

"And did you know these breeders are stripping them of their coats, chopping off their paws for key chains, saying they've got magical powers, and selling them to pad their pockets? It's despicable."

"I didn't—"

"But Furry and Free simply won't stand for it." She taps a pin with the logo on her chest. "We're organizing, lobbying. The Board *will* face our demands, you understand?"

I nod, stuffing another cookie in my mouth.

"Her mom's not a witch, Mom." Ash rubs her temples, mouthing, "Sorry."

Ashley's mom is befuddled at that. "Well, can I count on *your* support for Furry and Free?"

"Furry and Free has my vote." I give her a thumbs-up.

Her smile widens as she flicks her wand, and a pin like hers appears on my chest. "Well, good talk . . ."

"Kyana."

"Kyana, lovely chat." She pats my shoulder. "And

welcome." She pokes Ash's cheek, a keen expression on her face. "You should bring your friends around more often, dear. I'm off to make more flyers. You two let Lou know if you need something." She takes the box of colorful streamers, chanting "You have to dream to believe . . . believe to achieve . . . believe in the dream" under her breath as she disappears down the hallway.

Ash wears a sideways smile. "She gets intense about her magical creature activism stuff. Thanks for not making a big deal. Hopefully the bribery cookies were good at least."

"They were perfection."

We laugh.

"Now, where were we?"

* ✻ ✻ ✳ ✻ * ✻

When the sun dipped low, Lou—who, I learned, is the stove—reminded the lights to turn on and then spit out some dinner, which reminded me it was probably about time to go. I texted Momma that I was ready to be picked up, and now she is on her way. Ash showed me the shoe charm a few more times and left me to practice on my own.

She's across the room hunched over her own spell book, arguing with a digital clock.

"Casorti clo-toe-toe-tum," I say, giving the shoe charm one more try. But the shoe tries to wiggle away. I set it aside. *This is a bust. I'm no good at this.* What *am* I good at? Ugh.

"No, don't . . . !" Ash bangs the clock with her wand, blowing a rogue strand of hair.

"What's up?

"Spirits are just so stubborn. And when I actually manage to connect with an Available, I sound like a blubbering idiot. One of them was listening to me for a solid two minutes. But when he asked me to convince him the properties of blue-ringed octopus venom are only fractionally understood, I froze. And I know that answer like the back of my hand."

"Just be yourself, Ash."

"I did. That's the problem." She sighs. "Any luck on your end?"

"Nope."

We plop down on the couch and I sip the dregs of my milk.

"I keep telling myself it's gonna get easier," she says.

"It will for you. You're brilliant, Ash." *Now, me? That's a different story.*

"AACHHHOOO!" Ash's mom shouts, popping up out of nowhere.

I yelp, milk splashing over the edge of my cup as something shoves me from the couch. My bum slams to the ground. Where there were plush cushions, a shiny plastic coating gleams. The milk spillage rolls down the plastic sofa cover and disappears.

"The splaukens are blooming," Ash's mom says, blowing her nose. "Gets to me every year. Sorry, honey, didn't mean to scare you. Ran out of tape." She smooths a hand over the couch before digging in a drawer.

I blink, and the sofa's not plastic covered anymore.

"Mom keeps SofaSeal on at all times," Ash says. "It's better than the actual plastic cover my grandma had."

Ash's mom shoves a twenty into her hand. "Go see Russell and grab me another SofaSeal, will you, Gerty? That was the last one."

"Sure thing, Mom." Ash turns to me. "That's Russ's one redeeming quality—he actually makes useful stuff. Wanna come?"

"Wait, Russ lives near you?"

"Yep, just a few houses down."

"And your mom is a *client* of his?"

"Yeah. I mean, the boy has talent. And then there's . . ."

"There's what?"

It's cool outside and Ash lets the door close good before answering. "You'll see."

Evening light kisses the street and kids ride their bikes up and down the sidewalk, parents at their side. Russell's house is like the other cookie cutters, but his has a red door. A couple boys I recognize from school huddle in Russell's driveway. Is that Calvin from the basketball team, and his teammate? Calvin's not a wizard, is he? He lives by me. If he was, he'd be hanging at PRMA, right?

Russ steps outside and his eyes dart in our direction. He chews his lip while exchanging something with Calvin, angling his body so we can't see. Transaction done, he disappears inside and they leave.

As Ash and I approach his door, a herd of cats loitering on the porch scatters, leaving a sweet, peachy scent in their wake.

"This is what I was talking about," she whispers, pointing to the cats before knocking at the door.

Russ pokes his head out the door. "More SofaSeal?"

"Yes. Just one," Ash says.

He disappears inside a second. Then he hands her a box with yellow-and-blue ribbons like I saw at PRMA and she gives him the twenty.

"That's it?" he asks.

"Yes." Ash talks to her shoes.

"Okay, well, thanks for your business. Tell your mom I appreciate it." His door clicks shut.

"You gotta work on eye contact, girl," I say as we walk away. "That's the first thing we're gonna do with you."

She leans in, whispering, "Those groits on his porch . . ."

"The cats?"

Ash snorts. "Groits are not cats. They were imported en masse from Winzhobble after that virus thing got bad here. Their diet consists of flowers and any remnants of bad germs they can find, and their gastrointestinal system turns them into antimicrobial waste. Basically isopropanol. So when they spray . . ."

"Like a skunk?"

"Yeah. They emit a flowery fragrance and actually disinfect anything in a quarter-mile radius."

"Lysol cats? Honestly, didn't see that coming."

She laughs. "But when some man in a small town in Texas started breeding them, calling himself GroitKing, they were outlawed as pets. So conservationists transfigured them, disguising them as cats. I'd bet money those are groits and not stray cats around his house. Keeping them captive is illegal, you know."

"So I've learned." I tap the Furry and Free pin on my chest. "So you think Russ's family is breeding and selling Lysol cats?" I ask louder than I mean to.

"Sssh! Yes, which could get him in huge trouble."

"I'm pretty sure Calvin isn't a wizard and he wasn't there borrowing a cup of sugar. I bet Russ was selling Calvin a charm," I whisper.

"You think so?"

"Yeah! I wouldn't put anything past him if it makes him money."

"You'd think someone with so much to hide would be more careful being so rude to people," she says.

"You'd think. We could take him down a peg if we told someone." *I'd love to see that.*

"Well, being on his sort of good side sucks already," Ash says. "I don't wanna know what it's like to be on Russ's bad side. And even if we wanted to, I don't have any proof he's doing anything against the rules."

I cut a glance at Russ's house behind us and spot him staring from a window.

Our eyes meet. No proof *yet*.

He snatches the curtain closed.

CHAPTER 11

＊✳*＊*

Monday was a typical start of the week at first, until I tripped and face-planted while trying to sneak-read my spell book walking to fifth period. Tuesday was a little better because we had a pep-rally half day, which meant no afternoon class. Hashtag winning!

Wednesday was when the world started to rotate off its axis. It started when I overslept, which snowballed into me being late to school, which turned into me waiting around in the main office for a hallway pass. And who else did they assign to escort me to my class but second period hall monitor *Russ*?

I could feel him staring at me the whole time, waiting for me to say something. But I glued my mouth shut. You don't get to be mean to Nae but play nice with me. Nope. Friend Rules 101.

"Nothing to say, huh?" he said before I stepped into my class.

"About what?"

"You know about what. What you coming around my house for, you and Ash, whispering and whatnot?"

Ooo, he thought I saw what he gave to Calvin. It *must* have been magic. Why else would he be so defensive? "I can walk around where I choose. It's a free country." I opened the door to class and turned back before slipping inside. "And if I were you, I'd be careful who you're mean to."

"That a threat?"

I didn't dignify him with an answer, closing the door on his clenching jaw. And for a moment I was on top of the world.

Until Thursday.

Thursday was a tornado.

Like literally, we had to do the tornado drill for real, and that was scary. Classes were shorter too and we spent a lot of time in the gym. Russ and his boys gave me side-eyes the whole while and now whenever I pass the basketball team, the hallway explodes in a swarm of whispers.

Friday morning came finally and just when I thought I'd get through the week at Thompson by sticking to the shadows, I smashed a pen all over my shirt in front of the whole class. The girls' bathroom is always empty between third and fourth period. Right before lunch, teachers act funny about letting you take a bathroom break. But with this inkblot all over me and my hands looking like I'm 'bout to fingerpaint, Ms. Rios practically shoved me out the classroom.

The water is cold as ice and the bowl's coated in blue. I have half a mind to pull out my wand and try a spell to get this stubborn stain off, but who am I kidding? The spells I've tried have been hit or miss. Mostly miss.

I feel for the lump in my backpack, just to make sure it's still there. Ms. Mo said not to let it out of our sight, so I don't. My spell book—all my magic stuff, in fact—stays with me all the time. Sometimes I peek at it, pinching myself to be sure all this is actually real.

I grab another paper towel and blot my shirt. I kinda feel bad for even thinking about investigating Russ. Getting people in trouble isn't my style, but what he's doing could get out of hand and expose us all. Then what? Magic is the best thing that's happened to me and even though I suck at it currently, I don't wanna lose it because he's being careless. I sigh. As much I want to dig into Russ's business, my stomach still flips at the idea.

I scrub my hands until the blue stains are hardly noticeable, then pull a sweater out of my book bag. A snapback falls out. It's turquoise leopard print and *so cute* I couldn't resist grabbing it from Ms. Mo's stack. I set it on my head and pose in the mirror for a quick second. I'm wrapped up in stringy fibers one moment, and the next, robes flutter at my feet in jungle shades of green. My hair tips balayaged honey blond.

Creak.

I dash into a stall. Crap! My bag's still open, wand poking out. I snatch it up and slip back inside the stall, where I rip the hat off my head. In a blink my clothes are normal again.

"Ahem." I flush the toilet to make it extra believable and come out the stall, to find Nae.

"Oh, hey," she says.

"Hey!" I hug her. "Cute! Where'd you get this?" She snatches the snapback and plops it on her head.

"Nooooo!" I tackle her and we tumble to the floor. "I— Sorry . . . it's, uhm, not ready yet." I shove the hat in my backpack. Her transforming into robes *cannot* happen. "I'm bedazzling it for you as a belated birthday gift."

"Uhhh, okay, weirdo. No need to linebacker rush me. Geez."

"Sorry!" I brush us both off and throw my sweater on over my shirt.

Rrrrriiiing. In seconds, the restroom floods with foot traffic.

Nae and I slip out the door and make our way to the cafeteria. Once we have our trays of obligatory, unidentifiable cafeteria food, we veer through the crowd to a table. Without a word, she takes my fruit and I take her chocolate milk. It's just our thing.

"So," she says with a bright-eyed look. "I'm thinking about a way to make up for my party." She piles a stack of glittery notebooks, all in mermaid print, on the table. "I have an idea. I wanna see what you think."

"Nae, I told you 'bout—"

"Hear me out! I'm thinking BIG and I'm not even planning to invite Russ. I just thought I'd get some good popularity cred if I have people over for a little themed party thing to launch my"—she drumrolls on the table—"class president campaign. I'm calling it Nails and Mermaid Tails! What you think?"

"Class president? I mean, I can't think of anyone better, Nae, but what's your motive? I think this popularity thing might have gone to your head."

She rolls her eyes and flips open a notebook. "So, the Math Club will all be there because I'm the president, duh. And this time it won't conflict with a game or anything so no excuses." She flips her journal around to face me. "I even made this little invitation. Figured you could help with the nail art. You're so good at that."

I survey the book in front of me. It's scribbled on both sides, with color-coded notes and dates. She hasn't just designed an invitation; she's made an entire political campaign.

I fold my arms. "Nae."

"Don't give me that look. I hardly see you anymore! And this is gonna be fun. Come on."

She's right. I've hardly seen her this week between keeping my nose in my spell book and trying charms with Ash after school.

"You know I'd be a good class president. And, I mean, do you want Shelby to get it? Word is, she's the only other person running."

"Ugh, no. Okay, *fine*."

She gives a little applause. Any more excitement and she might burst.

"Oh, look who it is," Russ says, passing by with his boys in tow. I wave my hand in front of my face just in case. Not wanting to get caught up with any of his magically altered auras. I swat the air in front of Nae's face, too, and she crinkles her eyebrows.

"What's up, Nae? Kyana?" He closes the notebook Nae's doodling in and his boys snicker.

So he's showing off? What a turd.

"Still feeling super full of yourself, Kyana?" he asks.

"Me? You clearly live on a different planet."

"Go away, Russ. We don't talk to people who lie about coming to a party," Nae claps back, snatching her notebook open.

"You have some nerve. I told you not to mess with us," I say, angling my back to him. Not even worth the conversation.

"No, *you* have some nerve," Russ says to me. A crowd is

forming around us. "You think you can threaten me? That's not even cool for . . . for a lot of reasons."

I hop up. "I didn't threaten you. I made a recommendation, which you're clearly not listening to."

"Key, sit down," Nae says. "Don't even bother with him. Nobody wanted you at my party anyway, Russ. We're having another event and you're not even on the list."

"Oh, I'm so sad," he teases. "Is it even a party if I'm not there?" He pops his collar and backs away. "Ain't nobody coming. That's a bet." The crowd dissolves as fast as it came.

That's it! I flip out my phone and text Ash.

Me: Mission Prove Russ Is Spilling The Beans On
Magic is officially on. You in?

"I could pinch that smug grin of his until he squeals," Nae says. "He makes me so mad. What's his beef with you, anyway?"

"I don't know." My phone buzzes.

Ash: OMG, really??? Ok ok. Let's do it. 😬

Nae sucks her teeth. "Key, you have no idea, really?"

Where would I even start explaining? At *I didn't hang out with you last Saturday because I hung with another friend and we happened to see our nemesis, Russ*? Or at *Hi,*

I'm a witch and Mr. Popular is secretly breeding magical creatures and selling charms to regular ole people? Feigning ignorance is easier.

"I don't know, Nae," I say, tucking my phone away, wheels already turning on how I can catch Russ in his hustle.

"You wouldn't keep nothing from me, would you?"

I hesitate, the truth on the tip of my tongue. What would she say if I told her? Would she be mad? Understanding? Both?

I can't be all about Russ breaking the rules if I'm gonna tell this major secret to my best friend. What if it gets out?

"Nae, come on. I don't know what his deal is." *And I don't, not entirely anyway.*

The longer I'm around Russ, the more his cockiness seems like a shell for a chip on his shoulder. But I don't care, somebody's gotta teach him. Once I dangle some hard evidence in his face, he'll shut up then. Bet.

"If you say so . . . Lately I just feel like you're not telling me everything. You've been distant or something."

Or something. Ding ding ding. Survey says, "CORRECT!"

"I'm going to do better at making time to hang out. I've had so much going on with . . . everything." Hanging with Ash is time I used to spend with Nae. Maybe the solution is hanging out together? "And oh, there's this girl I met that doesn't live too far from us. She's real cool. I think you'd like her. I thought maybe we could all hang out. Plan the Nails and Mermaid Tails thing together?"

Nae raises an eyebrow. "This a new friend or something?"

"Yeah, she's homeschooled, so she doesn't know a lot of people at Thompson. *And* she's no fan of Russ, either. You wanna get together maybe this weekend?"

Nae opens her mouth to speak but closes it. She picks at her nail polish, pursing her lips, and the silence hangs there for several minutes. "Sure, all right. I'll meet your new friend."

CHAPTER 12

*∗∗✳∗∗

The Saturday crowd's a little thinner at Ms. Mo's when we arrive.

I'm in the chair first. Fishman Stan's already made his run—early today, I guess. I grab a plate from the tower of foam on the coffee table.

"Thanks, Moesha." Momma slips a twenty into her apron.

Going natural today. She has me out the bowl, my twist-out done in no time, and next thing I know I'm hugging Momma goodbye.

"Be on your best behavior." She pinches my cheek and I pull away.

"Momma, I'm not three."

Once she's out the door, I say what's up to Lucy and she

lets me on through. Two people I don't recognize from last time are in the classroom, stacks of giant boxes in their arms.

"Where do you want them?" asks the taller of the duo—the mother, maybe?

"Over there is good." Eric points at the supply closet behind me. "Oh hey, Kyana!"

The mother follows Eric's directions, blond bob swaying. A girl in a pleated skirt and blazer sets down her box then retrieves another. Who dresses like that on a Saturday? We meet eyes but they don't say anything. I crane for a peek at what's in the boxes. Jars and pouches in all different sizes and colors. Some are half full, others look brand-new and unopened. A few books and a canister of green sickle-shaped somethings are also in a box.

"What's all this stuff?" I ask no one in particular.

Ash slides up next to me. "Some donated things from the Magick academy over in Berkeley Oaks. Guess we're running low? I don't know."

Berkeley Oaks? That's one of those neighborhoods Momma says I'm not ever allowed to go to without an adult. She said Black folks going over there, especially kids, doesn't usually go well. We drove through once and it looked like a bunch of houses big enough to be ten houses in one, with security guards and fountains out front.

"They have a magic school, too?" *Of course they do.* There are witches and wizards all over Rockford.

"Oh yeah," Ash says. "You've probably seen it."

"Nah, we don't drive over there much."

"You ever heard of the Rockford Arts and Learning Center?"

"Uh, yeah." It's like a giant museum full of arts and crafts, space station models, virtual reality manipulation chambers. It's like a kids' dream play place. "My school visited there on a field trip one year."

"Yeah . . . *that's* their magic school. After hours, of course."

"Wow!"

Mo thanks the blond duo as they set down the last few items, and the class shuffles to their desks.

"Of course," the mother says, tucking her purse tight to her body. "No problem. Hope it helps. Come along, Perstefanie."

Pleated Skirt looks Ash up and down and smirks. "See ya later, polka-dot panties."

Her mother turns pink and pulls her along quickly. Everything inside me runs hot.

"Her name's Ashley!"

But they don't look back.

"Ash, I'm sorry—"

"Don't worry about it." She picks at the band of her watch, avoiding the eyes of everyone probably wondering, like me, how she knows Preppy Girl. "She's just like that. And all her friends. I used to go to school with her."

"You went to private school in the rich neighborhood?"

"I had a full scholarship." She picks at her nails. "I scored off the charts on their placement test or something. Anyway, Perstefanie was class president like every year. So, everyone listens to her. And well, I mean, I did leave my extra undies out that one time after gym. So I guess I earned the nickname. Whatever, it's fine."

"No, it's not," I say as everyone else goes back to minding their own business, curiosity satisfied apparently.

Except for Eric. He comes over, hands in his pockets. "Sorry, Ash. I didn't know kids were like mean to you like that. Don't listen to Perstefanie or whatever her name is. She's probably jealous because you're so smart."

"Right," I say. "I'm pretty sure you're the smartest witch here. She's clearly just hating."

"Yep!" Eric and I pound fists.

Ash blushes and tucks a green strand behind her ear. "You guys are nice."

"We're honest!" I nudge her with my hip and her smile grows. I scramble for something else encouraging to say to make sure Ashley knows how great she is. I don't want some popular rich witch getting her down on herself. But Mo's voice booms across the class before I can get another word out.

"To your tables, please. We'll do some warm-up, review, and then hold our specialty exams for those who have chosen to participate."

The class groans and most of us are on the edge of our seats, but a couple folks are completely chilled at their desks, content with a Gen Spells designation. *I want to at least try.*

"If you're not sitting the exam, hang tight. We'll be presenting community project ideas afterward! Always helpful to see where your mind is at while I'm putting finishing touches on specialty designations."

Mo's words are a sucker punch. My community project. I haven't even given it a second thought. And it could have helped me make a case for getting Charms. Shame twists in my gut.

After practicing wand posture and wrist motion in unison for what feels like forever, we move into a quick warm-up of a basic General Spell for extracting beetle juice. Ms. Mo watches all of us carefully. I grab a bug from a jar at the front of the class and bile hovers in my throat. I'm just thankful it's not still alive. I shudder and pick up my wand. The spell on the board is half smudged, so I squint to see it.

KO NO LASIUM

General Spells aren't about speed, so I take my time to follow each step and do it right. I mean, how can I make a case for Charms if I can't even get basic spells right? I set the beetle in the middle of the petri dish and press him flat. His papery belly is soft like a pimple that needs to pop. "Ugh."

As I look away to gulp down air I catch sight of Ashley. She's wearing a mask and gloves. Why didn't I think of that?

The next step on the board says to angle the wand at its belly, then tap twice while saying the spell. Here goes nothing.

"Ko no lasium," I say with fairly clear pronunciation the first time, tapping once, then twice. I suck in a breath and hold the bug there, willing my puke back down as yellowy liquid oozes out of the beetle's insides onto the dish.

"There!" I throw my hand up. "I did it." I drop off my dish at the front, trying my best to ignore my bubble guts, and notice Ash had enough to fill two dishes. Magic comes so naturally to her, I swear.

With warm-up spells over, we move into stations for our first test: Potions. For a split second I consider throwing the test, so that by comparison I would do better on Charms. Then I see Momma yelling at me on the back of my eyelids. That's *not* how we do things.

My cauldron waits for me and I flip to the potion for today. The instructions seem clear enough and I go through the motions. But without disgusting bug guts to distract me, my mind flits back to my community service project. My shoulders slump. I can't believe I *forgot* to brainstorm a community project.

Maybe I can come up with something quickly? On the fly? Momma always says we do our best and at least try.

I scan my brain for an idea or something. I won't have anything written down, but if I could at least think of something
to say, surely that'd be better than nothing. My potion bubbles under my nose and I sift in a handful of Potion Base and
squeeze a few drips of wig glue like the instructions say.

What kind of project could I use charms for?

I wind my wand backward, then forward, then set my
cauldron over a fire for twenty seconds. I let it cool down
and repeat the process, half distracted the entire time.

Think, Kyana.

Potion complete. But the brew is watery and stinks like
sweat. That can't be right. My fingers hover over a stock of
ingredients and lion's mane twinkles at me or something.
I take a few strands and put them in. I turn up the heat
because . . . I don't know, it feels right. My potion simmers.
Ms. Mo passes by, silently jotting down notes.

"Doyanas yeti zorum," I say, aiming at the pot with my
wand. It rumbles and the mixture thickens.

"That's looking almost right, Kyana," Ms. Mo says,
peering over the edge of my cauldron. "Excited to hear what
you got planned."

I didn't even look at the Potions section of my book until
today. But I don't burst her bubble. I'm just so glad this brew
is coming together somewhat. I smile and Ms. Mo disappears to fawn over a sock puppet Russ has charmed to do a
jig. If I roll my eyes any harder, they'll get stuck in my head.

I pour my potion into a container, stopper it, then clean my pot. At least that charm I know pretty well. I rack my brain for an idea but come up with nothing. All I can think of is food. And how is food relevant in any sort of way that matters? Or Potions? Charms is where it's at.

A candle floats to each desk as Mo writes on the board.

Charm: Pyrominus tranquantum

"For your Charms test, you'll be attaching a calming aura to this candle," she says. "So that when it's lit, anyone around it feels relaxed."

I tighten my grip on my wand.

"You have fifteen seconds. Go!"

"Pie-row-miny-us," I say, winding my wrist, my heart lodging in my throat. "Trantum."

Nothing happens. My shoulders cinch and I open my mouth to try again, when I hear Russ next to me muttering something different entirely. *What in the—?* He catches me staring and winks as his candle lights.

"Two seconds," Mo says.

I bite down, ignoring him, and shove the words out. "Pyrominus . . ."

"One second."

"Tran . . ." *Don't mispronounce!*

"Time! Wands down."

"Tranquantum!" Purple powder shoots from my wand

136

tip and my candle flickers with flame. Judging by Ash's desk, I did it right. But was I fast enough? I bite my lip.

"Russ," Ms. Mo says. "Clever, but I noticed you used a modifier. Those were *not* the instructions."

"But the modifier works more efficiently, to—"

"Following instructions matters, Mr. Watkins. A lot."

He snaps his lips shut, sullen.

"Kyana, good job, but you finished right after time." She pushes her mouth sideways. "Still, pretty good." She turns to Ashley. "Simply superb, Ash."

I sigh, shoving my spell book aside. First I fail at my big homework assignment and then I basically mess up on my Charms test.

Is that what I do—fail things?

Apparently.

What if I blow my chance and Mo thinks I'm not taking this serious and kicks me out?

With stations cleaned, a girl named Tiffany is up first to share her project idea. I resist the urge to bury my head in my arms on my desk and try to pay attention to Tiff and the others after her. But after Brandice's invisible-braces idea and Leah's grocery-gardening concept, my eyes glaze over. One presentation blurs into the next until—

"All right, girls," Ms. Mo says, and all eyes are on me and Ash. "Kyana, Ashley, who'd like to go next? You two are the last ones."

My time to think of something on the fly is up.

"Ashley?" Ms. Mo says.

Ash is probably over there about to have an anxiety attack about speaking in front of the class. "I'll go, Ms. Mo," I say.

Ashley smiles in thanks, savoring her last few minutes sans the spotlight.

"The truth is . . ." I'm not shy about public speaking and even I have bubble guts right now. "I didn't have . . . I didn't *make* time to do my homework. I don't have any ideas of what my project could be yet." I try to hold my chin up, but the look on Ms. Mo's face casts my gaze right to the floor.

"That's very disappointing, Kyana. I know how much this means to you, so I expected you to be putting your all into this opportunity."

"Well, I mean—" Russ starts.

"No commentary from you is needed, Russell, thank you." Ms. Mo cuts him off but doesn't hide her disappointment.

Ash is up at the front and I couldn't feel any more small. Magic is supposed to be my one special thing. Ash clears her throat and I try to at least artificially perk myself up to give her any confidence juju I have.

She taps a rolled-up scroll with her wand and it sprawls open, larger than the whiteboard. On it is a picture of what looks like a science lab: lab tables, microscopes, pipettes, and a Bunsen burner spring to life right there.

"So . . ." Her cheeks go rosy. "I'd really like Charms as a specialty so I can go into Summoning. And I think my idea makes a great case of why I'd be good at it." She taps the presentation. "I want to create a bio research lab that can investigate and test all sorts of potentially hazardous diseases like that virus we had a while back, but using tethered Availables instead of people. That way the research staff isn't at risk of getting infected. I'd like to tether spirits to microscopes, pipettes, vacuum pumps, glassware, centrifuges, stuff like that, and let it all operate hands-free."

What a cool idea! Ash catches my eye and I point to my eyes, then back at her, to remind her about eye contact.

"Ashley, that's an absolutely ingenious idea." Ms. Mo beams.

Ash lifts her chin and addresses Ms. Mo. "Thanks. I've actually been able to hold an Available for a full seven minutes, but no luck tethering yet. I—I've been practicing every day."

Ms. Mo checks off something on her clipboard. Okay, Ash is getting Charms. She *has* to be. Which means there's one other spot. It can't go to Russ—it has to go to me!

"Well, I can't wait to see what all you do as a witch in our community, Ms. Ashley. I'm so impressed." She turns to the class. "I think I've seen enough. Who's ready for their designation?"

My stomach drops. The whole class gathers in a circle

and Ash and I grip hands, fingers crossed. I even put one foot over the other so my legs are crossed and tangle my arms up. All crossables crossed, I await the news. Ms. Mo flips through papers on a clipboard once more.

"All right. Deep breaths. Remember, no area of focus is more important than any other. You'll all come to love your skill. I tried to consider your preferences where I could, but the tests did weigh heavily in my decision. And in many cases confirm my leanings."

I'm going to pee my pants from sheer nervousness. And probably fall over because standing cross-legged is harder than it looks.

"Tiffany Boyden . . . General Spells."

Everyone claps. Russ makes a big to-do. Tiff looks genuinely pleased, smiling as she takes the paper Mo gives her.

"Is that what you wanted?" I whisper.

She nods.

"Congrats!"

Mo calls another several names. My surname is Turner, so I'm used to being last. Everyone's gotten General Spells and most seem fine with that.

"Ashley Martinez," Ms. Mo says, and Ash's nails dig into my arm. I yelp.

"Sorry!"

"Charms," Ms. Mo says.

"Ahh!!!" We jump up and down. There's actual applause coming from somewhere, too.

"Geez, excited much?" Russ says. "Watch it, Turner, hanging out with Weirdo One is making you Weirdo Two."

"Ignore him," I say to Ash, who is so overcome with joy at her designation she's hardly paying any attention to Russ. "He's just jealous you did better than him on the Charms test."

There's a few more names before we finally near the *T*s. The only people left are Russ, me, and one other girl who wanted General Spells, I'm pretty sure.

"Chassidy Rayne . . . General Spells."

Chassidy thanks Ms. Mo and takes her paper.

And now it's Russ or me.

Ash squeezes my hands and I squeeze back.

"Kyana Turner," Ms. Mo says.

Please, oh please, oh please, say "Charms."

"Potions."

Russ snorts a laugh, takes his paperwork from Ms. Mo, and holds it up like he's showing off a WWF wrestling belt.

Did I even hear right? I stare, sure it was a mistake. I didn't get Charms? The one thing I wanted. It was my whole plan. I know my test wasn't great, but he didn't even follow the instructions.

"Kyana, I'm sorry," Ash says. "You're going to be great at Potions, though, I know it."

I try to thank her, but the only thing that comes out is a squeak. I can't cry in front of stupid Russ or anyone here. I kick the floor. Why would she give it to him? Why?

"Kyana?" Ms. Mo taps my shoulder. "Can I have a quick word?"

Ash gives my hand another squeeze and I follow Ms. Mo away from the crowd saturated with revelry.

"I know you're disappointed, but listen . . ."

Cracks in the wood floor sure are interesting.

"Look at me."

I sigh, but meet her eyes.

"I've never had a student show such an astute affinity for Potions. I couldn't ignore that. Trust me when I say you will excel at many things. And Potions will only be one of them."

She doesn't get it. This isn't about me excelling or making a name for myself like the bird lady or her Wriggly friend. This was for Momma. Everything's foggy and I don't want to talk anymore. I want to curl up with triple chocolate toasted-hazelnut brownies and vanilla ice cream.

"You can still learn charms here and there, too."

"Here and there won't land me a Charms job." Or make me more useful around the house.

"Kyana."

"Thank you for helping me do this at all. It is really special. I can see that. But I just . . . I'm so disappointed."

Ms. Mo leaves me to my feelings. As class adjourns, she hands us another parent notice, probably announcing my specialty. I stuff it in my bag, not even trying to read it. Eric offers Ash a high five as she packs her bag. Everyone stops by her desk, congratulating her on such a cool idea. Except Russ. He doesn't say a word when he passes. But I know I saw his jaw drop at her presentation. Mr. Arrogant doesn't like when *he's* not the center of attention.

"You are a friggin' genius, Ash, seriously," I say, trying to not sound deflated.

Her smile is bashful, but she manages to not thank her shoes this time.

"And congrats on Charms! You deserve it."

She shoves her assignment paper away. "Thank you. I'm sorry, Kyana." She hesitates before meeting my eyes fully. "I know how bad you wanted Charms. And you certainly deserve it more than that guy."

"Yeah, no kidding."

"You know, when you come over again, we can keep practicing. Even if it's not your specialty, you can still work on charms. Get good at them for your mom like you wanted."

The thought pricks my disappointment. I didn't think of that.

"Oh, and here." She pulls out Momma's work shoes. "You left these. I went ahead and put the charm on them. So they should be good."

"Oh, man, thank you so much." I survey the shoes and I can already see Momma's crinkly smile. "She's gonna love these. Her feet are always hurting." Maybe if I can still practice and use charms, like she's saying, it won't be a total bust? Assuming I can get better at them. And that's a *big* assumption from the looks of it. That reminds me. "I was gonna ask, actually—my best friend, Nae, and I are getting together to plan a Nails and Mermaid Tails party. You wanna join?"

"Oh . . . uh, no. I—I better not," she says.

"Ash. She's really nice."

"I'm sure. I just . . . no thanks. Maybe some other time."

"Hey." I throw an arm over her shoulder. "I understand."

"You do?" She exhales. "Thank you."

"I do." I grab my bag and we say goodbye to the others. I don't get nervous talking to people, but I know that feeling of thinking you're gonna screw up somehow and never live it down.

Thing is, Ash is way more capable than she realizes.

Me on the other hand . . . screwup is my middle name.

CHAPTER 13

˙✳˙

Home from magic school, I pull the envelope from my bag and slip the paper out, my curiosity getting the best of me.

PARENTS, I AM HOPING IT DOESN'T . . .

"Excuse me," Momma says, taking the paper out of my hand. "That envelope said 'parents.' Get on up there and get your homework out."

Memaw's banging around in the kitchen, so I peep my head in before going upstairs. She has piles of celery, onion, and bell pepper chopped, which means we're making some yummy comfort dish today.

"All right now, wash them hands and get me that mixer out. You're on the dessert today."

"I gotta get my math done first, Memaw. Then I'll be down."

I hurry upstairs. The worksheet I pull out has percentages and fractions on it and I go cross-eyed. My phone vibrates.

Ash: I got something official on Russ.

Oooo! I start typing back, but stop and set my phone aside. Gotta focus.

I huff an exhale and start. That's the hardest part, but the minutes click by, my timer goes off, and I managed to finish eight questions. Not bad—I could only finish six last week. I check through the questions and by some miracle they're actually right.

I change into more comfy clothes and hightail it downstairs, answering the scent of cinnamon calling me. The wood groans under my steps and I slow up when I hear talking—*whispered* talking.

"Earlene, don't be getting in my business now." Memaw's words are stern.

"Mom, your business is my business. Did the doctor say it's official?"

"He said that it's not uncommon around my age. That—"

"Mom, enough!" Momma's upset.

Goose prickles dance up my arms. I hold in a breath and ease down a few more steps to hear better.

"Enough beating around the bush. Is it Alzheimer's, officially?"

Silence. I can't see, but Momma sniffles and I hear Memaw's voice softer now.

"It's okay, baby. I'm just fine. Don't you get to worrying. He said it can take a long time sometimes. So that's what we'll hope for."

My shoulders sink. We suspected that's what it was. Why'd this all have to happen *now?* I don't want anything to happen to my family. I just . . . I want everything the way it was. Only a little better because I'm a witch now and I can help everyone. My eyes sting, but I blink back the tears.

If Momma's sad, I gotta be strong. I clear my throat and join them in the kitchen. They break their hug and Momma smooths a finger under her lashes quick, turning her back to me. When I see her face again, she's all smiles. But I know Momma.

"How'd it go?"

"Got 'em all right," I say. "Did eight in ten minutes!"

"That's my girl." She grabs her bag. "I'm off to meet with your teacher, finally. Hope she will have some positive updates. Since you've been doing your practice."

The knot in my stomach twists.

"Key, keep your eye on things in here. I'll be back."

147

By "things" I know she means Memaw. Seconds later, the screen door claps shut. I settle at the table and Memaw hovers over me, necklace dangling.

"Finished up this lil snack." She passes me a slice of banana bread with extra nuts, just the way I like it. She slides a chair up to the table, tucking her necklace back inside her shirt.

She wears that necklace literally *every day*. Its leather strap is brown and tattered, and something hangs from it, but every time it falls out her shirt, she tucks it back in so quickly I can't see what it is.

Her eyes follow my every move as buttery banana flavor melts on my tongue and a toasty nuttiness swirls all over my mouth. She always pops the walnuts in the oven a few minutes first. That's the secret to the world's best banana bread.

"How it taste?" She always asks. But she already knows the answer. She just likes to hear it, I think.

"So good! How about cobbler for tonight? Peach?"

"Oh yes, yes," Memaw agrees. "Sounds good."

With snack done, I pull over our mixing bowl and pile in canned peaches with the juice, flour, and sugar. Memaw is standing at the stove, staring blankly.

"It's the crushed tomatoes next, Memaw." I hand them to her. "Two cans."

"That's right." She pours them in and the scent of savory

goodness curls my toes. I grease my glass baking dish and slice my piecrust dough into strips for a lattice top, careful to keep an eye over my shoulder at Memaw.

"So how's that magic stuff going?" She grabs a bag of shredded carrots and I quickly take it out of her hand, replacing it with a bag of cheese. She blinks a bit, stunned, then breaks into a smile. "Thank you, baby. That's what I thought I had." She piles the cheese into a casserole dish and adds steaming rice and broccoli from a pot on the stove.

"It's going all right."

"You don't sound too excited." She pops the broccoli-cheese casserole into the warm oven and tops up the étouffée on the stove, then covers it with a lid. "Show me some of the stuff you learning."

"Uhm."

"Don't be shy now." Memaw's eyes are warm with a grin so big it could broker world peace. I can't let her down. Especially not today, with the news she just got.

"Okay. I don't know a lot yet." The one charm I *do* know might go decent. I've done it a bunch of times, so I shouldn't botch it. I hope. "There *is* this one charm I know." I take the pot she cooked the rice in. "Ready?"

"Ready."

I check my posture, steady my wand arm, and hold my wrist at the right angle. I aim and flick. "SKUH-REET-ZEE-LA-PLOO."

The pot tries to jump out my hand, but I hold on tight. It sparkles clean.

"Well, I'll say." She plants her hands on her hips and the sun seems to shine brighter in our kitchen. "My grandbaby, a Charms witch," she says, a lilt of surprise in her voice.

"Actually . . ."

"Key!" Momma rushes in through the door and my heart jumps. She wrestles me into a hug and waves a paper in my face.

I take it from her and realize it's the last math quiz I took—with a giant red *A* at the top. "What? I got an A? On a math quiz?" I can't be seeing this right.

"Your teacher said ever since she requested that meeting, you've been doing a lot better on your homework and quizzes. Your grade is officially passing again, baby. And not barely! A solid C, almost B."

Oh my goodness! I think of Nae and the knowing grin she'd give me if she were here. I have to text her.

✳ ✱ ✴ ✱

I was up until *late* reading my spell book. I skimmed the Potions section and actually found out that several of the ingredients needed for potions can be grown, like in a garden. Memaw loves her flower beds. I wonder if maybe we could try some stuff? I also managed to find a Charms spell for attaching relaxed auras to objects. I'm almost sure that's why I felt so serene at Scooter's. I practiced enunciating it over and over until my eyes wouldn't stay open anymore. I'm going to try it out with my wand soon. If I could pull that off, attach it to the front door, Momma would flip!

But all that studying meant I woke up *late*. So late, I overslept and Momma fussed at me all the way to the library. "Being on time says something about a person, Kyana. You not 'bout to be out here embarrassing me."

The library comes into view and I dash out the car. The building's doors glow green and swish open. I wonder what sorts of secret magical rooms the library has? I tingle all over from the thrill as I squeeze between a cluster of people perusing the sale books and another line snaking to the snack cart. Groups wait for computers and I skirt around them to the return dispenser, craning for any sign of Nae. I texted her I was running late. She answered cool but something 'bout her one-word response made it seem like anything but.

I drop my books in the dispenser. It answers with a puff of glittery green smoke and spits out a receipt. I always thought that was some techy special effect, but I bet it's someone's community project.

Nae's at the table on the third floor, our usual spot. But what I don't expect is to see Ash skimming a shelf behind her.

"Hey, girl, hey. Sorry I'm so late. Overslept."

"Nice pin." She points to my Furry and Free badge from

Ash's mom, which I was messing around with and must've forgot to take off. When she turns around to pull out her art box, I snatch it off fast. She passes me a poster and glitter markers. "Thought we could work on some campaign signs today. *Anyway*, you overslept again?"

"Again."

Ash gazes in our direction and I wave. She flails her arm back and I remember her text. What did she find out about Russ?

"Remember that girl I told you about? She's here."

"Oh." Nae twists in her chair. "Did you wanna get started on—"

"Let me go grab her and introduce y'all." I rush across the study area, and Ash's nose is in a book about lab equipment. "Hey, Ash! I got your text. Sorry I never responded."

"It's fine. So, about Russ!"

I hang so hard on her words I'm not sure if I'm still breathing.

"I was taking out the recycling the other night. It was real late and there was an unmarked van outside his house. I immediately cast a Veil charm on the blanket I brought, obviously."

"Obviously." *I don't even know what that is.*

"So he can't see me."

"Oh!"

"And I snuck closer. Kyana, he handed the guy a box of

kittens. A *whole box* of kittens. *And* the guy gave him an envelope in exchange."

"This is so good. You get a picture?"

She flips out her phone. "You know I did." On her screen is Russ and a guy in plain clothes with a hood shading his face, taking a box with a furry head popping out. In the next photo, Russ is going indoors with an envelope hanging out of his pocket.

"We got him."

"Wait, who should we tell? Not like the Magick authorities? I mean, we just wanna scare him, right?"

I didn't think about what to actually do with any information. "Uhm . . . yeah. I mean, I don't want him to get in any *real* trouble. Let's only tell Ms. Mo?"

"Yeah, that seems smart. She can take it from there. She wouldn't tell anyone, right?"

"Wait," I say. "Are we sure they're those illegal magical creature things?"

"Groits. I mean, not entirely, unless I can grab one and check. But I'm pretty sure."

"Hmm. We need to be sure they're not just stray cats. Because then we'd look ridiculous."

"Okay, so let's hold these cards to our vest and try to snag one to be extra sure."

"Deal." We shake on it.

"You here much longer?" I say. "Would you want to

maybe meet my bestie, Nae? Just say hi? We hang here every Sunday."

Ash fidgets. "Uhm—"

"No pressure. But I better get back. If you wanna, stop over and just say hi. I promise she's really chill."

She agrees and I make my way back to our study table. Only, Nae's gone and so is all her stuff. I pick up the folded note on the table.

My mom's here. I guess I'll catch you later. If you have time, that is.

CHAPTER 14

*˟**✳**˟*

I call Nae over and over but she doesn't answer.

I feel terrible about leaving her at the table for so long, especially after being late. *What was I thinking?* I wasn't thinking.

Me: I'm sorry, Nae! Call me.

I toss my phone aside, and it buzzes again. I whip it up but it's not Nae's name on the screen.

Ash: Stakeout to steal a cat tonight?
Me: I'm in!

Momma takes some convincing, but she drops me at Ashley's for a movie night. I make sure to wear my Furry and Free pin to avoid any more of her mom's talking-tos about where my magical creature loyalties lie.

"Take this." Ash hands me a mask. "In case you get sprayed. You don't wanna breathe that stuff in. He lets them out at night. That's our chance to catch one. You have your wand?"

"Always."

"Loshiva umen," she says, and her wand lights at the tip. I copy her and, by some rare aligning of the stars, mine lights up, too.

"Use *Tocana Voblem* to snatch one."

"Tocana voblem, tocana voblem," I whisper, practicing, as we sneak through the neighbors' yards and hunker down beside the car in Russ's driveway.

"Invisio canto." She brandishes her wand and a weight settles on my back like someone's thrown a blanket over us. "That should keep us veiled." She checks her watch. "For at least ten minutes." She squeezes in closer to me so we're fully covered.

"Tocana voblem," I whisper, practicing. "Tocana voblem."

Russ's door cracks open and a herd of cats scutters out. I wait for the door to creak back closed, but it doesn't. Instead, footsteps clack our way. I press against the car tire.

Russ throws a pizza box in a big trash can and heads right toward us. *Please oh please, don't let the veil wear off.*

156

"Meow." A cold nose touches my finger. The cat paws at me but I'm too scared to move.

"What is it, Pixy?" Russ scoops up the kitten, his feet no more than an inch from bumping into me.

Ash's eyes are bugged out of her head. She presses a finger to her lips and I hold my breath.

Thankfully, Russ keeps walking toward the door and I can breathe again. Another kitten creeps up to me to sniff and I snatch it under our veil. It purrs in my arms and Russ's door clicks shut. I exhale.

"Tocana voblem," Ash says, and a kitty slides toward her like it's being pulled by an invisible string. It wriggles in her grasp, clawing. "It's okay. Calm down."

"Meow!" It claws its way up her. *Riiip.* A cloud of pink smoke chokes me. It tastes like perfume and my nostrils sting.

"Ugh!" I say, coughing. The cat in Ash's hands skitters away but she's too busy hacking up a lung to grab it back. The kitty in my lap still purrs. I stroke its tummy, shoving down another cough as the pink cloud dissipates.

"No—" Ash coughs. "No n-need to check them. Definitely groits."

* ∗✳∗ *

Monday came but Nae wasn't at school. She usually tells me when she's sick but she still hasn't even texted me back.

I collected her homework from her teachers like I usually do when she's out and sent her another text. That got a response, but it was just a simple thanks.

The rest of the week was more of the same. Turns out Nae was sick and missed Tuesday, too. And on Wednesday, when she returned, she had a Math Club meeting during lunch. Thursday, she held another makeup club meeting because they had a big competition coming up on Friday. And I mean, that made sense, but I couldn't shake the feeling that she was avoiding me.

When Saturday rolls around, I wake up with Nae instead of magic school on my mind for once.

Things don't feel right so I shoot her yet another text, which she probably won't respond to. I pull myself out of bed and drag myself to the kitchen.

"What's that stuck-out lip for?" Memaw asks, skillet in hand.

"It's Nae." I plop down at the table. "It just feels like something's . . . like we're off."

My phone vibrates, and to my surprise it's Nae.

Nae: You got a minute?

I grab the phone so fast I almost fumble it. Maybe she wants to finally talk about the other day. I owe her a huge apology but in person seems best.

Me: Nae! Hey!! 😃 🖤
Nae: Can we meet today instead of tomorrow for
 library?

Today's magic school and I have a bunch of practice I
was hoping to do after, but I can't say no. She'd feel slighted.
And I'm just happy she wants to keep tutoring me at all,
given how last time went down.

Me: Yeah. That's fine. Is like in a few hours ok?
Nae: Yeah, see you then.
Me: K. What's up? What you been doing?

I hold the phone for several minutes but nothing happens. My shoulders slump and Memaw sets an omelet in
front of me.

"Eat up, baby. You two are thick as thieves, I'm sure
you'll work it out. Sometimes giving it time is all you need."

I hope so.

Momma drives me to magic school and tells me I can go
to the library after but she won't be able to take me so Mo
will. At the shop I make my way to the back, say hey and
"Ooweppe d'yo" to Lucy, and when she swings open the
door I enter the classroom. Ash is already there, but Mo's
not teaching. Instructions are scribbled on the board and
she's nowhere in sight. I grab my pot and get started. The

PotLuckImmunity potion comes together well and I tuck it away. Momma is gonna love this one. She's always talking about going to potlucks to be polite but getting side-eyes when she doesn't wanna try people's Pinterest-experiment version of macaroni and cheese. Potions are pretty useful, I guess.

My potion jar near runs over. I head to the supply closet to grab another and spot Mo, arms folded and watery-eyed. A ferret—not her Link but another with blond fur—stands at her feet, holding a clipboard and crossing off things. Another ferret sifts through Mo's shelves. It grabs a bag of unicorn hair and our entire supply of mermaid scales and troll venom and drops them all in a box.

"Mo?"

"Kyana, hey."

"I need another potion bottle. What's going on?"

"Oh, just . . . the Board's confiscating some of our more hazardous supplies. Sent out their team to sort through our stock."

"But why?"

A ferret crawls up to Ms. Mo's shoulder and taps a spot on a clipboard.

"Excuse me a second, honey."

The ferret pulls a pen from I couldn't tell you where and Ms. Mo signs the form. Closer now, I catch a glimpse of shiny metal on his chest.

Section X
Investigatory Security Squad

He dips his chin to her, then me.

"Uhh . . . have a nice day?" I say, scooting out of the way. The ferrets lift the box of supplies above their heads and march out.

Mo hands me a potion jar. "That all you need?"

"Y-yeah . . ." Russ flashes through my mind. "I mean, I could use some advice if you have a minute."

"Sure."

I lower my voice to a whisper. "If I knew someone is doing something that could negatively affect a lot of people, should I say something?"

She stares a moment, tucking her lip. "Yes, you should absolutely speak up, dear. Saving bad news isn't going to make it hurt any less."

"I—"

"You're absolutely right." She pats my shoulder and walks away.

Uhm, okay. Good talk? I scratch my head.

I find Ashley eyes-closed with a giant grin on her face. Her mouth's moving but I can't make out the words. Sparks shoot from her wand as she bats her eyes open.

"I DID IT!" She grabs my hands. "Kyana, eleven minutes! I told him about the thirteen molecular differences between dragon and faerie blood and he asked questions. And I did exactly what you said—I pretended like he was you or Mom and I said whatever came to mind. And he stayed listening!" She jumps up and down.

"Ashley, that's wonderful!" Ms. Mo's eyes are puffy, puffier than a second ago, and a stack of envelopes is in her hand. "Next is Tethering, but you've done the hard part, dear."

"I'm gonna grab a bit of dragon belly and try the tethering charm." She squeals.

"*Womp, womp*, no one cares," Russ says, handing out tiny boxes. "Check out these. Made 'em last night."

"Where he gets the money for all these bells and whistles I couldn't tell you," Ms. Mo says. "But your presentation is very professional, Russ. This box is so cute."

Oh, I know where he gets the money, all right. Why'd he have to come and shade Ashley's parade?

Everyone opens their little boxes, except Ash and me. I refused one; so did she.

Pops of light flash with each box opening and one by one, the class looks a wrinkled mess. Shirts looking like they were crumpled up wet and left to dry like that on purpose. I laugh behind my hand, glad Ash and I didn't take one.

"Now tell me whose momma is gonna make them go *anywhere* looking like that?" Russ smiles and his teeth sparkle as a wave of "aha"s spreads through the crowd. "In seconds, get out of wherever your fam is trying to make you go by wrinkling your wardrobe. I'll be giving out free samples all weekend. Tell your friends." The crowd ogles Russ as he whips out more samples.

Russ's attitude doesn't seem to faze Ash but it's all the way under my skin. He struts away like he's a gift to the magical world and it takes everything in me not to toss his little wrapping paper at him. I can't take this anymore.

"Oh yeah? Well, we'd probably all have extra money to make something cool if we were selling charms to a non-Magick on the basketball team."

The entire room gasps. Even Lucy at the door.

"And breeding groits to pad our pockets."

"Kyana." Ms. Mo's eyes are wide. "That's a serious accusation."

Russ's stare burns into me and he balls his fists.

"Admit it." I stare right back at him. "You'd do anything to make money and tote around this Mr. Cool persona." I pop my collar. "Look at me, I'm Russ, I poop charms, and I'm so cool."

His mouth falls open at that and his nostrils flare. But there's something in him I can't quite place. His eyes tilt at the corners and his lip quivers before he stomps off. Lucy doesn't even speak to him, she just swings open with a "*hmph*."

Ash's hands are clamped over her mouth and our classmates are staring in a mix of shock and awe.

"Well, since we're already rattled," says Ms. Mo, "I too have an announcement I need to get off my chest." Ms. Mo heaves a big sigh and a dark cloud settles over me. The stack of envelopes in her hands shoots around the class distributing itself. The note's addressed to parents again, but I rip it open.

REGRETFULLY, I MUST INFORM YOU . . .

No . . . It can't be . . .

"You guys," she says. "I'm so, so sorry . . . but PRMA is being closed."

CHAPTER 15

✴

I slip the letter from the envelope. The words **P.R.M.A. PARENT NOTICE** are in bold black letters across the top.

OUT OF FUNDING . . .
CANCELED . . .
LAST MEETING . . .
GIFTED KIDS IN PARK ROW . . .

I blink faster, willing my eyes to make sense of the words on the page. Back at the top, I'm read each word carefully.

New policies passed down from the City of Rockford's Magick Board have imposed funding limitations on our

location. Due to these restrictions, Park Row Magick Academy will be closing effective Nov. 11.

That's in . . . two weeks?!

Maybe I'm misunderstanding. Maybe there's a different PRMA. Maybe . . . My eyes sting.

Waivers will be granted for students to attend mandatory training at a different campus for a fee. Fees start at $3,000 for the required 6-month training period. Enrolling a student at an alternate campus without paying the appropriate fees may make you subject to a $5,000 fine or jail time.

OMG, that's so much money. We don't have that. And no way Momma would take me across town to go to another campus. They're closing our campus and the only way they'll let us go somewhere else is for a fee? How is that fair?

Untrained students with abilities unable, or unwilling, to complete training may schedule an appointment to be sanitized Mon.—Wed., 10:36 a.m.—7:43 p.m.

That's real? Kids can have their magic stripped? Just taken, forever? I want to throw up.

Wand carrying, for those who have completed training, is still permitted.

I *have* to get the mandatory six months of magic training done or my magic will be taken away? I can't breathe. What about Ashley's big plans? She's made so much progress. And all the projects people were planning—aren't they important? We need our school. *I* need our school. It *has* to stay open.

There has to be a way Mo can fix this, right? If she can't . . . somebody has to.

"We have fourteen days, so two more Saturdays, before we are closed," Mo says. "But in that time the regulatory board will be visiting to get a record of each enrolled untrained student's decision. So weigh these choices with your family and let me know soon, what you decide to do."

No one speaks. No one moves.

Mo takes a deep breath. "Let's try to enjoy the rest of today, okay?"

Everyone returns to their desks sullen. I move into my desk, set up like a potions station, and flip to the intermediate-to-advanced section. My head and heart are half in it, but out of nostalgia or sheer determination that this can't be over, I make a series of potions in succession. The room is silent but for the occasional scrape of a chair on the floor, the bubbling of my cauldron brewing, or a screech from an ingredient.

I glance at Ash and she gives me a sideways smile, disappointment hanging on her shoulders. Hot tears streak my cheeks as I stopper up a GreaseCleaner potion I know Momma will love and turn to another page. Three frog legs, an umpher root, and a tuft of eweglie fur later, another brew is ready. This one for reupholstering small leather items.

Someone calls my name but I tune them out. I don't want to hear whatever it is or think or anything. I just want to work on my magic. I flip for another potion, something that sounds useful, exciting, but my potion book suddenly feels twice as dense, packed full of possibilities I'll never experience, like a cookbook full of recipes I'll never taste. Still, I wipe my face, biting down, and put one ingredient, then another, in my gumbo pot.

Finally, Ms. Mo dismisses us. Ashley's all tears when she tells me goodbye. Lucy is in a state, arguing with Meryl—the Available attached to the closet door—about if only one of them gets to stay who it'll be. My head hurts.

I hop into Mo's car and am watching her lock up the shop, when my backpack vibrates.

Mom: I'll be working extra late tonight.
Me: K
Mom: Please keep an eye on Memaw after the
  library tonight. A closer eye than usual, baby.
Me: K

Mom: Love you.

Me: K

The phone vibrates with Momma's face. She's calling. "Hello?"

"K?" she says. "What kind of response is that?

I try to sift the disappointment from my voice. "Sorry. I mean, I love you, too, Momma."

"What's wrong? Magic school go all right today?" There's a note of suspicion in her voice. I can't tell Mom. Not yet. I don't need her stressing, trying to figure out how she'll make it work, when I know there's no way.

"I'm good, Mom. See you tonight."

"Okay, honey."

We hang up as Mo slips inside the car and all I can do to keep the tears from flowing is look away from her.

"Kyana, if there's anything you wanna talk about, you can talk to me."

I twist the ends of my hair around my finger and fix my gaze on something, anything, outside the window. I do want to ask her more about the letter. But she's white-knuckling the steering wheel, "old-school" jams playing. Last thing I want to do is add more to her plate.

"When you're ready," she says. "Mind if we stop at the corner store before I drop you?"

"Sure."

Stopping is a relief. Buys me a few more minutes to think about what I want to say. I notice the time and shoot Nae a text in case we're a few minutes late.

Me: On my way

My hand vibrates.

Nae: K, I'm just getting here. Tables all taken in the usual spot. I'm on the 2nd floor.
Me: 👍 Excited to see you.
Nae: I'm excited too. Made a whole pinterest board of campaign ideas for us to go over. Playing around with slogans. "PICK ME & HEARD YOU WILL BE" or do I lean right into my platform "SWEETS & STYLE, PICK ME & 6TH GRADE YEAR WILL BE WILD"?

My fingers can't type fast enough. Maybe time really does help.

Me: 😍 The second one! Shelby is going DOWN #NaeForPres

My message sends with a swish. *Sigh*. One minute everything is amazing and now this. Could my life get any more complicated?

I tap my foot, waiting on Mo. The sign above Lu's Cleaners glows green. It should excite me but everything's sour in my stomach. Not completing training means I lose all this. I'm just unspecial me again.

I have to ask. Did she do all she could? Is this for real? Has she appealed to . . . whoever magical people talk to—the Grand Council of Magicians or whatever they called it?

Ms. Mo finally comes out of the mini mart. She tosses a plastic bag in the backseat and we back out the parking lot.

"Isn't there something we can do?" I ask.

"*We*." She smiles to herself. "Girl, if the world had a heart as big as yours, it would be a better place."

I want to help if I can. Magic can make life easier on Momma and from what it looks like, my whole community. I need this witch thing to work. My family needs this. Park Row, too.

"What happened?" I ask.

"I did what I could for as long as I could." She sighs and it's long and real deep. "They redrew some lines on a map and the costs—license fees, liability insurance, all that—are just more than I can do. We have no choice, Key. I don't have the money to keep the school going. Park Row kids don't have it either. The best I could get the Board to agree to was a payment plan for kids who have some money to attend in a district across town."

That won't work for my family. I hate that the only answer is *taking* our magic or paying a bunch of money. It could be free and I still couldn't go. All that bus fare? Gas money? No way. We need PRMA *here*. In Park Row.

"I wanted to keep it as close to free as possible for you all," she said. "I've done all I could, truly. I even appealed to my friend Mr. Wriggly, but his hands are full dealing with trouble in Winzhobble. I can't think of any other options, Kyana." Mo's expression fractures and I can tell she's trying to be strong. But this saddens her, too, very much. "I guess our time's up."

I can tell she doesn't want to talk more about it today. But I need to talk more. I wish I could talk to Nae about this. I wish I could show her everything. She's who I go to for everything, and this one tiny secret is a giant snowball taking over my entire life.

Gah, why couldn't Nae be a witch, too?

The library comes into view and I zip up my bag.

"I don't want to get your hopes up, Kyana, so I won't say much, but I will say that I'm still talking to some people on the Magick Board to see if there's any way they can work with me." The car rolls to a stop. "I've done and will keep doing everything I can to see if there's a way around this, I promise." She's looking at me, but I refuse to look up. "This isn't your problem to fix, Kyana. Try to enjoy the next couple weeks while you can."

I don't see it that way. We supposed to support Black businesses. This is sort of like that.

I'm *going* to fix this. Somehow. Some way.

"I have a few errands. So, I'll pick you up at—"

"At five. I remember. Thanks, Ms. Mo. You're the best." I hop out the car to Naomi beaming behind the glass entrance door, poster materials under her arm. I try to pick up my chin.

She barrels into me, handing me things.

I don't know where all this renewed enthusiasm came from, but the olive branch is like chicken noodle soup when sick; just what I need right now.

"I picked teal and orange as official campaign colors," she says. "Didn't want to be cliché, you know?" She's squealing and talking a million miles a minute. "What you think?"

"Yeah, that's cute." It's only been a few days since we really talked, but it feels like years have passed.

"Okay, okay, but!"

"Uh-oh, what?"

"Shelby got word I was running and her dad called my mom to offer her money if I dropped out."

"No she did *not*." I slip my books into the return drop and we head toward the elevator.

"Yes! So you know she thinks I have a shot at winning."

I'm cheesing so hard my cheeks might pop and it feels

good. I've missed this. We head up to the study rooms upstairs where we can actually talk in normal voices. Inside the elevator I realize she hasn't stopped to breathe. Something about Toya's new friend being shady and Roderick—the class clown at Thompson Middle—acting a fool as usual.

The doors slide open and a familiar face, Tommy Bushnell from Thompson, staples up a poster on the wall. I forgot he volunteers here on the weekends. Nae points out a table in the corner and we head that way.

"Sup, Kyana?" Tommy pulls his earbuds out.

Not in a talking mood, I wave and keep on moving. Only then, I notice what Tommy's actually affixing to the wall. I stare speechless. There posted on the wall is the answer to my problem on a bright blue poster:

City of Rockford Harvest Fest Baking Competition
FIRST ROUND: NOVEMBER 4
FINAL ROUND: NOVEMBER 11
Cash Prize: $50,000

Fifty. Thousand. Dollars? OMG!

I can practically smell the browned butter my peanut butter cookie recipe calls for and the toasted hazelnuts I sprinkle on my chocolate torte. I might suck at magic, but I *know* baking like the back of my hand. And that's a *lot* of money.

With that kind of money, I could save Park Row Magick Academy.

CHAPTER 16

✳✳✷✳✳

Monday morning the clock on the wall is slowing down intentionally, I swear.

The longer I stare at it, the slower the seconds move. My foot's jittering under my desk. When I got home from the library, Momma still wasn't in from work and Memaw was asleep. Sunday Momma was gone *all* day. So I have to wait until after school today. I *cannot* wait to tell Mo my idea! But I need parent permission to sign up first. And with the competition this weekend, I don't have much time to prepare.

Ms. Wisseman's talking about the Spanish Inquisition and the words are a dull noise compared to the *ticktock* of the hand on the clock. My brain is still whirring with ideas for this baking competition. *Could I actually save Park Row Magick Academy?* Nae's next to me jotting down notes every few minutes. I keep looking over, but she's throwing major shade.

"Hey," I whisper. "You aight?"

She glances at me over her shoulder with pursed lips. "Sure."

Well, that's not convincing at all. "What's up?" I ask when Ms. Wisseman turns around.

"Nothing."

She's obviously upset. "Just tell me."

"Don't mind me. You got so much going on, clearly."

Oh my gosh, the guilt trip. I was distracted in the library yesterday, she's right. I just . . . With all this magic school closing business and now the cooking competition . . . I don't know how much I can say. "Nae . . ."

"Nah, it's cool. You hardly said two words after you saw Tommy at the library. I showed you my Pinterest board with all my campaign plans and you hardly responded. Ever since missing my birthday party you've been weird. I mean, who are you these days? I mean, is it Tommy? Is tha—"

"Nae, *what*? No! That's not it. I ain't worried about no Tommy Bushnell." I laugh, but that seems to upset her more.

She folds her arms. "So then there *is* something that has you distracted? Something you won't tell me?"

Sigh. "I didn't mean there's an *it*. I—"

"You *said*, 'That's not *it*.' That means there's an *it*. Don't try to play me, Key."

"Girls!" Ms. Wisseman raises an eyebrow. "Whatever's so important needs to wait until after class. Quiet."

Throbbing behind my eyes makes me close them. The seconds drag on and finally the bell rings. Nae's walking fast, but I catch up to her.

"Nae."

She turns around, planting a hand on her hip. "Uh-huh?"

"I—" *What do I say?* "Your birthday party . . . there was the theater and I—"

"You know, you on some next-level lying these days. Last night I told my momma how things have been weird with you and I mentioned your day at the theater because I still ain't seen no pictures. And she said when she called about last-minute tickets, the show was *canceled*."

Oh crap!

"I had hoped you'd at least have an excuse," she mutters to herself. "That it was some misunderstanding." She takes a deep breath as if whatever she's realizing might shatter her into pieces. "But no, you never went to the theater, Key."

My heart stops as I scramble for words.

"You didn't come to my birthday for some reason and you won't tell me. And that's what hurts the most. Not that you didn't come. But you won't tell me why. And you've been giving me this second-rate treatment since."

My heart's a brick in my chest. "I'm so sorry, Nae. I—"

"I thought we were best friends, Key? But you're lying to me and I feel like I don't even know you anymore." She walks off and my eyes burn as I rush outside. Thankfully, my school bus home leaves soon so everyone at Thompson Middle doesn't have to watch me cry.

* ✳ ✴ ✳ *

The screen door slams shut.

"Kyana, that you, baby?" Memaw's voice rings from the kitchen.

I let my bag fall to the floor and don't even bother moving it. Nae's words haunted me the whole ride home. My brain's a confused mess. I need to be focused on this competition in a few days and give that my all, assuming Momma says I can do it. Regardless of what's happening with Nae, our entire community's magic school depends on me making this work.

I push out a slow breath and let go of the Nae drama with it, for a moment at least. I'll fix it up somehow. We've been friends for too long to let this get between us.

Right now, this baking competition needs my full focus.

The clock says 3:45. Momma will pop in between her day shift and night shift soon. When she gets in, I'll talk to both her and Memaw. Convince them I *have* to do this competition to save our school.

"What we making tonight, Memaw?" Scents of rosemary

and garlic suggest it'll be something with potatoes. My tummy rumbles.

Memaw pulls off her gardening apron and sets her gloves by the back kitchen door. She lives in the garden out back or the kitchen. Flowers and food. That's her jam.

"I was thinking some baked chicken, macaroni and cheese, string beans, maybe?" she says, setting some fresh peach-colored roses in a vase by the sink. "What you have a taste for, baby?"

"That's fine." I try to make my words sound a bit more upbeat. Memaw can always sense when something's wrong. Cool air slams against my face as I look for the butter, bacon, and beans. A warm palm rests on my back and before I know it my head's on Memaw's shoulder.

"All right, che. What happened? Tell me what's wrong."

I don't have words, but tears flow easy. Her arms are tight, strong.

"Whatever it is, baby, I promise you it ain't as bad as it seem." She hugs tighter and for a moment I feel like somehow I might make it through all this without losing my best friend. Her shoulder's soaking wet by the time I finish, and I wipe my nose on my sleeve.

"I'm okay," I manage through sniffles. "I just wanna bake. Can we bake today? Maybe something chocolate."

"All these tears ain't about some sweet tooth, but I'll pick it up if that's what you putting down." She squeezes my hand. "Remember what I said, che. Whatever it is. Give it time."

We get the bacon in the pan and the kitchen's smelling like heaven. In minutes, Memaw's shimmying around dancing as she cooks, mumbling the words to some song I ain't never heard.

"That's Sam Cooke, baby. Way before yo' day." Her joy's contagious. I don't even know who Sam Cooke is but my feet are lighter. Next thing I know I'm singing along, throwing beans in the pot. The grease fills in the backdrop with a sizzling crackle and pop. Momma creeps up on us and before I know it, dinner's on the table and I'm tired from hip-bumping and sidestepping.

"So how was your day, Key?" She's only home for a couple hours before her next shift. If I'm doing this, *now's* the time.

"It was fine, Momma. Actually . . . there's something I wanted to talk to you and Memaw about."

"Oh?" Momma looks up. Memaw does too. Their eyes burn my skin.

It's now or never.

Sensing my hesitation Momma puts down her fork. "It's okay, Key. What is it?"

Park Row Magick Academy needs you. I take a deep breath and spill.

I tell them everything—from the way I didn't get Charms

even though I tried my hardest, Russell selling charms to non-Magicks, and the stakeout to steal a Lysol cat. Momma gave me side-eyes at that part. But she perked up when I told her about how I cleaned my pot with magic. And she was *real* interested in the PotLuckImmunity potion, like I'd suspected. I didn't mention how I lied to Nae about missing her birthday and she found out. That's a whole 'nother can of worms.

I explain that the baking competition is this weekend and that it doesn't require baking on-site. I can make my entry dessert at home, with Memaw's help, and bring it in. I beg and plead to participate, making it clear this may be our *only* chance to save our school. For several moments they don't say anything. Momma starts to speak, but Memaw touches her arm and speaks first.

"Your heart is bigger than this world deserves. If I never see you grow old, knowing my grandbaby loves deep and wide makes me *so, so* proud." Her eyes glisten and she looks at Momma. "I say let her do it."

I gasp, hanging on the silence. Momma leans back in her chair and folds her arms.

Say yes! Say yes!

"*If*..." She stresses those two letters so hard. "*If* I say yes, you can't let your grades slip. You've been doing so much better. This week you have a big test if I recall correctly."

OMG! OMG! OMG!

"Yes, ma'am! I won't! I promise!" My insides are so tight they might burst.

"And *if* I say yes, you will do your homework first before any baking practice."

I nod like a bobblehead, biting my nails.

She's gonna say yes! I can feel it!

"And one last thing. *If* I say yes"—she winks—"you *gotta* use one of your memaw's recipes!" Her lips split in the biggest grin I've seen on Momma's face in a long time.

I throw my arm around both their necks. "So that's a yes?"

"That's a yes, baby. I'm so proud of you. For caring enough to try."

Ahhhhh! "If I win, maybe we could even keep some of the money. Maybe you wouldn't have to work so much."

She pulls my face into her hands, her eyes soft but stern. "It's not your job to take care of me, baby. It's my job to take care of you. And we getting by on grace just fine. If you win that money, you use it to bless them magic kids, you hear?"

"You mean it?" I squeeze her.

"I mean it." She squeezes back.

She's the best! The kitchen bursts into commotion in an instant. Memaw's shuffling through her shelf of recipe books trying to find one in particular. Momma's clearing the table and pulling out the baking goods.

I can't believe it! I'm entering. I slip out my phone and

text Mo. We need to have a meeting with everyone. She's going to be ecstatic.

"How does that thing work, anyway?" Momma asks, nodding at my wand as she scrapes food off a plate. I want to impress her. Let her know when I get good, she won't have to wash another dish.

"You just sort of flick it." I snap my wrist and the spice rack on the wall explodes in a cloud of seasoning.

Oops!

Momma massages her temples.

"Maybe a bit more practice, baby," she says, wiping the paprika from her face.

Thankfully, I'm better at baking than I am at spells. Relieved I get to compete in the contest, I'm smiling, which feels good.

Now, I need to win.

CHAPTER 17

﹡✻✳✻﹡

5 days and counting

Neon lights play on the ceiling of Scooter's retro diner as PRMA kids pile in. Trays of something sweet and peppery like paprika, with basil and thyme, pass under my nose and my stomach doesn't even rumble. Since that conversation with Memaw and Momma, I've been seeing word about the competition *all* over the news. It's gonna draw a huge crowd, I bet. Just the thought makes my stomach knot.

But so much is on the line. I have to do this. Scooter was happy to open his restaurant after hours for us to have a meeting about a plan to save Park Row. Mo, on the other hand, didn't respond as enthusiastically. But she agreed to come to the meetup and hear me out.

Scooter glides through the crowd serving more plates than we could ever finish in one night. Beside me, Ash's thumbs move a mile a minute tapping on her phone. Eric and a few others squeeze into booths and pluck crab-stuffed mushrooms from a tray. Kids slump in their chairs, lips turned down. Occasionally a giggle breaks through the somber haze, but most of the chatter hovers like a cloud heavy with raindrops.

Ash heaves a sigh and puts her phone down, tapping her foot. "Who's all coming?"

"Everybody."

"*Everybody* everybody?"

"Well, everyone but Russ. Why?"

She hesitates. "Nothing."

"Speaking of Russ, he acted *weird*. Like, I figured he'd be mad, but he was . . . something else. I don't know."

"Yeah, I saw that, too." She glances at her phone.

"You tell your mom about the groits yet?"

"Not yet."

Why not? But before I can get the words out, a hand sets on my shoulder.

"Kyana?" It's Ms. Mo. "Thank you for putting all this together but you don't have to do this."

"We have to do something," I say.

"I . . . I don't know what to say," she says with a heavy sigh.

"Don't say a thing." Scooter hands Ms. Mo a caramel-glazed cookie the size of my face with a hill of vanilla ice cream on top. "These kids here aren't the only ones who love Park Row, Mo. I wanna hear this plan to save it. Now, gon now and have a seat. See how you feel after a bit of that." He dusts a purple powder over the top of her sundae. Ms. Mo takes the advice and melts into a chair.

"So I did some research, and like everyone who's anyone on the chef scene is talking about competing in this contest," Ash says. "Like professionally trained people."

I gulp. "I don't know, I could be out of my league, but I have to try."

"Can't we try to figure out a way to make money grow on trees or something instead?"

"I'm not trying any sort of magical nothing. Uh-uh. No way." This is my best shot. I may be a mediocre witch but I'm *good* in the kitchen. Something about cooking just makes sense to me. I can almost feel it . . . like somehow cooking is part of me. Memaw says it runs in the family.

"That was a joke anyhow, money trees aren't a thing. Some witch a long time ago tried to make one using some illegal spells and her tree blossomed all right—into a bunch of bills."

"Okay, definitely not trying that. I read that the judging will include the crowd favorite, too. So if we can convince everyone we know to come and support, I'll have an even better shot at making the final round."

"It's a good plan. If anyone can do it, Kyana, you can."

I'm glad one of us believes that, because my track record ain't great these days. My only hope is that my cooking gene comes through.

"This sucks," says one girl, cleaning under her nails with the tip of her wand.

"Sis, seriously?" I say.

"What?"

"For one, that's gross. For two, I have an idea to fix this. That's why I called this meeting."

She sits up and the buzzing conversations quiet.

I stand up and face the room. "First, I want to say thanks, Scooter, for letting us meet here."

He tips his hat and I go on.

I explain the competition prize and how we need as many people to come out as possible. Taste-tester spots are limited, so arriving early to get a seat in that section will be key. There will be hundreds there if the news reports are right. Philanthropists and Big Money Folks have put their dollars together for the grand prize.

"Rockford hasn't had a competition like this in a long time," I say. "But the last time it did, half the city was there."

Scooter rubs his chin.

"Man, this don't sound like it's gone' work," someone shouts from the back. "How you gone' beat all those people with like real culinary training?"

"I—"

"When cooking is a part of you, it's what you do," Scooter says. "The year I entered, I didn't expect to win. I just knew I was good with clever food pairings. It wasn't pastries that year. And my potions background might've helped a bit." He winks.

"Wow, you won?" I ask.

"Yep. That was *years* ago, though. But I took that money and put it right here into the Row. Built Scooter's Skewers."

"I say go for it!" Mo shouts from her chair, spoon in her mouth, her whole vibe full of joy.

I flash a suspicious glance at Scooter, remembering that purple powder, and he winks.

"We'll have to cancel magic school that day. But I don't think anyone will mind," Mo says.

With Mo on board, more in the group agree. Eric is tied up that day helping his uncle but says he will try to get out of it early. A few others have conflicts, too, and all of a sudden my foolproof plan looks like Swiss cheese.

"What if we get more of the Rockford Magick community to come?" Ash asks. "Like those kids donating supplies, for example. Or I mean, there's magic academies all over Rockford, right?"

"Yes, true," Mo says. "They tend to keep to themselves, though. I don't know that we'd get very far with that." She licks the last bit of caramel from her spoon and hops up, shouldering her purse. "I think it's a great idea, Kyana. But don't you get your hopes up if it doesn't pan out. Try. But remember, this isn't on you, dear." She waves to everyone. "I better be going." She shakes Scooter's hand. "Thank you for that sundae, it's by far the best I've had in years. I haven't felt this relaxed in a long time."

A bell jingles as Ms. Mo leaves, and the mood has perked up a bit when bottomless globs of sherbet in floating bowls make their way around the room.

"So then, it's settled," I say. "As many of us as possible will be at the competition early to vote for crowd favorite."

"What if we like someone else's better?" Eric asks. "I kid. I kid." He slaps my hand and we put a twist on the end. "This is really dope, Kyana. Even if it doesn't work. Means a lot."

The crowd finishes up their plates and some people leave. A few stop by to show support, promising they'll be there. Worms wiggle in my tummy, but it's better than the sinking pit that was there when I held that closing notice in my hands.

"I wish Mo was willing to reach out to the other schools. We need to come out in big numbers in case, you know . . ."

"Okay, we're not gonna think that way," Ash says. "Confidence is a powerful potion. But you're right." She taps her chin. "What about Russ? He knows everyone."

"I can't be hearing my ears right."

"I know, but he's really connected."

Ugh. She's right. "I don't want to talk to him. I just . . ."

She picks at her nail. "What if . . . I mean . . . maybe I could do it?"

"Do what? Talk to Russ? You're gonna talk to Russ?"

"He's so connected and we need as much support as we can get." She rolls her eyes. "He also lives on my street, so it's not exactly out of the way."

"You really don't mind?"

"Oh, I'm going to hate it. But I'll do it. If you're gonna go up there and bake to save our school, I can force myself to have a conversation with Russ." She glances at her phone again.

"What's with you and the phone?"

"Okay, he might have texted me."

"Texted you what?"

"Just that he was really upset about the groit thing. And he can't believe as his longtime neighbor I'd think that."

"Russ is trying to give *you* a guilt trip? Wow."

"I don't know. It was weird. I didn't even know he had my number. I just told him that no one was trying to get him in real trouble. Which is why we told Mo and not like the police."

"I didn't mean to say it in front of everyone like that. Russ just gets me so mad with his—"

"Russell Watkins?" Scooter takes the plate I didn't touch from in front of me and Ash sets her dishes on top.

"Yeah. You know him?"

"Do I? That's a fine boy there. Real nice kid."

Ash and I glance at each other with quizzical expressions.

"I keep a few of his charms in stock 'round here. Makes busing and cleanup, even prep work, twice as fast. Real bright, that kid. Tells me he makes them charms himself. Charms was never really my thing." He stacks plates from the other tables, most of the crowd gone by now. "Oh, and be sure to tell Mo, I'll put some feelers out to a few wizard-owned businesses around the Row, see if we can pull together any funds for PRMA. Business been tight since the pandemic, but we're in this together."

"Thanks, Mr. Scooter," I say, and turn to Ash as he walks away. "Okay, Russ *literally* knows everyone."

"Clearly."

"Okay, so you talk to Russ about coming to the competition and telling more people and I'll find the best darn recipe to enter that the judges will drool over." We fist-bump on it.

Working with Russ is the last thing I wanna do, but every vote counts. Will he see it the same way? I just hope he doesn't do something catty to sabotage this or embarrass me . . . like I embarrassed him.

CHAPTER 18

˙✳*˙*

4 days and counting

Momma pulls out of Glenda's Grocery's parking lot. The store's glowing doors grow small in the distance. I pop a Kietchy Square in my mouth and lean back on the headrest.

The spell book Memaw gave me sits on my lap. I flip backward and forward mumbling spells under my breath, making sure to say them correctly. But every few seconds I can't help but glance at my phone.

I haven't seen or talked to Nae since the blow-up at school. I sent her a text with a pic of the baking competition flyer, told her I was entering, hoping that'd spark a conversation. It didn't. I got a meager good luck in response.

I don't know what to say to her to make it better. And I've been spending every possible second between classes with my nose in a spell or recipe book. I'm learning so much.

There's a spell for almost anything. And potions, hundreds of types of potions. But outside of the supply closet at Park Row Magick Academy, most of the ingredients would be impossible to find.

Charms aren't math . . . but I'm as good at them as I am at algebra. *Ugh.* Late last night I tried a laundry-folding charm from the first chapter of my spell book. First chapter means it will be easy, right? Wrong. I enunciated as clearly as I could and my shirts folded themselves all right—then floated up to the ceiling and stayed there. Getting dressed this morning involved climbing—one foot on my bedpost, another on the top of my dresser—and snatching the lowest-hanging shirt I could nab. The jeans were out of reach and no amount of coaxing brought them back down. So I wore yesterday's. Classy, I know. No idea how I'm going to get my clothes down.

"Learning anything cool?"

"Oh, so much, Momma."

"Stee-jay," I say under my breath. A lifting spell could be useful.

"You look happy." Momma's hands are on the steering wheel at ten and two.

"I just really hope I can win this competition. I don't want to lose all of this. If they close down, that's what happens, right?"

Momma does that smile where she tucks her lips but doesn't say anything.

"For real, Momma? Can I at least keep my spell book?"

"Anything school issued has to be returned, I'm afraid. Only students who complete training can continue to wand-carry, if I'm understanding that letter. But try not to put too much pressure on yourself. I'm proud of you whatever happens." Momma sighs. "And, Key, I want you to know I'm doing everything I can to try to get the money together for you to finish your six months somewhere else. Just in case. I'm doing my best, baby. It's just . . ." She looks out the window. "A lot of money."

Momma never likes to tell me she can't afford things. She'll tell me "maybe" or "we'll see" but I know that means no. I'm not mad at her for it. She works so hard and it's all for me. She always says that. I wish I was old enough to work. To help Momma out. I *was* able to get the dishes put away the other night with a spell. I only broke two cups. She wasn't home to see, thankfully.

"Don't worry about it, Momma." I reach for her hand and she wraps hers around mine. "I'm *going* to win this baking competition."

Her cheeks push up her eyes. "I bet you will, baby."

Speaking of keeping PRMA open . . . I slip my phone from my pocket and text Ash.

Me: Any word on Russ?

* ∗ ✳ ∗ *

Memaw's fast asleep in her recliner when we get home, but is quick to shout "I'm awake" when Momma's grocery bag hits the floor.

She eases up. "Key, baby, I was thinking, we could do one of my grandma Mamie's recipes for this competition." She slides a book over to me, its cover holding on by threads. Its yellow-stained pages are curled at their corners. A mothy aroma joins the nutmeg scent in the air.

"Memaw, you have something in the oven?" I ask, taking the recipe book.

Her eyebrows jump.

"Mom!" Momma rushes into the kitchen and the oven clangs open. "Momma, no more cooking when we not home! We agreed."

Memaw huffs, pursing her lips. "All right, Earlene. Don't start to fussing." She turns her attention back to me and her frustration melts like butter. "Now, lookie. These here recipes are over a hundred years old."

"WOW!" My fingers graze the scratchy pages. I need to make and bring nine dozen of whatever dessert I pick, so it needs to be something I know I can nail and make look good one hundred eight times.

"I watched my grandmother in the kitchen," Memaw says. "She never wrote anything down. But over the years when your momma was coming up, I started jotting down a thing here and there." She curls her slender hand around mine. "Next thing you know, I had all this. And now I'm giving it to you."

"No way? Really?"

"Really. Took me all night to find Mamie's, that's *my* memaw's, recipe book." She chuckles to herself. "Had it tucked away real good under a bunch ole junk in the closet."

I slip my shoes off at the door before Momma realizes I forgot and flip through the recipe book as delicately as I can. My knack for baking could *save* my school. How wild is that?

Gingerbread
Chocolate Cake Brownies
Tea Cake Cookies
Banana Cupcakes
Vanilla Buttermilk Cupcakes

Memaw watches in silence, her eyes smiling. I'm definitely using one of these recipes. If it's been baked for that many years, it's gotta be more than good.

"I think I like this one," I say, pointing. "But maybe I should try a few different ones . . ."

She squints. "Ohhh, yes. Chocolate-raspberry cupcakes sound wonderful. Yummy one. But yeah, you best make a batch first, see what you think." She blinks a few times. "One question, sugar."

"Yeah?" I sit down at the table.

"Wherever did you find Mamie's recipe book? I've been looking for it for years."

I . . . She just . . .

Her watery eyes fill every cracked crevice in me. I kiss the back of her hand. "It doesn't matter, Memaw. I'm just glad it's found."

* ✳ ✳ ❋ ✳ ✳ *

With groceries and a few potion ingredients I was able to find at Glenda's put away, dinner prep creeps up on us. But tonight I'm gonna bake some cupcakes as a practice run. I wash my hands before joining Memaw at the counter. She preps a chicken to roast and I set out the eggs and butter to bring 'em down to room temperature. Memaw says that makes a real difference. I grab the measuring cups and preheat the oven, checking that the rack is in the exact middle. Something else Memaw says matters. I portion out the dry ingredients in a bowl and peek at the recipe book again to be sure. It says room-temperature butter and eggs, but something funny about the milk. I glance at the scraggly handwriting.

Buttermilk from scratch

That's right. I grab a lemon and some whole milk and join Memaw, who is shelling some shrimp. The more you make from scratch, the richer the flavor profile, she always says. I wrinkle my nose squeezing lemon in a cup of milk. It feels wrong, but the minute the juices separate, I grin. Perfect. This'll give it a unique tang.

"Not too much now, watch it. It'll go sour on you."

I smile and pull back from pouring, then give it a stir.

"That's it. So, how's that magic stuff going?" she says. " 'Bout every night I hear you bumping around in that room of yours until the wee hours of morning."

My cheeks burn. "I'm learning a few things." I pull out my wand and aim it at a kitchen towel. "STEEEE-JAY." It lifts in the air. "I did it!" I flick my wrist and it flies right to Memaw's lap.

"Look at you. And what about potions? You been practicing them?"

Telling Momma and Memaw I didn't get Charms was a bigger deal to me than it was to them. And all my disappointment was of course overshadowed by the school closing and the baking competition. I'm surprised Memaw remembers I was assigned Potions.

"Not really."

"Any reason?"

"Nah. I don't know. I found all these charms I wanna master to help Momma, so I've been focused on that."

"But don't you have to master that potion stuff to finish your training?"

"Yeah, I guess I do." I didn't think about that.

"And since we know you're gonna win this competition, PRMA won't be closing."

Her confidence makes me smile.

"So shouldn't you be working on it?"

This is turning into a whole talking-to. "Yes, ma'am."

"Come on, up from the table." She cleans her hands and moves the pot simmering on the stove. "Let me see one of them potions."

"Wait . . . Memaw . . . I don't . . ."

She points to my books. "Open it on up. Let me see what you can do."

I sigh, grabbing the spell book Memaw found and gave me weeks ago, which is as hefty as it is ancient. I flip to a page with something that looks fairly simple.

GrowthGoo
{for plants}

To Potion Base add a handful of rotted parsnip, three eel ears, one dragon scale, and two tablespoons earwax. Set it on fire and boil.

Sprinkle in phoenix tears and stir until the mixture is pale.

Then, counterclockwise-stir while chanting "bellioso moratwix" 41 times.

I stomach the urge to barf as Memaw narrows her eyes in concentration, tugging at the necklace around her neck. She pulls out our gumbo pot and a low flame flickers underneath it on the stove.

I take a deep breath and put the Potion Base Mo gave us in the pot. I throw in the few ingredients we have on hand.

"I don't have any dragon scales or any parsnip. This isn't gonna work."

Memaw bites her lip. "Well, can you use sweet potatoes for that? It's a root, too. Ain't that the same thing?"

"I . . . I don't know. We can try it, I guess." I toss in the potatoes and a carrot substitute for the parsnip and stir, winding my wand. The mixture is sticky like peanut butter. Memaw takes my arm and winds it backward, then forward, then backward again.

"Try stirring like this. Get all of it from the sides and corners like you would mixing anything else."

The mixture folds over on itself, smoother with each turn. I set it on the fire and sprinkle in the phoenix tears. *Pop.* Purple sparks fizzle above the pot and Memaw lowers the fire. The picture in the spell book is crackled with age, but I can't miss the green color, deep and forest-y. The pot on the stove rumbles quietly with that same color, and notes of sandalwood and pine fill the air.

"I think we did it? That was so easy." I ladle out a bit. "And if it's as useful as it says . . ." I pour the ladled amount on Memaw's aloe vera plant and the pot cracks; soil spills everywhere as its leaves stretch to the ceiling, tripling in size. "WOW!"

Memaw high-fives me and I pour the potion into mason

jars since that's all I have. She screws on the lids and labels them with a marker.

GrowthGoo
By Kyana, Nov 1

"That's my girl," she says.

I clean up the potion stuff and, with Memaw's help, lug the giant aloe vera plant outside. Then I take my recipe and the old spell book Memaw gave me to my room for safekeeping. She sure knew a lot about helping me pull that potion off. I guess it is a lot like cooking. I open the rickety spell book and flip to the first page.

This Guide to Spellcasting Is Presented to

But the rest of the page is ripped out.

CHAPTER 19

* **✳** *

3 days and counting

I'm surrounded by triple-tiered cupcakes topped in glitter buttercream with a gooey ganache center. Everyone in the crowd at the competition has a unicorn horn sprouting from their forehead. I serve my cupcakes and the crowd raves, then doubles in size. I scramble to ice more, but I only have a few left. My breath's quick. The judges say everyone has to get one or I can't win. And right there, in the middle of City Hall, a kitchen appears and I start baking more.

But the oven is too hot. The icing too runny.

My heart's thudding in my chest and I'm slick with sweat.

"She can't hang." The judge's tinselly voice echoes like

through a megaphone. *"It's just too* much *for her. Nice try, though."*

No! No! I can do it. *I try to shout, but words stick in my throat and tears sting my eyes.*

The crowd's smiles droop and I'm swallowed by a sea of sad faces. I reach for my wand even though I know it's wrong, but with magic I could whip things up so much faster.

"Wait," I yell, wand in hand. The spell. What's the spell? I can't think. "Wait!"

But the judges turn their backs on me and the crowd dissolves.

"WAIT!!!!" I sit up, gasping, paper stuck to my face. *A* dream. *It was just a dream.* What time is it? What day? I yawn. Thursday? My wristwatch confirms. School bus comes in a couple hours. The competition is in three days! Last I remember, the streetlamps were buzzing as I flipped through the potion part of my spell book. Seeing Memaw so excited about GrowthGoo got *me* excited and I've been sucked into all the possibilities with potions since. I peel a piece of paper off my face—it feels like being wrapped as a human Christmas present.

Ash's name lights up my phone screen. *Finally.*

Ash: Actually, no Russ updates 😬

Rats. We need as many people there as possible.

Me: Really? Wow

Ash: He's being real . . . Russ-like. You know? He
wants an apology.

Me: HE WANTS . . . OMG. Tell him we ain't trying to
be friends. Just come support PRMA. That's what
this is about.

Ash: 👍 I'll be attributing that quote to *you*

Me: It's the truth! He can't possibly be THAT self
absorbed that he doesn't wanna help save our
school?

Ash: . . .

Me: That's 😖

Ash: Will keep you posted.

Ugh. I pull off the covers and scrape the crust from my
eyes. My laptop's still open and I tap it. The screen glows,
eighteen different search windows still open, each with
another article on perfecting a ganache filling.

I throw on clothes and get downstairs. Everything's quiet
and Momma's already gone. *Which sucks.* I grab a bowl and
am stuffing down some cereal and milk when a folded note
with my name on it in Momma's handwriting catches my eye.

Good luck on your math test today!
Love, Mom

That's today? Crap!

I should have spent the night reviewing formulas instead of baking techniques. Maybe I can catch some study time on the bus. My luck is the worst. If I fail this test, will I even be able to compete? Momma was clear: I *have* to pass.

The bus ride to school gets me twenty minutes or so, but by the time the sun is bright enough for me to see my paper, we're pulling up to school. A quick scan of my spell book and best I found was a memory charm. I chant it to myself three times, hoping, pleading I pronounced it correctly and that it works. Then I take a hard glance at my math formulas. *Please remember them.* Off the bus, up the steps, down the hall, and the first-period bell rings as I slide into my desk.

"Good luck." Nae's seat is right next to mine.

She's hardly spoken to me lately. I study her face. No hint of sarcasm. She means it? Maybe things *will* be okay?

"Thanks," I say. "You too."

"What's with that competition thing you're doing?"

What do I say? Or how much, rather? "Oh, I'm doing it for charity, sort of. Like if I win I want to donate the money . . ." I'm just so happy she's talking to me again.

"To?"

"Uhm."

"Girls, if you want to take a zero and finish your conversation in the hall, be my guest," says Ms. Sameer. "Otherwise, zip it."

We face forward.

"I really hope you do well, Key," Nae whispers. "Doing it for charity is cool."

"Thanks, Nae."

"I'm still annoyed I don't know what's going on with you." She flashes me squinted eyes and I catch a glimpse of a smirk. "But I . . . I hope you win!"

She's such a good friend.

"You should come!" But before I can say any more Ms. Sameer is hovering over me.

The test flies by and I'm lucky that eight of the ten questions *actually* look familiar. Maybe my ten minutes a day is helping. Or maybe I'm better at spellcasting than math. *Highly doubtful.*

The bell rings and I feel okay. Good, even. Nae's waiting at the door for me, but I let her know I'll meet her in the cafeteria. This last question is taking forever and the teacher was nice enough to let me finish it before I leave for lunch.

After a few minutes staring at the test, I feel that the formula I need for the last question is like a dimming light. I grasp for it, trying to remember if the *A* goes before the *C* and if I multiply that two times? I chance a guess and pick *C*. Then, press submit on the screen and turn in my scratch paper, grateful at least enough of them looked familiar that I should have passed. The rest of the morning is a blur.

Lunchtime rolls around and the cafeteria is buzzing with cliques of kids in every corner. Trays slap tables amid a hum of a million different conversations. I don't see Nae as I scoot to the pizza line. I bump into Tommy, who was the one put-ting up the baking competition posters at the library.

"Oh, hey," he says.

A tickle in my nose makes my head fuzzy. "Wa—wa—wassup." It comes out more like a violent sneeze and the space between my eyes throbs. Another one. "Achoo!"

And another. "Achoo!"

Buzzing whirls through me like electricity as another sneeze—a great big one this time—sneaks up on me.

"Aaaaaacho!"

The lights flash and everything goes dark. Students gasp and silence umbrellas the space.

Wait, d-did I do that?

I feel for the wand hiding inside my sleeve.

"Oh snap!" Tommy laughs. "Power's out. Maybe class'll be delayed."

"Achoo?" I whisper. *Was it my words? Did they sound like a spell?* I knew keeping my wand in my sleeve was a risky idea.

Sneeze again? Maybe that'll undo it. How do you fake a sneeze? I move my lips in wide circles, trying to make my nose tickle. I look ridiculous. Mo said magic is stubborn. I steady my feet and say it a little louder this time, making sure my wand is pressed tight against my arm. It's gotta have skin contact to work, pretty sure.

"AHHH-TSU."

The lights flicker back on.

Okay, that spell needs a different name.

"Ah, guess not," Tommy says.

I wipe the sweat from my forehead, no longer hungry. I really need to spend *more* time studying my spell book. I didn't even know that was a spell.

"I'm going to grab a tray," Tommy says.

"I'm just gonna grab a seat and catch some study time, I think."

Settled at a table by myself I can't help but look for Nae again. No sight of her as I pull out my hefty magic book with a grunt. Last time I saw Ash, she put a cloaking spell on the cover so from the outside it looks like an algebra book. Studying spells is way more interesting than figuring out what the heck a hypotenuse is.

I flip through the pages to the tab on reversal spells.

To reverse a cast spell, simply cast it again with your mind set on undoing. If your magic is particularly resistant, use *Aga'thrut megaya*—the General Magic Reversal Spell—three times in a row within 64 seconds after the original spell was cast. Make a counterclockwise motion with your wand and backwards-flick. If that doesn't reverse your spell, see a certified Wizarding Instructor for reversal oversight.

See Appendix XICII for more info.

Also see section Potion Antidotes for Spells.

Reversing a spell is probably a good one to know given the lights snafu. "Aga'thrut megaya," I whisper a few times, practicing the wrist motion. "Aga'thrut megaya, aga'thrut megaya, aga'thrut megaya."

"This seat taken?" Tommy's back with a goofy smirk on his face. I slap my magic book closed, hoping he didn't see. Ash only bewitched the cover. He furrows his brow a moment, then slips into the seat across from me.

"So how'd Ms. Sameer's test go?" he asks, setting down his tray.

"We'll find out soon," I say. "It felt okay. She said she'd have grades up during lunch. Fingers crossed."

"I bombed it. I just know it."

"You know Nae's a math whiz, right? You're already at the library volunteering on Sundays. You may as well join our study group."

"Really?" His cheeks flush. "You think she'd be cool with that? I mean, I don't wanna crowd or anything?"

Nae thinks Tommy Bushnell is the cutest boy in the entire sixth grade, so I know for a fact him being there wouldn't be a crowd.

"She won't mind. I'm sure."

"Speaking of the devil!"

Nae sets her tray down. I reach for her chocolate milk and she slaps my hand away.

"Hey!"

"It's strawberry today. I actually like that."

I fake a dry retch. "Strawberry, *ewwww*."

"Yeah, see! Always looking out for you." She isn't lying. I hate strawberry milk. It tastes like rotten eggs soaked in Pepto-Bismol. She laughs, sliding on the seat next to me like usual.

Finally things feel normal between us.

Ding. Nae's phone chimes.

"Grades." She pulls it out even though we all know she passed.

"I'm scared to look," Tommy says. Nae's tapping her phone extra quiet. Which is the norm when Tommy's around. She's never outright said it but I *think* it's because she likes him, but I'm not trying to put her on front street like that.

"You passed," Nae says without looking at me. (We have each other's passwords because hashtag besties.)

"What? *Yes!*" I nudge her playfully. "You're the best tutor ever!"

Tommy's face glows blue in the light of his phone. He sighs and I already know.

"Dang, I'm sorry," I say. "But really, study group on Sundays will help."

Nae snaps her head around at me, eyes bugged like I have three heads or something. "What?!" Her eyes dart from him to me and back to him.

"I told him he could join our study group on Sundays," I say under my breath. "Figured that was cool."

She sucks her teeth and something tells me I've messed up. Again. Tommy's lost in his phone, raking his hands through his hair. I whisper, making sure he doesn't overhear. "What's wrong?"

"Nothing. Nothing at all. You know what? I'm not hungry anymore. I'll catch you later."

"Nae?"

She doesn't answer. I dig circles into my scalp. I swear the more I try to help, the more things blow up.

∗✳∗

At home that night, Memaw isn't feeling well, so I make dinner (an easy-peasy chicken pot pie) *and* dessert.

I wanted to practice baking, so I got out the banana cupcake recipe. My bananas weren't ripe, so it was almost a bust. But then I remembered I could brown them in the oven and voilà. But they were meh.

I sit slumped at the table, staring at them and Memaw's recipe book, and finger the half-heart charm at my neck. I haven't been able to stop thinking about Nae since that exchange, especially since I hardly saw her at school after. I bury my head in my hands. How am I going to fix any of this? PRMA? Now Nae? I'm the literal worst.

I allow myself a few more moments of self-pity before dragging myself upstairs and plopping on my bed. I have ten thousand things to do before I can earn some phone time from Momma to try to call Nae. I sigh and pull out my assignment sheet. Reading log, a math fact sheet, and finishing my science lab. Three things. Not bad.

My phone vibrates, but I know the rules and turn it on Do Not Disturb. I fold my legs underneath me and tuck my favorite pillow at my back and start with the fact sheet. My fingers work over the math page as my mind wanders to the bananas, buttermilk, and milky chocolate with tangy raspberry. I'm almost sure those would be the yummiest option, right?

I tap my pencil and notice my math page is done. Wow, that was . . . suspiciously painless. I set it aside and grab my copy of *The Autobiography of Alice Walker*. I need to be completely sure about whatever I choose. The chance to win fifty thousand dollars isn't likely gonna fall in my lap again. So, my dessert needs to slay. I set a reading timer and for a moment the world of flour, sugar, and butter quiets.

After what feels like forever, my reading is finished, lab notes are done, and I glance at my phone. It's blowing up from people apologizing that with the day off from magic school, they've made other plans. I sigh and put away all my homework, zip up my backpack, and lay out tomorrow's clothes, which I am lucky enough to get from the ceiling using a yardstick.

I check my phone again. Still no definitive word on Russ and I'm just over it. Looks like it'll be me, Mo, Ash, Eric, and maybe a few others there Saturday. My shoulders sink. *Is our plan falling apart?* I set an alarm to get up early to practice baking before school and bury myself in bed, hugging tight to my pillow.

CHAPTER 20

*₊∗∗✳∗₊∗

2 days and counting

Friday morning comes entirely too soon, mostly because I set my alarm early. But Nae is the first thing on my mind when my eyes bat open. I need to try talking to her. I didn't know she'd bug out about Tommy like that. My alarm blares again, prying me out of bed. The house is quiet and dark and the baking competition dissolves my woes about Nae for the second. The competition is *tomorrow* and I still haven't settled on what I'm making. Ugh. *Stress!* My stomach is a bed of eels. I have an hour before school and I want to make one more trial batch before the real thing. Just to be sure.

I click on a lamp and run my finger down one of the old recipe books, eyeing the ingredients for Mamie's cupcake recipe. *I think we have some of this, but I'm still gonna have to buy a lot of stuff.* I glance at the porcelain panda on my dresser with a sigh.

Low tunes from Memaw's record player pulse through the walls. Memaw is already up? That tugs my lips in a smile. I chew my lip a moment, then, trusting my gut, grab Mamie's cupcake recipe. I book it downstairs to find clouds of flour in the air and the whir of the mixer.

"You're up?"

"I wouldn't miss helping you practice, baby."

The pressure is on. I wipe the morning crust from my eyes. "Let's do this!"

* ✳ ❋ ✳ *

The school day was a blur. We had a field trip to the African American History Museum today, which was bittersweet because 1) hello, no classes, which means no homework, but 2) we were split into trip groups *all* day by last name, which meant other than waving at Nae from my bus's line, I didn't get to talk to her at all. Without Nae on the brain, all I could think about was getting home to make the however many dozen cupcakes I need to show up with tomorrow. Nine, I think? *Yes, nine.* That's a lot of cupcakes. I'm so glad they're cool with us bringing the cupcakes. I can't imagine baking on the spot like on those shows! Too much pressure.

I haven't felt this antsy since the first day of magic school. Thankfully, Mamie's recipe this morning came out *chef's kiss* perfect. Duplicating it this evening should be a cinch. If I'm focused. I hurry into the house and throw down my bag. Only to turn around and pick it up and put it away properly, hearing what Momma would say if she came in and saw it like that. I peek for Memaw, hoping she is feeling up to helping. That's double the hands!

"Kyana, that you baby?" she shouts from the kitchen.

"Yes, Memaw." Nervous anticipation hurries my feet to the kitchen, where Memaw has all the ingredients laid out and the oven preheated. "You ready? We got a lot of dozens to get through."

This is it. I better do the best baking I've ever done in my life.

"As ready as I'll every be." I grab a bowl as she dunks her giant measuring cup in the sugar. I almost remind her to slide a knife across it, level it off. But I remember she said sugar always needs a little extra.

"Pass me that there." She points to the baking powder.

I'm fancy today, wand in hand. "Stije." I wind my wrist slowly and the tin can lifts in the air. *Now go. Go to Memaw.* My tongue pokes my cheek. The can bobs a moment, then moves through the air to Memaw's hand.

"You getting good at that, che."

On my side of the kitchen, the table's covered in extract, nutmeg, more bags of chocolate than we actually need, and frozen raspberries. We're going to be at it for hours. The competition rules say there will be three finalists chosen and a shot to compete in a final round. My body tingles with excitement. Second and third place get some sort of prize that's not money. Momma said it sounds cool, classes somewhere or something. But first place gets the grand prize money.

Scents of warm chocolate swell in my nostrils and seconds later the oven *ding*s.

First batch ready.

"Stije!" I say, wand pointed at the oven mitts across the kitchen. They lift, hover a moment, and fly through the air toward me, then slip right on my hands. I am getting *good* at this.

The oven opens with a creak and a gush of heat like a breeze in the desert assaults me. Scraping metal cries as I slide out the baking pan. "They are absolutely perfect!"

"Now set 'em down over there," Memaw says, pointing to the rack on the counter. "Get 'em cooled down."

"I remember," I say. "Can't ice 'em until they're *completely* cooled."

"My girl knows her stuff."

I set them down and get the next batch in the oven. With all in order, I chance a glance at the phone. It's after 9 p.m. Momma will be home soon. She's strict about my bedtime usually but tonight she said I can stay up as long as I need to prepare for the competition.

"We don't half do things," she said. "If you're gonna do it, do it the absolute best you can. No exceptions."

Sounded like a good excuse for a later bedtime to me. Memaw switches the record on the record player.

"You know we can just use Spotify on the phone?"

"Spot-a-what?"

"Never mind."

She blows the dust from the black disc and sets it on the record with a scratch. Her shoulders start bouncing to the beat and before I know it we're both jamming and icing cupcakes. My buttercream frosting tastes like sunshine chasing away rain on a cloudy day. Vanilla with hints of berry cartwheel on my taste buds. *Mmmmmmm.*

"The trick's using salted butter," I say.

Memaw winks. "That's it!"

Another *ding.* Next batch done.

"One more to stir up and we're done," I say.

Empty butter wrappers are piled on the table, a thin pool of grease underneath.

"Flej'err stije." I twist my wrist and flick, flick, flick. The wrappers crumple in a tight ball and zoom to the trash.

Another spell, executed perfectly. *Eeeeeek!*

"Watch out now, y'all," Memaw chides, hunched over an icing bag. "Kyana think she knows a thing or two." Circles of pearly frosting from Memaw's piping bag stack higher and higher on each fluffy brown surface. *Dozens* more need to be frosted. We're gonna be here literally all night.

I'm managing the ones coming out the oven, but I bet I can help frost, too.

I flip through my spell book with a sugar-crusted finger and find the spell for mixing. It's in the cooking section. How convenient! There's a million words on the page, warnings, and boxes of notes with added information.

Where's the spell? My finger slides down the page until . . . *Aha! There it is.*

Wand in one hand, I tap my icing bag twice and rotate in a circle above a naked cupcake.

"Rontom milyon," I whisper. The bag rises and contracts, like an invisible hand is squeezing it, an even stream of icing pouring from its metal tip.

Yesssss!

It swirls around the cupcake in the same motion I made with my wand and in seconds a perfectly iced chocolate cupcake stares back. *Yippee!*

"Better pick up that jaw off the floor before somebody steps on it." Momma's voice makes me grin even harder.

"I did it, Momma. Look!"

She watches as I hold my wand steady and the piping bag ices another cupcake, then another, like a magical assembly line.

"Oh goodness! I'm impressed."

"Mom, how you feeling today?" She kisses Memaw, who's standing in the middle of the kitchen all of a sudden, her hands in her pockets.

"Earlene! Hey, baby, where you been?"

"Work, Mom."

"Work on a Sunday?"

"It's not Sunday, Mom. It's Friday. Kyana's baking competition is tomorrow."

"Don't try and tell me it ain't the Lord's day." She's feisty now. "That preacher just came by here trying to tell me how good service was."

No preacher's been by. Memaw and I've been baking for hours.

Momma kisses her again. "Okay, Mom."

Distracted for a minute, I look back and my wand is piling circles of buttercream on the salt and pepper shakers.

Oops! Okay, uhm . . . how does the reversal spell go?

"Aga'threw migi yoya."

My wand trembles. *Uhm, no. That's not it.*

"Aga'thrut mago ya."

Tiny sparks burst from the tip of my wand. Momma yelps.

That's not it either.

"Aga'thrut megaya." *That's the one!* "Aga'thrut megaya."

My wand jiggles a moment and a flash of purple light bursts from its tip.

Uh-oh. What was that?

I blink, and streams of creamy buttercream pour from the piping bag in circles like before back on top of the cupcakes and I exhale.

Guess it was nothing.

"It's all good, Momma."

She throws her hands up. "I'm getting outta here before y'all blow this place up." She pinches my cheek. "Going to bed."

"Night, Momma." I don't even ask if she can make it tomorrow. I know the answer.

"Get in bed at a decent hour, please." She points at Memaw. "And get her in bed, too."

"Yes, ma'am."

"We leave here tomorrow at eleven a.m. sharp."

Wait, what? "We? You took off work?"

"I sure did. I wouldn't miss it for the world, baby."

I could scream, I'm so excited! Tomorrow is going to be *the best* day of my life.

CHAPTER 21

* ✳ *

At a certain point of tossing and turning trying to sleep, it really is pointless.

So, at 3 a.m.—only two hours after we finished icing all seventy-two cupcakes and cleaning the kitchen—I finally gave up on trying to sleep. Bubble guts are a real thing. And even though my spell book says swallowing a slug remedies a nervous tummy, I'll just keep the quivering tummy, thanks.

Instead of sleep I practiced spells and somehow managed to bewitch my old ratty stuffed elephant (from way back when) to make pig noises. And I only cracked one picture frame in the process. Calling that a win. My clothes are still hovering at the ceiling, but hey . . . baby steps.

Around 6 a.m., I texted Mo, reminding her of the time to

be there. All adults get up early, I'm pretty sure. (And judging by Momma, I'm not sure if they sleep at all.)

Then I made sure Momma and Memaw were ready, and we loaded up the car carefully and made our way downtown.

Momma's spent the last ten minutes of this car ride gushing over a letter from school. Time has flown by ever since starting magic school and learning it's being closed down. I hardly even remember going to my regular classes. But apparently I have been going and doing quite well. I saw the envelope, but I'm so used to this not being a momentous occasion I didn't even open it. But Momma did this morning and I have an A in *all* my classes including, you guessed it, math!

"That's my baby! That's my baby!" She's full-on dancing in the driver's seat and I'm just hoping we don't wreck. "I'm so proud of you, Kyana!"

A stoplight turns green and the car juts into motion. Memaw's in the back humming to herself and looking out the window.

"Thanks, Momma. I'm going to keep it up. I promise." And I mean it. It feels good seeing Momma smile like this. I don't think I've ever pulled an A in math before. And sure it's an 89.5 so barely an A, but I'm still counting it. I can't believe it. All that practice, I wasn't even sweating math because of everything else going on. And I have *an A?*

Maybe practice does make perfect. A thought needles at me and I shift in my seat. Maybe it's the same with magic?

My lap is weighed down by my spell book. I fan through its pages to distract me from the fireworks in my gut. I flip each page, reciting aloud, practicing enunciation.

ADD FRAGRANCE
Say once: Nasateree
Then name the plant you'd like to emulate.
Do: Wind wrist and flick once when you say the spell
and again when you say the plant.

Hmm. I pull my wand from its pocket and hold it up. The car stutters to a stop at a red light and I snatch my hand below the window when I spot a balding man in the car beside us staring *hard*. I roll the wand in my hands and read the spell again until the light turns green. When cars move past us in a blur I raise my wand again.

"Nah-sah-tah-ray." I flick. "Lemon." A puff of air spits from my wand. *Wait!* Why not something flowery? Why on earth would I say lemon? But it's too late, the car smells like someone's been bathing in Lysol.

Momma's nose curls as she veers onto the highway. "Kyana, what in good creation are you doing over there?"

"Sorry, Momma, just trying to . . ." *Keep myself from*

thinking about anything but this competition. "Practice."
My stomach's in my throat.

"Okay." She rolls down the windows a minute.

I shield my hair from the wind. Last thing I need is to be
nervous and look a mess. Ms. Mo would get one look at my
hair and be as embarrassed as me.

"Well, maybe try ones that aren't so strong."

I smirk, nodding, then turn a page.

RAISE SPOKEN VOLUME
Say: Qworiuntum
Do: Tap throat.
Raise hand to desired volume.
Tap throat again.

"Let's see," I mutter, but Momma doesn't hear me over
the radio. I sit up in my seat. "Qwar-ree-un-tum." I poke my
neck with my wand. Then flick my wrist up just as a burp
bubbles up my throat. "BURRRRP!!!!" The car rattles like
we've driven over an earthquake.

"KYANA!" Mom jumps, startled. She corrects the steering wheel.

"Qwar-ree-un-tum," I whisper, but even that sounds like
a wind storm. I tap my throat again, tilting my wrist down,
down. "Sorry," I say, and it comes out normal volume.
"Sorry, Momma. Just . . . trying to practice."

"Well, practice a different one."

I stuff down a laugh and turn another page.

FORGETTING

Say three times: Vergeetsa

Do: Tap. Tap. (Downward wrist motion)

Hmm. "Vergeetsa," I whisper, practicing. Simple. But why would someone want to forget something?

I turn a few more pages but Memaw's shout from the back of the car startles me.

"You think yo' daddy will be here too, Earlene?"

Paw Paw—Momma's dad—has been dead for years. I have one memory of him. He wore overalls and I sat on his knee. He had a big booming laugh that scared me. That's literally all I remember.

"I don't think so, Mom," Momma says.

"Hmph," Memaw huffs. "Well, that's a shame."

I guess forgetting could be useful. I shift in my seat. But I don't know. Somehow that doesn't feel right. I reach back behind my seat for Memaw's hand. She laces her bony fingers between mine and I squeeze. "Love you, Memaw."

"Love you too, baby. Don't be mad about yo' Paw Paw not making it. I'm gonna get on him about working so much."

I cheese. So that's where Momma got it from.

* * * ✳ * *

City Hall is much busier than it was on our field trip. We roll past Areala's Aviary and I tell Momma about the Link Ms. Mo introduced us to and the beautiful song her birds sang. We park on the street outside of high-rise homes that tower as tall as the sun, each hugged in wrought-iron balconies and single-pane glass doors.

"You have everything?" Momma asks.

"Yes, I'm sure." Thanks to my insomnia I checked my things twelve times at least. Parking is bad, I guess, because we circle the building three times before settling in a spot. A bus roars by as we get out. I tap my pocket, rolling my fingers over the lump there. *My wand.*

Carrying 108 cupcakes requires a magic of its own. Momma used to be a waitress, so she juggles most of the boxes like a pro. I take what I can. Memaw loops her arm into mine. Best to keep her holding on to one of us. Downtown's a busy place, full of noise.

Indoor walkways arc over us like bridges from one building to the other. We pass under one, then another, washed for a moment in their shade. The area opens up to a square patch of grass outlined in pavement. City Hall's many buildings tower on all sides. Red banners with white letters that read Rockford Baking Competition sway in the wind.

The buzz of the crowd swells. People that were dots far away grow larger and far more intimidating. My feet are heavy. I have to present my cupcakes in front of *all* these people?

227

"I don't know if I can do this."

"If anybody can get up there and wow these judges, you can," Momma says.

I nod and force my feet to keep walking. But each step speeds up the tempo in my chest. I didn't know there'd be so many people here. So many eyes. A table on the far end sits under a sign for competitors to check in. We head that way and I swallow, my entire stomach hovering in the back of my throat. A man with sprigs of gray hair waves us his way. A petite woman next to him hurries over to meet us like she's had too many cups of coffee. She takes some of the boxes from Momma's hands as a gust of wind whips past, almost knocking her off her tall pointy shoes.

"You can set that over here." Mr. Wispy Gray Hair is beaming ear to ear. "And whom might we have here?"

Momma nudges me with her elbow.

"My name's Kyana Turner, from Thompson Middle."

"Ahhh. Our youngest participant."

Ash was right, I'm the only amateur entering. Momma must sense my panic, because she shakes her head at me like *don't even start.*

"What are you, about twelve? Thirteen?" He folds his arms across his chest.

"Yes, sir."

He pats my head. *Why do people do that?*

"I'm impressed with you, young lady," he says. "Winner

or not, it takes a lot of courage to enter this competition against *real* pastry chefs."

I gulp. *What have I gotten myself into?*

Momma's still shaking her head, reading me like a book, apparently. "She's just as excited to be here," Momma says. "She's going to give these chefs a run for their money."

He stares a moment in disbelief. *Yes, mister check-in dude. My momma is serious. She's my number one STAN.*

"Ha! Well, I'm excited to see it." He extends a hand. "I'm Steve. I'll be one of the three judges on the panel."

Oh crap! He's a judge? I stand up straighter, smoothing my hair, and shake his hand back. Momma always says a good handshake tells something about a person, so I hold his hand firm. My wand slips further down my pocket when I raise my arm and for a split second I can't breathe. Thought it slipped out. *That'd be awkward.*

"Nice to meet you. Julie here will take you over to the tent with the other contestants. We'll call your name when it's time to come up and tell the judges about what you baked."

"Oh, okay." I glance at my cupcakes, walking faster. *Get those out of the heat, please!*

Julie leads us across the courtyard, past rows and rows of white folding chairs. In the center is a stage with a microphone. I didn't even think about public speaking being involved.

Steps away from the tent entrance, Julie points. "You're welcome to wait in there with your family. About ten minutes before things start, we just ask that everyone is inside the tent to hear the judge's instructions." She smiles. "Then we'll begin."

She says that last part like it's not the scariest words I've ever heard. *What was I thinking?* My feet stick to the ground like cement, but I urge them forward.

Just as my heart feels like it might burst from trepidation, I spot a gang of familiar faces across the field, and practically break into a run.

"Ms. Moesha!"

She hugs me tight. Eric and Ashley are steps behind her. No sign of Russ, so I guess that's that.

"You made it," I say. "I'm so glad you made it!"

Somehow having them here, having friends here who *get* the reason I'm doing this, makes it feel all the more possible.

"You are amazing, Kyana." Eric offers a fist bump.

I bump it back. "Hey, I haven't won yet."

"You will, though," Ashley says. "You're the youngest person in the competition. That's going to go over well with those judges."

"I think so too," Mo says.

Ashley nods. "I wish I had your nerves."

I stand a little taller.

"We won't keep you." Mo ushers them on. "We'll be over there, near the front!"

Momma, Memaw, and I retreat inside the tent and it's loads cooler. I lift my curls from my neck and fan. Memaw makes her way to the refreshments table as a man in a white chef coat clears his throat. I recognize his coat as one of those fancy kind chefs wear from the TV show *Best Chef*. Memaw and I watch that sometimes to get ideas of stuff to try in the kitchen.

"If everyone would gather around." He gestures and glances at his watch. "We'll go over the rules in just a minute."

People snap to the center of the tent like magnets. It's hard to tell who's competing and who's not, but it's crowded.

"Ma'am?" A helper with rainbow-streaked hair and an armful of blue lanyards approaches Momma. "I need all contestants wearing one of these." The helper offers to slip it over Momma's head.

"Oh, thank you. But I'm not the contestant." She points to me. "She is." She nudges me to introduce myself.

"I'm Kyana," I say, reading their name tag and pronouns. "Thank you, Tae."

They offer me the lanyard, eyes wide. "Wow. Well, best of luck." They smile with a wink. "Trying out something like this at your age? You're *already* a champ in my book."

I smile, unsure of what to say to that. Maybe that's true. I don't know. But I wanna win!

"Oh, and doesn't look like you've reviewed the rules and signed. Or had your mom sign, I mean," they say, skimming a clipboard. I look to Momma as they hand me a paper on a clipboard. I take a seat and read carefully, Momma over my shoulder, pen in hand.

The rules aren't what I expected at all and the further I read, the clammier my hands get. Three finalists will be chosen today, and next weekend those three will compete in a final round. But only first place gets the cash prize.

So I have to prove myself today and then if I make it—*if*—I have to do this all again. I gulp, nails digging into my chair before Momma signs. She hands the clipboard to the helper and they smile. I remember their words and repeat them to myself. *I can do this.*

I gaze around at the tent *full* of people, many more than I expected. There are thirty-eight entries. We're all numbered. I'm #37. The lanyard dangles from my neck and I needle my toe in the grass.

My knee won't stop bouncing and at this point I don't expect it to. One by one, contestant numbers are called. Moments later they rush back in here covered in sweat but smiling big. Relieved, I guess.

"Number thirty-two," Julie, the assistant, calls. *Getting close.* An older man in a Hawaiian shirt and a grass skirt huffs a breath, mumbles, and leaves the tent.

"You okay?" Memaw pulls me into her, and I nod. I'm *determined* to win. *Determined* to save PRMA. Ash and Mo are right, me being in sixth grade *has* to impress them. I'm gonna lead with that.

"Number thirty-six." Julie and a red-haired girl with a top knot disappear from the tent.

I'm next. OMG.

I hop up, pacing.

"Key?"

"I'm good, Momma. Just need to get some energy out."

"You're gonna do fine, baby. Just fine."

What I wanna say is, "If I don't stand up and move around my chest will explode." My heart's racing twice the speed of my feet. The applause outside dies down and I know any second it'll be my turn if I don't faint on the spot. Julie's pointy nose and auburn hair slip between the tent flaps.

She looks around and her eyes settle on me. "Thirty-seven, we're ready for you."

CHAPTER 22

✳

The stage is only steps off the ground, thankfully, because as woozy as I am with nerves I might fall off.

The judges' table is to my right, a podium on the far end of the stage, and the gawking audience to my left. A few clap when I step out, but I study my feet. Behind me, Momma's standing in the flap of the tent, gesturing for me to keep walking.

"Over this way." The emcee beckons for me. And right there, smack dab in the middle of the stage, is a table with four of my cupcakes. One for each judge and one for the emcee. Serving waiters stand on the outside of the aisles in the audience with piles of my cupcakes on their platters. There aren't nearly enough cupcakes to serve the endless sea of chairs. But a sign in the back says the first hundred guests to show up get a taste. The seats are *filled* with people, adults and kids. I recognize a few faces from Thompson Middle.

In the second row, next to a woman in a business suit jotting down notes, I spot two faces and my heart skips a beat. Russ and Nae. *They came!* I wiggle my fingers at Nae, waving, hoping she sees.

"This is Miss Key . . . yan . . . y-yay . . . ney Turner," the emcee says.

It's "Kyana." That's not hard to say, bruh.

"Ms. Turner is a sixth grader at Thompson Middle School over in the south side of Park Row area," he continues, and whispers erupt from the crowd.

"Sssssh! I'm tryin' to hear." Ms. Mo says to the chattering folks behind her.

"Miss Turner, if you would, tell us a little bit about your cupcakes."

The mic's a brick in my hands. I find Nae's face and she's grinning so big, the knot between my shoulders eases.

"It's okay. Don't be shy. As much or as little as you want to say."

"I—" My voice booms all around me and I shuffle my feet. "My grandma and I like to cook together. This is a recipe her grandma taught her and she taught me."

A few swoons from the crowd slow my rattling pulse.

"Isn't that sweet? And tell us, why do you think this recipe will win today?"

That's easy. "Because Memaw's the *best* cook in the hood!"

The crowd breaks out in applause. Waiters move through the first few rows offering cupcakes. Nae gets one and winks up at me. I can't believe she's here. She's the best friend anyone could have. Russ grabs one too but stops himself right before taking a huge bite. Julie motions for me to head to the tent. I walk toward her but can't keep my eyes off the crowd. Do they like it? My fingers are crossed so tight behind me, I'm holding my breath as I step off the stage.

Back at the tent, Momma throws her arms around me and slams a sloppy wet kiss on my cheek. *Ew.* I pretend to try to pull away. Across the stage, the judges are munching into their cupcakes.

Moment of truth.

Please love it!

I rise on tiptoe for a better view as Julie disappears inside to grab the last contestant. One judge nods his head, jotting down something on a square note card on the tabletop in front of him. Another one taps a pen on his chin a moment, then writes. The last one is still chewing. He takes another bite and from all the way across the stage, he meets my eyes. Still . . . no writing. He sets down the cupcake, still staring.

Uh-oh. He hates it. Shoot! He hates it!

Just before scribbling something on his paper, he winks at me and cracks the tiniest smirk.

OMG! OMG! OMG! Was that a good wink? It looked like a good wink. My heart thuds like it might burst from excitement.

Until the unthinkable happens.

The judge flinches a moment and purple sparks shoot from his ears.

I blink and blink again. But the scene doesn't change. *Sparks are coming out of his ears!* I've seen those sparks before . . . somewhere. I gnaw down on my lip. Besides a few chatters in the crowd, the event keeps going like no one noticed. I noticed! I saw! In seconds, a chair in the front row starts wobbling like it's going to take off from the ground. Oh my, *what* is happening?

I fumble for my wand, scrambling for words. Momma's saying something I can't hear. I don't know what's happening. But I know sparks don't fly out of ears and chairs don't float.

This is my magic. Somehow my magic did this.

Wand pointed, my mind's never been so clear. "Aga'thrut megaya," I whisper. The chair sets back on the ground, still. The people nearby are wholly befuddled, trying to figure out how the heck a *chair* was floating!

OH. MY. GOSH.

Don't panic. Think.

The forgetting spell!

"Vergeetsa, vergeetsa, vergeetsa." *Tap, tap.*

The creases of confusion in their foreheads dissolve, replaced by blank stares. Oh thank heavens. It worked! Julie has the last contestant up on stage. It's *almost* over and I'm *almost* relieved.

Almost.

Until a lady in the third row of the taste testers, still chewing my cupcake, hunches over like she might vomit.

Oh dear.

She hops up, gripping her throat. A waiter pulls her aside.

OMG. My cupcake is going to kill this woman.

This is *not* happening.

I bolt from the tent. Momma's calling for me. The emcee is asking the last contestant questions. It's all a blur of noise. I slip around the outside of the audience for a closer look. The choking lady reaches into her mouth and pulls out a wooden umbrella handle.

Oh god!

The waiter's eyes pop with shock and his tray crashes to the ground.

"Vergeetsa, vergeetsa, vergeetsa." *Tap, tap.*

His face goes blank.

This is a mess. A complete mess. People are looking!

The woman's tugging harder and the umbrella's coming out.

My life is officially over.

What spell do you even use to correct that? If I reverse it, will she swallow the umbrella? Tears sting my eyes. I duck behind a bush. *Think. Think. Think.*

In the distance a woman walks from the porta-potties, her hair lengthening down her back by the second—growing in plain sight and at warp speed, in shades of purple and orange, no less—until it's a long train behind her. She swats at her hair like it's a swarm of invisible bees. Poor lady probably thinks she's hallucinating. I point my wand her way.

First, reverse. "Aga'thrut megaya."

Now, forget. "Vergeetsa, vergeetsa, vergeetsa." *Tap, tap.*

The woman's hair stops growing. She looks around a moment, confused, then keeps walking, quickly.

Everything's falling apart.

A hand on my back startles me. Mo points her wand at the choking woman, now fully surrounded by a gasping crowd. More witnesses, more eyes! I could cry or scream or both. Mo mutters a few words and the woman's bugged eyes relax. Her mouth closes and she collapses.

I yelp, barring my mouth shut. "Is she gonna be okay?"

"Well, huh, I—" The emcee stammers over his words. "That—that concludes our event today, ladies and gentle-men. We'll, ah, announce the three finalists and have them back next week for the final round. Have a nice day!" He jets off the stage, pushing through the crowd to the fallen woman. "Excuse me. Out of the way. Lily? Lily? It's Roger!"

Half the audience rushes to the edge of the courtyard, surrounding the fallen woman.

Mo's face is stern. "She'll be okay," she says, sirens wailing in the background. Mo faces me at eye level. I've never seen her so serious. "What did you put in those cupcakes, Kyana?"

"I don't know, I swear."

"I hate to ask this. But I *have to*. You didn't use magic to win, did you?"

Tears are streams of fire on my face. This is a disaster. A complete disaster.

"No, I would never." The words come out a garbled mess. "I just did normal baking. I used my wand to help make things go faster. And then . . ."

The misfired reversal spell.

The purple sparks!

THE SAME SPARKS THAT CAME OUT THE JUDGE'S EARS!

"Oh, no." My mouth dangles open. "I should have been more careful. More practiced. I—"

"What? I need to know *everything* you did, step by step."

Momma rushes over, Memaw on her heels, faces riddled with worry.

I can't believe it. I thought the reversal spell worked fine.

"Kyana?"

Icing the cupcakes like normal. But that burst of light. Those misspoken words. Dang it!

"KYANA?" Mom's nails dig into my shoulder. "Say something!"

"I—" I'm a floating head and Momma's words are dull and fuzzy. "I think some magic slipped into my cupcakes. And half the crowd just ate it."

* ⁎ ✳ ✳ ⁎ *

Chaos is an understatement.

People swarm like bees. Workers disassembling the stage glance every few minutes at the elderly woman who "fainted." She's going on about choking on a wooden handle, but the paramedics told her that made no sense.

How many got away with a taste of the cupcakes? How many will be sprouting magic symptoms on their way home? A hundred guests tried those cupcakes, including the mayor himself. My palms are cool and clammy on my forehead.

This is worse than my dream. This is a nightmare.

Mo's off talking to someone in uniform and Ashley and Eric rush over.

"This is wild!" Ash leans in close. "Do you remember what spell you used?"

"It was a frosting spell, but I botched up the words and it came out wrong."

"Oh, yeah, spells are prickly," Eric says. "Last year

I missed a week of school because the spell I tried to use to cut my hair gave me a horse mane instead."

Ashley pats my shoulder. "Don't be too hard on yourself. You were trying to help all of us. We're not upset."

That's nice but what's going to happen if Rockford figures out magic is real? That witches and wizards are hiding all over the city? What will the Magick Board do if they find out I did this? "I mean, it's one thing to keep the school open, but now with magic sprouting up out of control like this, our entire existence could be uncovered. The Magick Board won't be happy. What if they want to do something harsh like sanitize the whole city of magic? Get rid of all our gifts. Forever."

"No way, you think?" Eric looks legit worried now.

"Don't jump to conclusions," Ash says. "It's like a puzzle. A challenge. We can figure this out." She opens her jacket and her wand peeks at me from the inside. "Together. A forgetting spell is the best we can hope for—that just erases the last several minutes or so."

"Yeah, I did that on the lady over there choking on the umbrella handle."

"Is *that* what was coming out of her mouth?" Eric asks, confused.

"Okay, well, the crowd's thinning out," I say. It's not foolproof but it's something. And frankly it's the best plan we have at the moment. "Let's wipe as many memories as we can while there's still time. Eric, you have your wand?"

He pats his pocket with a smug smile. "Of course."

"Let me help?"

I don't have to turn around to know who it is. Russ.

"I knew something was off when I smelled the cupcake. I can help. I want to help."

No time to argue. "Fine."

I tell him the exact spell I used that misfired and how I did it. With the info, he runs off. We disperse into the crowd but so many people have already left. This is hardly going to be effective if half the people who ate the cupcakes are gone. I can't even tell who was sitting where. A few people still nibble bits of baked goods over tiny plates. I flick my wand their way, muttering the magic words. If they forget the weirdness ever happened . . . that could work. *Right?* I bite my lip.

I slip around the outskirts where the tent is now being disassembled, looking for a good spot to hide. Since I'm, ya know, holding a magic wand in public.

Nae and Tommy are chatting and he's swaying on his feet. For good measure, I aim at him and mutter the reversal and forgetting spells. Nae's looking around in every direction, searching for me, I know it.

I duck when a pair of waiters walk past, arms full of discarded plates. I hide my wand quick, heart hammering in my chest. They're near out of sight but their whispers are still in earshot. "It's the strangest thing. Did you see it? I know what I saw. It was an actual umbr—"

"Vergeetsa, vergeetsa, vergeetsa." *Tap, tap.*

"You were saying?" the guy beside him asks.

"I wasn't saying anything. What do you mean?" He shakes his head like there's water in his ears and their voices dissolve in the distance.

This is terrible. I want to cry.

"There you are." Nae and Tommy greet me with smiles. I plaster on a smile, hands behind my back.

"You came!"

"Yeah, turns out my parents are like patrons for this thing or something. They donated to the prize pot of money." She points. "They're over there."

My wand pokes the back of my legs and I try *hard* to listen. People all around us are leaving, heading for their cars, and I'm like a magpie trying to keep an eye on each one, watching for some hint of magic that I need to snuff out.

"*Hellloooo?*" Nae waves her hands in front of me.

"I'm listening! Sorry. A bit distracted. Just the nerves." I twist my shirt.

Nae eyes me up and down. "Uh-huh."

"You did great up there," Tommy says. "And that cupcake must've tasted great."

"Didn't you get one?" Nae asks, brows furrowed. "We both got one."

"I—" He searches for words. "I don't remem—"

"Well, I'm saving mine for later," Nae cuts in. "I hope you win."

"You mean it?" I ask.

"Duh!"

Ashley catches my eye over Nae's shoulder. She's gesturing for me to come, worry painted all over her face.

"You said something about helping out some charity or something?" Nae asks.

"That's cool," Tommy adds.

"I, umm . . ."

Ashley points to the ground as if to say "Come now."

"Key?" Nae's voice is strained, but Mo and Eric have joined Ashley and they're discussing something in a huddle.

Something's wrong. Something's really wrong.

"Kyana?" It's Tommy this time, but I'm half hearing them.

"I'm sorry, guys. Thanks for coming. Nae, I love you. You're the best. I gotta go." I jet off before they can get a word in response. I can feel Nae's eyes burning my back but the look on Mo's face stills me like lead in my veins.

I catch up to them, panting. "What? What happened? Tell me."

"I got a lot of 'em," Ashley says. "As many as I could."

"But so many have left, Kyana," Eric says. "We tried but it's no use. Half of the crowd *at least* is gone."

Mo's eyes are glassy. "I talked to the Magick Board. One of the representatives was here asking questions." Her words are like a dagger to the heart. *The magical authorities know? They know what I did? It was an accident.* Tears well in my eyes.

"I didn't tell them anything. But I don't know, he didn't look convinced."

"No! No! Ms. Moesha, that's just another strike against us in Park Row. Another reason for them to close us down."

"Listen, Kyana. There's only so much you can do, honey. This is a serious problem. Much bigger than you. If non-Magicks find out witches and wizards are running around Rockford, we could all be done for."

I mean, she's right. Isn't that what I accused Russ of doing? Who'd have thought I'd do the same thing?!

Eric's mouth falls open. Ashley elbows him and he picks up his lip.

"This is all my fault," I say.

"It was an honest mistake, Kyana."

"No, it's my fault and somehow I *have* to fix it."

CHAPTER 23

*∗∗✳∗∗

I've read my spell book three times: once on the drive home, twice when we got here.

I've run through it over and over and there is no way to fix this without breaking a hundred magical rules and potentially disfiguring a camel. *I just . . . ugh.* This is so messed up.

My phone vibrates. I unfurl the five blankets I've nested into out of sheer restlessness and grab my phone. The news anchor's voice is a low hum in the background.

A text from Ashley. *Ignored.*

I'm not in the mood to talk—to anyone.

My dresser's full of potion jars, a dirty cauldron pot, tear-outs from my notebook with piles and piles of notes I've taken on everything I could about any possible way I can fix this. And the short answer is—there isn't one. Not without knowing exactly who tried the cupcakes. *Sigh.*

I grab my spell book again. Reading the same spells so many times makes you go cross-eyed after a while, and still no ideas are sparking. I shove the bedcovers on the floor and bang my head backward on the wall.

I mosey downstairs for a snack before dinner—I didn't get any lunch in all the hustle after the magic explosions at City Hall today and I'm hungry. I turn down the blaring TV so I can hear my thoughts properly. Why isn't there an erase-the-last-twenty-four-hours spell?

Another text. Nae this time. *Nope. Don't wanna talk.*

I rake my hands through my hair. *Think.*

"Arrests have been made in connection with the strange occurrences that have been happening across the city since this afternoon," an anchorman on the TV says.

Arrests? People are being arrested? I turn the TV up.

Memaw shuffles around me on her way upstairs. "Things in this world are getting stranger and stranger by the day, che, I swear," she says. "And I'll do that kitchen for you tonight, baby. You get you some rest."

I thank Memaw but can't peel my eyes away from the TV.

"Authorities have taken neuroscientist Dr. Cromwell Dixon into custody for questioning."

An elderly man with bushy white hair and rectangular

frames is led by two officers out of a funny-shaped house with a balloon-looking roof.

I know that face from somewhere.

They flash the scientist's face again.

Is that . . . ?

I grab the cord Ash gave me weeks ago and plug it into the back of the TV. The wizard with the pink vest comes in fuzzy at first, but clears up when I wiggle the cord.

"Benji Charles here with breaking news from Rockford. Dr. Cromwell Dixon, Chair of the Rockford Magick Board, has been arrested."

The same video clip of the bushy-haired guy being escorted out of his home plays again and I gasp. *That's* where I knew him from—the history section of my spell book.

That's the Chair of the Magick Board!

He's arrested? Because of me?

"He's suspected of being connected to a slew of magic symptoms in non-Magicks cropping up all over the city," Benji continues. "Dozens of accounts came Saturday afternoon, following a gathering near City Hall. Charges remain unclear, but Rockford mayor Applegate has a briefing planned for later. The Board encourages the magical community to remain calm during this time as next steps are developing. I'm Ben—"

My head's going to explode. I dig a nail in my palm and

fight down the tears threatening to choke me. *Think of something, Kyana!*

The doorbell grabs my attention, but when I rush to open the door, there's no one there.

Ding!

Uhm, okay. I open it again and a clipboard juts me in the knees. There at my feet is a whole gang of ferrets, the ones from PRMA with shiny badges and judgy stares.

"I—"

They scutter inside and scatter.

"Excuse me!"

The one with the clipboard and the shiniest badge claws his way up to my shoulder and taps a signature spot on a form. I take the pen but hesitate.

"I don't understand. I thought you were confiscating magical ingredients?"

Something shatters in the kitchen and somewhere upstairs Memaw yelps.

"Hey! What are they doing?"

The ferret taps the form on the signature line again, his brows cinched. I read, carefully. Momma says searches without consent are illegal.

I certify I am not in possession of any magical ingredients listed in Section XIV of Prohibited Magical Commodities. I hereby submit to this routine search and seizure.

"I don't have anything I'm not supposed to, I swear." I mean, I've never even seen that form, but everything I have is things Mo gave us to take home and ingredients Momma and I got at Glenda's Grocery.

The ferret's eyes are narrowed suspiciously. He taps the form again as his friends return, empty-handed.

"Told you!" I sign the form, open the door, and they scutter away. I slam it harder than I mean to. Last thing I need is more trouble for rule breaking.

Why would they even come here looking for . . .

Unless . . .

Could they know *I'm* responsible for the magic symptoms sprouting all over Rockford?

No. No, that sounds delusional. The form said "routine." It's routine since my school is shutting down, I guess? I am *not* being investigated by a band of security squad ferrets. I chuckle at the ridiculousness and check on Memaw. She was more tickled by the ferret invasion than shaken, thankfully.

Back in the living room the TV blares from the corner, reminding me the sky is in fact falling even if the ferrets aren't hip to it.

I can practically hear Momma's voice in my head. "Pouting won't get you anywhere," she'd say. "You got something to do? Get up and do it."

Yeah, I wanna say. *But how, Momma? How?*

The wall's firm against my back and I fold my legs under

myself. I pound my head again and again until my brain rattles.

I flip the pages in my spell book, the words a blur. My old spell book falls open to the ripped-out section. An assortment of written-in notes are there and I peer closer.

AN INTRODUCTION TO POTION MAKING

Prickly and precise at heart,
easy potions are the best to start.
From healing to hexing,
spell fixers and unraveling clues,
potions are the greatest muse.

Spell fixers . . . ? I turn the page.

SPELL ANTIDOTES

Below is a laundry list of potion antidotes to reverse any cast spell. *Hmmm.*

"And don't miss the finals—get your tickets before they're sold out," the anchor continues.

Even if I could make an antidote potion to reverse the spell, how would I get it to everyone who happened to taste my cupcakes? Tons of them were students from all over Rockford. My head throbs.

Okay, let's think about this.

It was first come, first served. How do I find every person who happened to show up first? How do I even find out who all came?

WAIT!

I turn the TV up louder. Did he say "tickets"? If there are tickets . . . there must be a guest list somewhere. Tommy was putting up the poster, maybe he knows something about who organized it. That's a good place to start.

I grab my phone to text him just as it vibrates again. This time a phone call. *Ashley.*

"Kyana?" Her voice is eager at the other end. "I wanted to make sure you're doing okay."

"Thanks, Ash. I just don't see a way to fix this. But I gotta figure this out without getting authorities involved—"

"I get it. If I'd done something like this, I'd have a hard time just letting it go. I'd feel responsible, like I need to help."

EXACTLY! This girl gets me. "Yeah. Well, thanks."

"Are you thinking potion or spell?" she asks.

"Uhhh, the only spells that seem useful are the Cleanso-Maximo spell and—"

"Ooo." She sucks her teeth. "Yeah, no. That'll wipe them of *everything*. And I mean *everything*, inside and out."

"Yeah. Well, and then there's the Blood Magic Sifter, which, I mean . . ."

"Where are you going to find a camel?"

"Exactly."

"And I mean, even if you found one. There are a whole host of complications with that one. The—"

"Ash!

"Not to mention the pretty penny ingredients would cost you. I just don't think—"

"ASH!"

"Yeah?"

"I'm not doing the camel spell."

"Okay, good." Ashley rambles on, thinking out loud. Something about seeing a few kids from her old private school after the event. One girl from her homeschool co-op apparently sneezed and sprouted a flower from her nose. "I mean, of course the minute I saw it, I took care of it."

A real friend right there.

"I take my wand everywhere with me now," she goes on.

Who knew someone so shy could talk this much?

"A quick Flora Morbidio spell and the flower was gone. But she *knows* what she saw. Poor girl must be so confused."

Oh snap! That's it. "Wait! You covered for me? You saw the problem at your group and you took care of it. Ashley, that's it!"

"What's it?"

"I'm gonna ask my mom to drop me at your house now.

Call any- and everyone you know at PRMA. Get them to come over, too. I know what I have to do!"

* ✳ ✴ ✳ *

It's not window-cleaning day, so Beverly was nice when I showed up to Ash's.

"Hey, you made it," Ash says. We hug as more people pile inside.

Half the crowd is already there, each wearing a Furry and Free pin. Ms. Janice, Ash's mom, sports a proud smile. I make sure to tap the pin on my chest when she says hello.

Lou's oven door hangs open and he coughs every few minutes, spitting out bubbling pepperoni pizzas one after the other.

"Thanks for letting us come over on such short notice. I've figured out what we need to do."

"So what's the plan?"

I whip open my spell book—the one Memaw found in a closet somewhere. It's older than the one PRMA issued but with all its handwritten notes, it's quickly becoming my preferred one, despite the random ripped-out pages.

"Spells have antidotes, " I say. "Fixes that undo them."

"Yep, usually a potion of some sort. But what of it?"

"At least half of the people who attended the competition were students."

"At least! But what are we doing?"

"We're going to get an antidote to every single student in Rockford School District. I figure—"

"Hey." It's Russ.

And even though I'm grateful for how he helped at the event, I don't want to turn around. I give Ash a look. I told her to invite everyone but we're here trying to *avoid* our magic being outed. So how is having a proven traitor here a good look?

"Why—?" I catch myself when I face him. His hair is fuzzy at the edges, unkempt. And his shoes are scuffed, which I've literally never seen. There's no superdupa fly aura about him either. He looks so . . . regular . . . I almost don't recognize him.

"Why are you here?" I manage.

"Kyana, I invited him," Ash says. "Just hear him out."

All sounds have stopped and every eye in the place is on Russ. They remember my outburst at PRMA, no doubt, and we're all looking at him sideways. I fold my arms as Russ turns to address the whole room.

He takes a huge breath. "Most of you know me for my charms hustle. My little thing I do on the side to make some money. But I—" He studies his feet and Ash steps closer to him. "I—I've never shared the whole of it. We live in this nice house down the street, but it's expensive. And when my dad lost his job after the pandemic, bills got tight. My momma's hair started falling out, she was so stressed. We barely had food in the fridge most days and our electricity got shut off for a whole week once. That was the last straw for me. So I started hustling, using my skills for charms. And sure, I mean, I use some of it to buy clothes and stuff but at first it all went to Momma. And even now most of it does." He exhales. "I just . . . after a while having the nice stuff, flyest shoes, dopest cuts . . . people starting paying more attention to me."

He has a point. I remember in like fourth grade no one even knew him. But last year, all of a sudden, Russ was on the *map.*

"The attention went to my head, I guess."

"You guess?"

"It went to my head, Kyana. I thought I was invincible. And then the groit accusation really hit home."

"Well, it should!" I'm upset and I'm not sorry for it. "*That* and selling charms to non-Magicks should get to you, too." I outed us on accident, which is terrible, but outing us on purpose is disloyal and that's despicable.

"I would never!" His eyes go all wide and something in his expression makes me believe him. "Calvin was picking up something for his brother, *who's a wizard* and one of my most loyal clients. But Calvin didn't know anything. I mean, maybe that wasn't smart, using a non-Magick to transport a charm, but I swear I'm not selling anything to anyone but our kind."

I purse my lips, more convinced than I care to admit.

"I know it's a bad look and that's on me. And sure, the strays at my house *are* groits . . ."

Ash's mom sits up at that, narrowing her eyes, and I'm shaking in my boots. Ten out of ten chance she gonna do something completely off the wall if Russ admits what I think he's about to admit.

"But me and Momma have been *rescuing* them," he continues. "We feed them and make sure they have a safe haven."

"So you're not selling them?" I ask.

"Not selling, not breeding, just caring for them. Did you know a groit is whisked away to captivity every 4.7 seconds?"

Actually, yes.

"I know how it all must look from the outside, but I love magical creatures and happen to be born into a family with an affinity for Charms."

Ash's mom is in the corner sobbing happy tears.

"So what changed, Russ?" Eric asks. "Why do you care all of a sudden?"

"I've always cared. The clothes, the shiny shoes, the swagger—all that's like a cover-up because when I was just me, I was a nobody. But when I'm flashy Russ, people pay attention. When we got the notice PRMA might be closed down, it hit me that everything I've built can be taken away if I can't complete training. If I lose my wand, who am I then? I didn't like the way that made me feel. That's not cool. But I gotta find comfort in my own skin, wand or not. So I took off all the charms, put my wand down, and I'm here . . . as just a guy at your school who loves Park Row and doesn't want to see it close. I want to help. Kyana, Ashley, I'm so sorry. I've been a jerk. I really have."

"You really have," I say.

Whispers swarm like locusts and Russ gets lots of sideway stares.

Ashley breaks the silence. "I can relate."

Every head in the room swivels to Ash and she's picking her nail so hard I worry she might pluck her whole finger off.

"I—I've always been different . . . and people made me feel like that wasn't okay." She gulps down a huge breath. "But I think what PRMA has taught me is that being different is what makes me *me*. We're good, Russ." She sticks out her hand and they shake. I blink in disbelief. Ash bossing up to defend Russ in front of a whole crowd of people? I'm so proud of my girl. She did eye contact and everything.

I offer a hand. "All right, Russ. We're good. *But—*"

"*But* I owe Nae a *huge* apology. I'm going to think of a way to make it up to her. Promise."

I smile, can't even help it. We do a twist on the handshake and pull it into a one-arm hug. Eric and Russ dap it up, followed by several others.

We've gotta get on the same page about this antidote

thing now. It's one of the few things I'm fairly sure will work. "So now that we're all gathered around . . ."

Lou coughs but it comes out like a sneeze and I duck. A charred pizza flies overhead headed straight for Beverly. Thankfully, someone in the crowd catches it. Last thing we need is them two fighting.

"Most of the tasters were students. Some adults, sure, but symptoms will be popping up all over schools, I would bet, and we can fix that."

Everyone sits up. We're truly in this together. And considering it was *my* snafu, I'm super grateful.

"I'm going to make an antidote and bake it into cookies. We can take them to each of the schools and pass them out. As long as everyone gets the antidote, it'll null the effects of the spell, according to the notes in my spell book."

Chatter erupts and I try my best to answer the barrage of questions that proceed.

"But most of us go to Thompson," someone says. I didn't think about how we could get it to other schools all over Rockford.

"If you guys have a sec I can grab my client list," Russ says. "I have contacts at magic academies all over Rockford. Maybe we can have a meeting with them? Explain what happened and get them to pass out antidote cookies at their schools, too?"

"That's a great idea. You think they'll be down to meet?"

"Oh, when The Russ calls, they *all* get excited to see what I've cooked up."

I snort a laugh. "Sounds like a plan."

We pound fists on it. With everyone in agreement I feel good for the first time in a long time. If I can correct this snafu and get things back on track, maybe, just maybe, I still have a shot at making it to the finals and saving our school.

CHAPTER 24

·✳✳✳*·*

The next day, before the sun is even fully awake, I wait outside Rockford Arts and Learning Center and a Mercedes pulls up.

The kind with really shiny paint and wheels like on the music videos. I dust off my pants and glance at Russ. He's standing tall, scruffy, but in that usual confident posture of his. If he's feeling some kind of way about this meeting, I can't tell.

Another few cars pull into the parking lot. Kids hop out and each takes a sideways glance at Russ. I mean, he does look like a different person, but eventually they all shake his hand.

More arrive and the parking lot's a stew of cars and people. Russ heads in my direction with the girl who just got out of the Mercedes, who is *way* too tall to be a middle schooler, if driving a Benz wasn't my first clue. I smooth my clammy hands on my pants. I expect Ash to be picking at her nails, but she's wearing her hair completely off her face and staring straight ahead like she's ready to fight a death match.

"This is McKenzie," he says. "McKenzie, this is Kyana and Ashley."

"Oh my gosh, hi! Your hair is like so cute." McKenzie reaches, but I'm ready for it and step back, offering her a hand instead.

"Nice to meet you."

"She goes to Berkeley Oaks High," Russ says.

Ah. That explains the Valley girl accent.

She clicks her key fob. But instead of a beep, her Mercedes sighs.

"If you want me to lock, then say so. I'm not some machine."

I blink.

McKenzie flips her blond hair. "No, I'm pretty sure like literally that's exactly what you are." She presses the key fob again. "Lock."

"Lock, *please*," the car says.

"Mercedes. Lock!"

Ash and I share a glance.

"We're not arguing about this in *front* of people anymore." McKenzie walks away from her car on her pointy heels and together we head toward the forming crowd.

"She's so moody, I swear," she says. "Tether an Available to the car, they said. It'll be so cool, they said. I'm gonna take her back and get another one that's not totally demented."

"I heard that!" Mercedes shouts.

"I'm glad!" McKenzie shouts back.

"Uhm, wow," Ash whispers to me, and we cackle behind our hands.

The glowing doors to the Arts Center open and the cluster of witches and wizards in the parking lot funnel inside. I've never seen so many Magicks in one place. Snapback caps on people's heads morph into robes as wearers pass the threshold. McKenzie's hair (which I assumed was hers) wraps her in stringy fibers, then turns out in a denim robe with a red stripe between two green ones.

Wands in every color, some glittering, some shiny, others rainbow colored with swirls, swish and flick, transforming the art stations into a magic wonder house. I visited the Arts Center before on a school field trip but I've never seen it like this. The ceiling towers six stories at least. A gold-and-mint crest with a Pegasus wrapped in rosettes is painted *huge* on every wall above Old English letters.

Berkeley Oaks Magick Academy

Where there are usually tables with activities are floating chairs, moonlit canopies, a unicorn-riding simulation thingy, but without cords and wires.

"What is *that*?"

"Ever wanna ride a unicorn?" Russ smirks. "Or how about a dragon?" He points at a sign for baby dragon petting, which already has a line to the door. "They do egg incubation in there, too. They import them back to Winzhobble once they start getting too big, of course."

"Oh, right. Of course."

Two silver doors labeled Potion Fermentation Chamber are roped off with yellow tape. And in the furthest corner some kid in leopard robes is firing hexes left and right, tucking and rolling as he fights his way through some sort of wizarding obstacle course.

My feet stick to the ground, but Russ pulls me along. The back wall is a tapestry made of books instead of thread. Ashley rushes in that direction and we hustle to keep up.

"It's wild here, huh?" he asks.

"You've seen this before?"

"Yeah. They offer enrichment classes after school, so some of my charms money goes to that. That's how I learned to engineer charms. Found a really complex spell book and for $5.95 it was mine for two weeks."

I pat my empty pockets almost instinctively. "Must be nice. This place must cost a fortune." I run my fingers along the spines. How much better would I be at magic if I had access to all this?

"Making yourself at home?" It's McKenzie again and I plaster on a smile.

"Yep, thanks."

"Good! Just don't, ya know, take anything . . . I mean . . . not that you would . . . I have friends who live in Park Row . . . no judgment or anything. Sorry—I'll—uhm, go get the others so we can get this meeting started." She hurries off.

"Do I even want to know what kinds of charms she buys from you?"

"You don't."

We finally catch up with Ashley and she's inside a glass chamber catching waves on some kind of bewitched surfboard. A crowd's formed around her but she's having the time of her life and doesn't seem to notice.

"Are they even gonna help us?" Eric pops up outta nowhere. "I mean, look at all this. They probably think PRMA is a joke."

"Hey, you came," Russ says.

They slap hands.

"And true, fair question, but not everyone here's like McKenzie."

"All we can do is ask," I say. "And I mean, we're asking them to pass out cookies, not support our campaign for president."

Russ taps his lip like a lightbulb has gone off just as McKenzie comes back with a microphone.

"Okay, guys!" She speaks into it first. "Kenzy here, and

we're about ready to get started. Let's hear what Park Lane—"

"Row."

"Park *Row* Magick Academy has to say."

"Who?" someone shouts, followed by a sprinkle of laughter.

I swallow when she hands me the mic. "Hello?" My voice echoes and suddenly my face is plastered on the walls like giant TVs. "Uhm, hi."

McKenzie whirls a gold wand and a fuzzy feeling itches my knees. I'm rising off the ground and floating over everyone, trying to get my balance.

"Wh-wh-whoa!"

A platform sprouts from the floor and McKenzie swishes her wand and my feet land hard on top of it.

"Go ahead." She gives me a thumbs-up.

"Oh, okay, hi." I wish I brought Ash up here with me. There are hundreds of eyes staring back at me. I spot a few more faces from Park Row, including Mo. She waves and confidence flutters through—

"I want to thank you all for coming," I say. "We're from different schools all over Rockford, I know. Most of you probably didn't even know Park Row exists. B-but we have a school in the back of Ms. Mo's Beauty Shop."

A few snickers skitter across the crowd and Ashley flashes a look that way that could kill.

Ms. Moesha waves and a few hoot and holler.

"You see, I *just* learned that I'm a witch . . ." I say.

"Noob," somebody taunts.

My cheeks burn but I keep going, a little louder this time. "And we have this fantastic group of magical folks in our community—Park Row. Kids like me that wanna learn how to master spells and be contributing members in magical society. My best friend Ashley over here."

Her face turns beet red. She's gonna kill me for putting her on the spot.

"She wants to be on the Grand Council of Magicians someday and run their Medical Innovation Department. She's smart. Like *really* smart. The smartest person I've ever met. And that's Eric over there."

He does a pageant wave, grinning big enough to show all his teeth.

"He wants to open his own magic school eventually, too. Teach kids how to use their magic and learn to control it."

"And you?" Russ shouts. "What do you wanna do?"

"Well, right now I just wanna convince you guys to listen to me."

A few laugh and the tightness in my chest loosens up a bit.

"Our school serves the witches and wizards of Park Row." I wait for the insults, comments, something, but they never come. Just stares—lots of silent stares. "And in Park

Row, there's a lot of other things we could be doing with our spare time on Saturdays. But we choose to spend them with Mo learning magic. It's a safe space to explore our skills. Be ourselves. It's *our space*. And it's being shut down."

Gasps erupt across the crowded room. Ms. Mo moves through the crowd and with some quick magic, stairs cut into my podium. She climbs them and stands beside me, her eyes glassy with tears.

"We don't want our school to close," I continue. "We don't want to lose our space because of someone drawing lines on a map a different way. But we don't have the money to keep the school going. We don't even have a school building." I take a deep long breath. "I wanted to stop the school from closing. That's why all this is happening. It's all my fault."

People look at one another.

"You heard about the city baking competition?" I ask.

"Uh, yeah," McKenzie says. "My parents own two 5-star spots downtown. My mom entered, trying to win that cash. It's a lot of money, I think."

"Yeah, fifty thousand dollars," I say. "And *I* entered, too. I wanted to win that money to save our school."

Silence.

That's when the tears come. I blink fast but it's no use. For all my good intentions, I still screwed up and now we're all at risk. "I made these cupcakes and they were amazing, but . . ." I glance at Mo and she nods for me to keep going. I swallow the bile hovering at the back of my throat. "Magic slipped in somehow. And since then, tons of non-Magick folks have been experiencing weird things." My chest is tight. So, so tight as the words claw their way out. "Now we're at risk of being discovered, all of us. But I have a plan to fix this, at least a *start* to fixing it, and I need all of your help."

I get a few angry grunts and lots of whispering. One guy flashes sparks from his wand, elbows his way through the crowd, and leaves.

They hate me. They're going to turn me in.

Ashley's beside me now and though she looks like she might pass out with all these eyes on her, she stands beside me and reaches for my hand. She squeezes and I squeeze back.

One clap. Then another. Until the entire room is a shower of applause. I exhale and make my way down from the platform.

I'm terrified of losing my shot at making Momma's life easier, of not having my own thing that's special and helpful and useful. I'm not brave or even sure this'll work. I'm terrified. But I have to try.

I smudge away the tears as I'm assaulted with hugs, high fives, people shoving my shoulders, noogies digging into my scalp.

"You're one brave noob, kid," a gargantuan high schooler says.

Brave. They've got it all wrong. But hey, if they are willing to help I'll take the compliment even if it is a lie.

"Takes courage," someone else says.

"And heart," says another voice.

They seem so sincere. I thought they'd be upset. Didn't even think they'd care. And judging by the way a few girls in pleated plaid skirts are whispering with their curled lips, some don't.

"So what can we do?" McKenzie asks.

People actually want to help!

"Okay, so first, I need everyone to tell me what school they attend. I want to make sure we have every school in Rockford represented."

I detail the plan of baking the antidote into dozens and dozens of cookies to distribute to all the schools in the city. The cover story has to be believable, so we all agree that "fundraiser leftovers" is the way to go. We'll say we have tons of extra and give them away, making sure every kid gets one. A cookie with an antidote.

Everyone bursts into a million conversations and papers fly every which way. Russ and Ash help me organize who attends where and thankfully after what feels like forever Russ gives me a thumbs-up.

"Every school in Rockford accounted for," he says.

Tommy's father's on the committee that organized the competition and he says he should be able to get a copy of the ticket buyers. That would be so boss for helping find the adults who sampled the cupcakes. Things are falling into place little by little and a smile tugs at my lips.

We might actually be able to fix this mess.

And if I'm lucky I impressed those judges enough to have a shot at the final round this Saturday. Announcements are delayed because of the whole snafu, but they should come soon—that is if Mayor Applegate doesn't do anything drastic like cancel it.

We have a plan. It's not perfect. It's not everyone.

But it's a start.

CHAPTER 25

₊✳₊

That afternoon, I caught a ride home with Ashley and her mom, who popped us into Glenda's for recipe ingredients. Heat from the oven has the kitchen at least twenty degrees warmer than the rest of the house. Momma's AC's been working double-time. She not gone' like that. I'm in the kitchen working like a fiend. Momma's off to work per usual.

A few folks offered to help make some batches at their house but I can't take any chances. I'm making *sure* these cookies get *done* myself. All eighteen hundred of 'em.

My pot swishes with the creamy antidote potion and I glimpse across the room the panda bank Momma gave me two summers ago, now broken next to the foot-long receipt for *all* these groceries. Momma told me to "put some change in there every once a while"—code for "save up what you can so the next time your BFF's family invites you on one of their fancy summer trips, you actually have some spending money." A couple dollars and a meager pile of change are inside the cracked open belly. The rest? All two years of savings worth? Gone. I sigh. *At least this still puts it to good use.*

Ashley's at the table, mixing a batch of tea cake cookie batter as I slip cookies from the baking sheet. We started after a quick lunch, when we got back from Rockford. Ash suggested magicking their quantity, but I'm not taking any chances with spells I haven't practiced. Not this time.

"This one's ready." Ashley hands me the bowl. "What's a tea cake, anyway?"

"Only the yummiest cookie ever." I pour a half cup of the potion carefully into the batter and thicken it up with extra flour and a little more butter. Once it's the right consistency, I scoop the antidote cookies onto a cookie sheet. "My grandma made them with her mom and now she makes them with me."

She licks her finger. "The batter's good."

"Ash, gross!"

She laughs.

"Don't lick the batter. People have to eat that. We're

making chocolate chip, too. Figured those would be extra popular."

"Oh, those are my favorite!"

I scoop another bit of potion and scrape the bottom. Time to start a new batch of potion, since this one's almost out. I pull over my spell book to triple-check ingredients.

Potion base. *Check.*

Croc saliva. *Check.*

Snail slime. *Check.*

Lace flies. *Check.*

Lion mane. *Check.*

Moth wings? All out of that. *Hmmm.* Scribbled in my ancient potion book is a handwritten note.

See substitutions.
Almost always works better.

Below that is a list of potion ingredients, most with a line through it and something else written next to it.

~~Spider Venom~~ Wig glue (any kind).
~~Beetle Goo~~ Kitchen Bouquet or similar
(the older the better).
Coconut oil (refined).

~~Dragon blood.~~ Kool-Aid powder (red only).

~~Thistle branches.~~ Neck bone.
~~Fish scales.~~ Sweet tea (from scratch)
                 + add aloe vera leaves

Each of the substitution ingredients is a thing Memaw keeps on hand. I crack a leaf of aloe in half, sliding my nail along its edge. Then I squeeze the clear gel into my cauldron and give it a stir. The tip of my wand answers with a poof of air and blue sparks. Then the mixture turns the familiar creamy texture. I watch carefully. Each batch, the same thing must happen. If I spot even a slight difference, that batch gets dumped.

The oven groans when I open it. I brace for the rush of heat as I slide the next cookie sheet inside. I heave a box of cellophane bags from underneath the table.

"I really think we could double these batches with a simple doubling spell," Ash says.

"No! I'm not trying that. No way."

"Kyana, we have like two hundred cookies made. We need *nine times* that. This isn't happening if we don't use magic. You're a good witch. I *know* you can do it."

I shift on my feet. "I can't take any chances. I haven't practiced that one an—"

"You made *one* mistake. You're a good witch, Kyana. Hard-working, too."

I roll my eyes.

"Fine, I'll drop it," she says. "But, I know the spell. I can do it." Her brows raise.

She probably can. But this is my mistake. I have to fix it. If anything goes wrong, it's on me. I don't want her to feel like a failure if this doesn't work out.

"Sorry, Ash, I have to do this."

"But I'm your friend—"

"No, Ash. I—"

"Kyana, we're in this together. Like it or not. You go down for this, I'm going with you."

I don't even know what to say.

"Come on. Let me help with this one little part. I swear it'll make everything so much easier. You trust me, right?"

"Of course I trust you. You're the smartest witch I know."

"Okay, let me do this. For PRMA."

She is right. This is going to take forever the conventional way. "Fine. But *please* know if something happens and it doesn't work—this is not your mess. It's mine!"

She laughs. "I don't have many other friends. *Any* other friends, really. You're the *one* person who talks to me and never makes me feel like it's wrong or weird to be different. You even called me your best friend *in public*. So, whatever, girl. I'm riding this ship to the ocean floor if *anything* bad goes down."

Her words warm me all over. "Okay, Ash. Thanks for being a great friend."

I think of Nae. She loves me the same way, too. Always willing to go to bat for me. How'd I get so lucky to have *two* priceless best friends?

I miss Nae. Haven't seen her since the competition. I need to call her . . . when all this mess is over. I take a deep breath and give Ash the nod she's waiting for.

She raises her wand over the piles and piles of cookies we've finished, enough crumbled bits on the floor to build a cookie sand castle. "Tweeyum kwixame," she says, winding her arm in a huge circle. Cookies dance, rising from their places, shifting in the air. Each one splits into two. She flicks her wrist and they split again. Another flick and where there was one cookie now there are four. *Wow!*

Tea cakes, chocolate chip cookies, recess thumbprints, and limoncellos rain from the air and I trip over my feet, fumbling for something wide enough to catch them. I need more pans! I dive headfirst into a cabinet.

She winds her arm around and we're basically in a cookie hailstorm. I balance Momma's widest cookie sheet with both hands, determined to catch each one. The cookie storm slows and other than a few warm casualties on the floor, we've gone from one corner of the kitchen stacked with cookies to every inch of Momma's counters, sink, stove, and table covered in piles and piles of antidote cookies.

Ashley's arms fall limp. "There!"

My wrist aches under the last pan. I set it down carefully and Ashley and I slap hands.

"We did it!" she squeals, tucking her wand away.

"*You* did it," I say, surveying the two feet of floor space that isn't covered by some form of cookie.

"Well, I'll say." Memaw's grinning from the doorway that leads to the living room. The feather on her lavender church hat flutters and her rhinestone brooch glistens in the overhead light. "You girls been working hard. How will we ever eat all these—cookies? I'm just—"

Ashley glances at me, brows cinched. Memaw knows the cookies are for the fake fundraiser to get the antidote in everyone.

"We're going to share them, Memaw," I remind her, again, sifting the annoyance from my tone. Because that's what you do when someone you love is having a hard time remembering. You tell them again, with patience and love.

"That's such a good idea, baby." She heads back toward the bedrooms.

"I don't remember her having it *this* bad," I mutter to myself. "Sometimes I wonder if . . ." My words trail off and Ash hugs me like she can read my mind.

"You can't fix everything, Kyana."

"I know." *It's just so hard not to try.*

* ✳ ✳ ✳ *

The rest of the day flies by and I have this feeling I'm forgetting something. I can't shake it, so I ignore it. Ash heads home and I package up the rest of the cookies in cellophane bags against the white noise of the TV. Russ is going to pick them up later today and get them out to everyone. He's being a big help.

The kitchen is a disaster—flour everywhere, dishes piled on top of dishes, and so many chocolate chips on the floor. Momma's on the graveyard shift tonight plus a double shift in the morning, so I have some time to get this kitchen together, which is great because I'm absolutely pooped. I plop into a chair still hopeful this idea of mine will actually work.

You have a plan. A smart plan. I force out a breath. Everything's riding on these cookies getting out tomorrow. This *has* to work.

Then we can handle the adults . . . somehow.

"Rockford's baking competition . . ." the anchor blares from the living room, and I raise the volume, half listening.

"AH!" Memaw yells from her upstairs.

"Memaw? You okay?" I rush up there and halt. There on her tiny TV on her dresser is the regular news anchor talking, a picture of three people hovering over his shoulder.

ROCKFORD BAKING COMPETITION
FINALISTS ANNOUNCED

Two of the people I don't recognize. But the one on the end, I do. *It's me!*

"You did it, baby!" Memaw yanks me into a bear hug.

I blink and blink again but the screen doesn't change. "I'm a finalist?"

Memaw turns up the volume and the anchor's voice is like a lull of soothing music. ". . . I mean, can you *believe* this kid? She's *twelve* and a *finalist* against actual pastry chefs! That's just plain impressive. That kid must have some sort of culinary gift." The anchorman's mouth keeps moving, but I am not listening.

I'm a finalist! One step closer to saving PRMA! My phone buzzes, over and over, going off like fireworks. I scroll through all the texts, my mind racing.

Eric: Did you see the news? You're in the top three!!! 😎

Momma: Turn on the TV, baby! The news. Go look. It's on the radio too! I'm so proud of you. Be home early if I can.

I may actually save Park Row Magick Academy. I could scream!

Tommy: Hey I got the guest list. You're right. Every person at the original event will be at the finals. Oh!

And sorry I couldn't make it to study group today!
Next time.

My heart stops.

That's what I was forgetting! Sunday library time with Nae.

She is going to kill me.

Or worse, never talk to me again.

CHAPTER 26

* ✳ ✳ ✳ ✳ ✳ *

Principal Gomez's office is freezing.

I fell asleep early *and* overslept. Woke up to the kitchen still a hot mess. I'm hoping Memaw gets to that kitchen before Momma gets home.

I slip my sweater on and loop my bag of antidote treats to distribute on my arm. Ms. Gomez's secretary is *clack-clack*ing on her keyboard, wearing a giant wool sweater. So I know it's not just me. The last time I was in her office, Nae was by my side. It was terrifying, but she was with me, so I knew it'd be all right.

I called Nae twice before nodding off last night, but she didn't answer either time. She wasn't in my first or second period today, so the soonest I can see her is lunch, probably. She's gotta be mad. No, pissed. I can't believe I forgot about our library meet-up. I'll explain myself the best I can. I hope it's enough.

"The principal will see you in just a minute." The secretary stops typing, resting her head on her wrists. "Saw you on the news last night. One of our *own* Thompson Tigers, a finalist!"

"Thanks."

"We're all rooting for you to take home the first-place prize!"

"Thanks." The final round of judging requires finalists to bring a cake this weekend. Haven't even started thinking about that yet.

"Any idea of what you're going to make for the final round?" She winks, whispering. "Or is it a secret?"

Lady, I'm just trying to make it through the day before someone pops up with bean sprouts for hair. "Uh, still deciding."

"Well, you're gonna do great. I know it." She hops up and peeks inside the principal's private office, then gestures for me to follow. I lug a giant pink gift bag that I'm reusing from some birthday a long time ago.

"Let me help you with that." She grabs the other end and peeks inside the bag. She wrinkles her nose, confused, but doesn't ask any questions.

Principal Gomez is on the phone when the door sweeps open.

"Uh-huh, I understand. But . . . well, yes." She waves for me to come inside and have a seat. "And what would that look like for us?" She tucks her lips and the line between her brows deepens. "Okay, well, send me what you have. I'll take a look. No promises, but I'll do what I can." The phone clicks in the receiver and she's all smiles. "And how can I help you today, Ms. Turner? I see you brought me cookies?" She chuckles. "I don't know if I can eat all those."

"Oh, no. Ha, yeah, I actually baked all these for a fund-raiser we did . . . a-and u-uh, these were the leftovers."

"Oh?" Her lips smile and her eyes do, too.

"Wondered if we could give them out here? We don't have to sell them. We just want to make sure everyone gets one."

"You probably could make some money," she says. "Sure you aren't selling yourselves short?"

But I don't care about profiting. She agrees to let me give them away in the lunchroom *and* she gives me special per-mission to visit each homeroom.

When I leave her office, I give her a cookie even though I *know* she wasn't at the event. "Here's one for helping us out."

She unwraps it and takes a bite. My shoulders tense. The last time someone ate something I baked, they started vomit-ing up an umbrella.

"*Mmm-mmm.*" She licks chocolate from her thumb,

smacking. "Where did you learn to bake like that?" She hands me a dollar. "I insist. Put that with the money you made on the fundraiser you did. And I'll take another. With all these wild news reports we've been having, homemade cookies are exactly what we all need."

I hand her another cookie. "Uhh, thanks!" Glad I made extras.

Her secretary gives me a hall pass and I pop into each of the classrooms during the homeroom period. My pink gift bag is crinkled on the bottom and ripped at the top, but it's half empty now. Kids in every classroom, teachers too, are munching on these chocolate goodies and I can breathe a little easier. I even caught a glimpse of Nae in the hallway when the lunch bell rang. But I don't think she saw me.

That's why she didn't look my way. That's all.

Lunch is super crowded as usual. I spot Russ across the cafeteria giving out samples. He waves and I make my way over, my bag of cookies weighing me down.

"Lunch lady has the rest of mine," he says. "She's holding them at the register. I told her one per student, principal's orders."

"Oh, good thinking," I say. I spot something furry darting across the cafeteria. "I . . . Is that . . . ?"

"A ferret?" Russ asks.

"Oh, thank heavens. I thought I was losing my mind."

He scratches his head. "But ferrets aren't *that* kind of rodent."

"I think it's the same ferrets that visited PRMA. And they're stalking me or something," I whisper. "Like they know I'm responsible for the magic getting out around town and are like collecting evidence?" This sounds preposterous. "They came to my house!"

"Oh, that's definitely weird." Something in Russ's expression tells me I *might not* be losing it, and that makes my neck sweat. He slips something small from his pocket and presses it into my hand. "Use this."

I open the box with yellow ribbon and it emits the tiniest puff of green smoke. For a moment, I'm tingly all over.

"That should make you undetectable by any government official, magical or otherwise, for at least the day. I hope you're wrong, but just in case."

A shorter kid with a pink buzz cut barges into us. "These are really good. You made these?" I recognize him from the cheer squad. "Can ya boy get more? My friends didn't get any."

"Oh, well, we gotta make sure y'all each get one," Russ says.

"Thanks." He and Russ slap hands. He offers me a dollar.

"Oh, no need to pay." Russ says as I hand the kid a stack of cookies.

"Y'all enjoy," I add.

The crowd disperses around us and every mouth in every corner of the cafeteria is chewing. Ripped-open cellophane bags are piled on several table centers. *It's working. They're eating it.* I mean, people are being complete slobs about cleaning up after themselves, but it's working!

I look for Nae as I slip my phone out of my back pocket. No sign of her. We *really* need to talk.

My shoulders are suddenly lighter as Russ pulls the gift bag with the few cookies I have left. He's immediately swarmed by a crowd, money in hand, asking for more cookies.

"No! Really . . ." Russ is harder to see, the crowd closing in around him. "It's okay . . . keep your money . . . I—" His words slip through like water through a crack. "Did everyone get one? We want to make sure *everyone* gets one." A waterfall of voices answers all at once, arms waving.

I hope we made enough.

My phone lights up and notice I've missed so many messages. I scroll through our group chat.

> Ashley: OMG, guys my co-op is flipping out over these cookies. They're going so fast!
> Emily: Teachers passing them out as we speak.
> Nathan: I can hardly keep up! People want more cookies. Ha Ha!

Rose: Roosevelt Middle is clean. Magic free. 😎
 Kyana FTW!
McKenzie: Berkeley Oaks High is golden!
Bobby: All clear at Gardner Middle. Every kid
 present has had one. There's
three people home sick, but I put cookies in with
 their homework packet.
Me: Thanks for all your help, everyone! We're doing
 great here, too. Antidote in the hand of everyone at
 Thompson Middle!

A smile tugs at my lips. We're really doing it.

"This is the last of it." Russ hands me two cookies and what's left of my pink gift bag. I ball it up and toss it. He offers a fist bump but I don't pound it back because I've finally spotted Nae. She's sitting with a pair of girls who I'm almost sure we do *not* like. Shantae and What's-Her-Face? Boujee and rude. Nae's talking to them? No way.

I get closer and Nae glances my way, but turns back around quick.

My tummy flips. *It's nothing.* I mean, I know I missed our study date, but no way would she act brand-new like that.

Shantae's face is all screwed up like she smells something stank. "Oh look." She flips her hair. "It's Kendra."

She knows my name is Kyana, but I'm not entertaining her attitude with a response.

"Nae?"

Her back is still turned. No response.

"Naomi Rosalind Jones. I'm talking to you."

She faces me and everything in her eyes that used to be soft and warm is watery and cold. "Yeah, I don't really have anything to say to you, Key. It's like you are in your own world lately and there isn't enough room for me in it." She stands up, tray in hand. The mean girl entourage stands up, too.

Nae's so close I could hug her. Would that say "I'm sorry" better than my words can? That she's still my best friend even though things are upside down right now?

I pull at our BFF necklace, dangling from my neck, my hands clammy. "Nae, I tried calling last night. I—"

"Save it, Kendra," Shantae spits. "She has *new* friends now that actually *want* to hang out with her."

"So that's it?" I ask, eyes stinging.

"Yeah, I guess so." Nae's gaze meets the floor and she walks off with her new friends.

That's it. She's done with me. In my efforts to save PRMA, I lost the one thing that matters to me the most—my best friend.

CHAPTER 27

＊✳＊

Brrrrring.

Nae doesn't usually have any practices or club meetings after school on Mondays. There's *no* reason she *shouldn't* answer.

Brrrrring.

"Hi, you've reached Nae . . ."

Sigh. I hang up. Pictures of me and Nae are *all* over my room and, because Momma loves her like a daughter, the house, too. A violet frame with glued-on hearts shows the time we went to a water park with her parents and I wanted to do the big slide *bad*, but when we went *all* the way up there I was too scared. We held up the line for ten minutes until the lifeguard told us I had to either walk back down or slide down, one slider at a time. Nae whispered in my ear and I pushed off and as promised Nae "slipped" and tumbled down the slide alongside me. We were banned from slides for the rest of the day, but I did something scary and Nae was right there with me. Like always.

I want her beside me now.

I try calling again, but she doesn't answer. I send a text, and finally get one response: stop messaging me.

She's really done with me.

I turn over the frame, and another, and two more, and make my way into the kitchen, smudging my tears.

Memaw hasn't touched a dish. She's been sleep most of the day, something about her new medication. I sigh, cookie crumbles crunching between my toes, grab the broom, and sweep a pile of flour into a dustpan.

The screen door *clack*s closed. *Shoot—Momma's home.*

I brace for the storm.

She pops her head into the kitchen and does a double take. "Kyana Lacreshia Turner, what in the world have you done?"

I can't even look at her.

"I come home early and *this* is what I find? How in the world did you make all this mess?"

I have words but they're glued to the roof of my mouth. "The antidote. I—"

Her nostrils flare. I'm a statue, brittle and crumbling like these cookie scraps all over the floor.

"Give me that wand." She snatches it from my fingers and sticks in her purse.

Tears gush down my face. I can't stop them. I don't even try to.

"Get upstairs right now before I lose my mind."

I tell my feet to move, but they don't listen, stuck in place like there's lead in my shoes.

"NOW!" Her voice booms and tears sting my cheeks, coming harder, faster. Momma never yells like this.

First I lose my best friend, then I fail the entire magical community, and now Momma's pressure is through the roof. Ever since becoming a witch I've screwed up everything.

I bolt up the stairs and bury myself in bed.

I can't do this anymore. I don't know how to fix messes, only to make them. I quit.

* * ✳ * *

A smoky bacon smell snatches me from my dreams Tuesday morning.

After a few blinks, the Beyoncé poster on my wall isn't nearly as hazy. The flickering streetlamp outside beats once, twice, then fades into the daylight. My clothes are all twisted around me. I stand up, straightening the ripped jeans and neon shirt I slept in.

The air is still. Quiet.

My door's cracked.

I'm almost certain I left it closed.

I came in here in such a rush, I'm shocked I didn't slam it. My phone's heavy in my hand and stays black when I tap it.

The bacon beckons me and my stomach rumbles. I wonder what else Momma made. She was so mad last night I'm surprised she cooked me breakfast at all.

And now I don't even have a wand, but if I'm honest, I don't deserve one. Not after the mistakes I've made. I plug in my phone and slip out of yesterday's clothes, listening for clanging pots in the kitchen.

Nothing.

Hmph. She must be getting ready for work. I listen for floorboard creaks, Momma or Memaw making their way up- or downstairs.

Nothing. The hair on my arm stands tall.

I slip into the hall. "Momma?"

Her bed is neatly made up, her work shoes gone.

"Memaw?"

Downstairs I round the banister, each step racing my pulse for first place. Down the hall the greasy smell grows.

Living room—empty. "Hello?" Silence hangs in the air like a guillotine. I rush into the kitchen and smoke swallows the stove. A piece of bacon as black as my hair is on top, sizzling. I shove the pot off the heat, coughing, and open the kitchen window.

And there, neck deep in her rosebush, is Memaw, pruning.

I burst out the door, book it across our lawn, and slam into her, almost knocking down. "You're okay!"

"Wha—" She hugs around me, wiping the sweat from her face. "Of course I'm okay, baby. You all right? Your lips as pale as ice, che."

"I woke up and couldn't . . . I didn't know . . ." I press into her. "I was just worried. And the bacon—"

"You made bacon?"

"No, I didn't . . . you . . . never mind. I'm just so glad you're okay, Memaw. With the way my luck's been going I was worried something *else* bad was gonna happen."

We settle on the ground. "What you mean, baby? Tell Memaw all about it."

"It's nothing." I play with the petals of a tightly closed rosebud.

She gives a knowing look but doesn't press. "I love flowers, you know."

I do.

"They're so beautiful when they fully bloom. So radiant. But watching them get there is the fun part." She snaps the stem of a robust rose, yellow in the center and orange on the tips, and puts it in my hand.

"It's so pretty."

"You gotta prune 'em to get 'em that way. They'll grow a little but to really get 'em to their fullest potential, you gotta touch 'em up time to time. Shave away what's dragging 'em

295

down. Going through the not so pretty parts is how they learn to shine."

She presses the bloom to my nose and my toes curl at the sweetness. "Don't you just love 'em?"

I nod.

She presses her shoulder into mine. "Is it about a boy?"

"It's . . . it's Momma, and Park Row, and . . . Nae."

"Nae? That's one of your friends, yeah?"

"Not one. *The* friend." My best friend for as long as I can remember. "And the kitchen Momma had to clean. That whole mess was because I made an antidote potion."

"Oh, look at you now, using that Potions gene."

I wrinkle my brow. "And it didn't even work. The potion I managed to make did, but we couldn't get it to *everyone*. And now all the Magicks around here could be exposed! I fail at everything. Everything that counts."

"You are not a failure, baby, because you made a few mistakes. Even big ones. Look at math. Some things gone' come easier to others, and that's okay. But if you work at it, you can do whatever it is you want to. Didn't I see you use that wand the other day to get that towel?"

"Yes, but that wasn't a hard one . . ."

She purses her lips. "And is that the only one you've done right?"

"Well, no. I mean, yeah . . . the ones I practiced went all right."

"See there. Charms might take a little extra work to learn and that's fine. You don't have to be good at what everyone else is doing. You have your own thing."

"I do?"

"You do. GrowthGoo?"

"Oh, Potions, I guess, Memaw, but that's because I'm good at cooking and it's kind of the same."

"You so right, baby, that you don't realize you wrong."

I laugh. "That doesn't make sense."

"Now let's see if this still works." She takes off her necklace—the one she always keeps tucked away—and presses the pendant hanging from it to her temple. The wooden locket glows green, as does the spot on her hairline where it touches.

"Memaw, what—"

"The core is gone by now, but I'm still about a 3C. They used wood back then, and mine was oak because Big Momma had a big ole oak tree in her yard. I kept a sliver of the wand, carved it into a locket, and had it bewitched with a remembering charm." She pulls the locket away and opens it, and a tiny roll of paper falls out. "Kept this in it."

She hands me the paper, and its yellowed edges crinkle as I unroll it. I recognize the page torn from the spell book Memaw found and gave me forever ago. The "This Guide to Spellcasting Is Presented to" is still in the book, but below the torn edge is written:

Amelia Espree

I gasp. That's Memaw's name. "I knew it! Memaw, you're a witch?"

She chuckles. "I sure am."

"You never told me!"

"Oh, baby, well . . . I wanted you to make the connection to your magic yourself. Magic, like anything else, you gotta put your heart in it. And I didn't want you doing it for the wrong reasons, just to make me proud or anything like that. This is for you, baby. My generation had our time. And yes, help the family, but you can't lose sight of yourself. *Your* dreams. For all I know you coulda come home wanting to bind yourself to a toad and I'd have smiled proudly 'bout that, too." She cackles and I hug into her.

I can't imagine what it would have been like to *know*. But I can see what Memaw means. I found my way to Potions with a bit of struggling, but all on my own, and that makes me stand taller.

She holds her necklace and sunlight glints on the metal holding the locket to the leather strand. "But this is all that's left of those days. I wanted to keep the memory even though I let go of the magic."

"What? Memaw, why?"

"Lots of reasons. But the biggest one is, I was scared. I didn't want to use a spell wrong or do something to hurt somebody on accident. Magic is prickly."

"You can say that again."

"And my sister, your great-aunt Pearl, was giving my parents a run for their money. So reckless. I wanted to be the good daughter. They rarely used magic in the house—"

"Wait, *they*? More than you and Aunt Pearl had magic? Big Momma and Big Daddy were Magicks, too?"

"All our family. We're descendants of the Balestrieuts, the most elite Potions witches to ever migrate from Winzhobble."

Winzhobble. The place magic originated.

"That's where that Potions gene you got comes from."

I *thought* she said "Potions gene" earlier.

"Oh, generations of civil unrest there, darlin'. Until our kind had enough. Our ancestors left in a mass exodus, generations ago, and settled here in the Americas."

"I do remember Mr. Scooter mentioning something about . . . covens?"

"Yep, we stuck together, kept our communities as tight as we could. This is of course cobwebs from what my own Mamie told me. It's in our Ancient History books somewhere. But over the years the covens have all but dismantled. I see 'em posting they events time to time on the Facebook: block parties, potlucks, family reunions are a big one. But that's more of an optional social thing. We been spread out for so long."

It's a shame the covens aren't together anymore. That would be so cool. To have a whole community right here together, all our distant magical cousins and aunties at each other's fingertips.

"So when I say you have your own thing, I mean it, baby. You not no everyday witch that knows how to swish a brew." She straightens. "You a Balestrieut."

My eyebrows press together like a jelly sandwich.

She chuckles. "The Balestrieuts were the most sought-after Potion folks ever existed. Now, history's not my thing really, but I seem to remember . . ." She squints and her temple pulses with green light. "Balestrieuts were famous in their territory in Winzhobble for brewing healing potions. Folks, including the king and queen, would pay pure gold for even a drop. To hold an audience of a Balestrieut was a privilege not many could afford. And to taste their food . . . *tuh*." She slaps her knees. "Forget about it. Once, a decade-long war was waged over the theft of a loaf of bread a Balestrieut woman made."

"*Wow*." I gape at my hands, small and lined, and picture my ancestors kneading magical pastries.

"Most settled in the South. Winzhobble being so cold, they wanted a change o' climate. That's why the best food you'll ever find is down south, che—it's remnants of our ancestry. That Potions gene makes folks good at cooking!"

"Wow, *my* ancestors. Potion witches."

"Baby, your ancestors could brew potions that would make the lame walk and the dead talk. Potions can do magnificent things. It's in your blood, boo. Don't sleep on that skill, you hear?"

"That's why it comes so easily!"

"That's *your* gift. *Your* special thing."

I was so focused on other people's talents I didn't even notice every time I sat down to do a potion, the ingredients almost sang to me. Like I could smell and hear and just know what went next. Even on my Potions exam, I didn't do perfect and yet Ms. Mo said it was the best she'd ever seen. Russ mentioned Charms runs in his family and even Mo said she'd grown up with Links around. I face-palm. How have I been so blind?

Potions is *our* family's thing. But why didn't I know?

"Don't be like your ole memaw, Kyana. I stopped going to Saturday magic school, had my teacher destroy my wand and give me this little keepsake. By the time yo' momma was born, she didn't have a clue 'bout my magic and that's my fault. She never showed no signs of magic. And besides what she saw, time to time, or heard whispered about with her cousins, she hardly knew anything about it." She sighs. "But, even just being around it regularly, knowing what it was, knowing how special her ancestors were, what they could do—I robbed her of that because of my own fear. I wonder what she coulda done? How might her life have been different had she seen my magic, her own mother? Would she have sparked some? I carry that with me. Your momma works so hard. I just hope somehow this home and the little bit I can do make it up to her somehow."

"Oh, Memaw, don't think that way. Momma is hard-working and that's because of all you taught her."

"Well, ain't you a whole pitcher of sweet tea." She kisses my hand. "My point, baby, is don't sell yourself short. You can make a mess of a kitchen, let me tell you. But you're also good at a lot of things. And like those roses there, the growing, pruning, and growing some more is all part of blooming into the witch you were born to be."

I turn the rose in my hand . . . it's so delicate, so pretty.

She taps my chest. "And listen—it sounds like them other Magick kids ain't holding a grudge against you."

"No, they were actually proud that I tried to save our school. I guess no one's been down on me for this but me."

"They forgave you." She takes my hands in hers. "But sounds like you need to forgive yourself. Maybe that's the first step in being the witch I know you can be. Fear will cripple you if you let it. You are not your mistakes, Kyana." She pushes hair out of my face. "And we Balestrieut witches aren't quitters. We fight for what we want—whatever it is."

Memaw's right—I'm not awful at magic, I guess. I just made a few mistakes—*big* mistakes.

What is it that I really want? The answer's so close, I don't have to reach far for it at all.

"You're right, Memaw. So, so right." I hand her locket back. "Mind if I run inside to make a call? There are *two* things I want . . ."

"Oh?"

"Yeah. First, I want my best friend back."

CHAPTER 28

₊ ✳ *₊*

Nae didn't answer. Big surprise.

And she avoided me all day at school. But when Momma got home from work, I begged her to take me over there, told her it had something to do with math. So she did. She even apologized for losing her temper yesterday and gave me my wand back.

I curl my fingers around it tight before slipping it into my sleeve pocket.

"I just . . . I have a lot going on, baby," Momma says. "I trust you, Kyana. More than you know. I didn't take your wand because you shouldn't be a witch. You're a darn good one from where I'm standing. I'm giving it back so you know—I believe in you."

"Thank you, Momma." I wipe my face with the back of

my hand. She had a talk with Memaw while I was at school, sounds like.

"Now gon in there and get whatever it is you need from Nae." The car doors click unlocked. "I'll be in the car, resting my eyes. I ain't dressed to be nobody's company."

I hop out the car and ring Nae's doorbell. Her mom smiles to see me at their door. I make my way upstairs to Nae's bedroom door. The rainbow KEEP OUT sticker we put on there years ago for her little brother glimmers in the hall light. And for a second I feel kinda weird . . . like it's referring to me. But I knock anyway.

"Who is—" Her hair is done up in some violet twists. It's so pretty. My cheeks hurt from smiling. I don't know what I'm going to say to her, but gosh it's good to see her.

She stares, looking more confused than excited.

"Can I come in?" I ask.

With a sigh, she cracks her bedroom door open a pinch. Sounds of her mom's heels clicking back and forth across the hardwood below float up the stairs.

"Please?" I say.

She rolls her eyes. "*Fiinnne.*"

The door swings open and Nae's mermaid comforter is piled with ice cream containers and tissues sprawled across the bed like she's been in here crying. Two poofs sit at the foot of her bed, one purple, one teal. I plop down on the teal one. It's been a minute since I've been over to Nae's, but the teal one's mine. We'd sit here, hunched over blankets and pillows, painting our nails, watching YouTube, gossiping about the latest Thompson Middle drama until we couldn't keep our eyes open.

I miss those days.

I miss her.

I miss us.

"So, what brings you over here so late?" She folds her arms.

"The reason I came up here is because . . ." *How do I make this sound right? How do I explain? That ever since she's stopped talking to me, nothing's been right. That she's my best friend, my other half, my girl, through and through. And whatever's going on between us feels like shoving a foot in the wrong shoe.*

"I'm listening. Or are you not gonna talk?" She turns her back, stuffing her homework into her backpack. The zipper's a mermaid tail key chain we got last summer when I went on vacation with her family to see the Lorraine Motel in Memphis.

Where do I even start?

"I . . . Nae, things have been off for a while." Saying I'm sorry don't cost nothing. That's what Momma says. Then why does it stick in my throat? "I just wanna fix it."

"Look, you've been acting weird ever since my birthday party," she snaps back.

She's right.

"And I don't know why you trying to act like I did something," she says. "I haven't been doing anything but trying to talk to you. *You* haven't had the time."

She's not wrong.

"*You* been hanging around with Ashley or whatever her name is instead of me."

Also true.

"*You* invited Tommy to our library days *without* asking me! You know I think he's cute and you bring him around like it's nothing, without thinking how I'd feel."

I didn't think about it that way.

"Lately, it's like I don't know who you are. It's like you've changed. You're different. And I just—"

"You're right."

"What?" She sets down her backpack.

"You're right."

"But?"

"There is no but." I can't keep skating around the truth. Lying to her was the first mistake I made. She's my *best* friend. And friendships are built on trust. "Nae, something really big—*life changing*—happened and I didn't tell you . . ."

Her expression softens.

"I wanted to tell you, but I couldn't. I couldn't tell anyone. So I started lying to cover my tracks. And one lie led to another and another and now I'm in so deep I can't even remember what I said and when."

She stares, speechless.

"It's the truth, Nae. And I'm done with the lying. I'm not supposed to tell you, but I'm just—" I bite my lip and warm saltiness spreads on my tongue. "I'm just gonna tell you."

"I'm listening." She sets down on the purple poof, eyes wide with curiosity.

The words are like pennies in my mouth. I want my friend back. If I don't trust her are we even best friends? "I— I'm . . ." *Just say it!* "I'm a witch."

My chest thuds loud enough I'm sure Momma can hear it in her car.

Nae bursts out laughing.

She doesn't believe me. That's fair. I wouldn't believe it either.

"I gotta say, your lies get more and more creative. I mean—"

I slide my wand from my sleeve and flick. Sparks fizz and the mermaid figurine on her dresser flies to my hand through the air.

Her jaw drops.

Oh gosh, please don't freak out.

She blinks, mouth hanging there.

I don't know what to say. I showed her. She's seen it. Her eyes fall to my wand.

"I . . . You just . . ." She reaches for my wand and I jerk back.

"Sorry." I hand it to her and she takes it delicately, mouth still wide open.

"So . . . I mean . . . how . . ." Her stutters don't stop, so I explain . . . *everything.*

I tell her about Park Row Magick Academy and my first day of class. I tell her about the notice for closure, Russ being there, suspecting him of illegally breeding Lysol cats. *That* got me a funny look. And I explain how I tried to beat him for a Charms spot with Ashley, how I'm a descendant of a long line of Potions witches and that's why I can cook so good, and how I entered the baking contest to win money to keep the school open, but how that blew up in my face.

She gasps at that part. "So *that's* why this competition was such a big deal. And *that's* what's been going on all over the news with people acting weird. It's because they got a taste . . ."

"Yep, a taste of magic."

Her eyes grow even wider as she hands my wand back. I stick it back in my sleeve and tell her all about the cookies laced with the antidote. How Principal Gomez let Russ and me circulate the cookies around school. And how they went out to all schools across Rockford.

"Uhhhh. Nae, you have to *swear* to not tell a soul!" I

take her hands, pleading. "We go through a lot of trouble to make sure non-Magick folks don't know we exist."

She draws a cross with her finger on her chest. "I swear, I won't." She squeezes my hands and I can breathe again. Feels good to have everything in the open. She rakes her fingers through her hair and turns her back to me.

Uh-oh. Something's wrong.

"Key, I don't know what to say . . . I had no idea you were—"

"Naomi!" Her mother's voice rings from the hall. "We're having dinner soon, and Kyana and her mother need to be getting back."

"Got it, Mom." The door clicks shut and I can see her face, hear her sniffles. "I was *awful* to you! The *worst* friend ever and you had all this *real* life stuff going on."

"Nae . . ."

"No, please just listen." Her face is streaked with tears. "You're usually so kind and nice and patient with me and I was so caught up thinking you'd let some stupid boy come between us." She throws up her hands, rolling her eyes. "Or . . . I don't know. I just felt ignored and I acted like a grade-A brat!"

"Nae, it's fine. I—"

"It's *not* fine." Her chest heaves up and down. "I was so selfish. You deserve a better friend. I'm so sorry!" She covers her face with both hands, muffling her sobs.

"You done with your acceptance speech for worst friend of the year?" I laugh, peeking for a glance of her cheeks. "I know you smiling under there." She smirks between sniffles. She's torn up about this and I mean, she is right. She had major attitude. But she's sorry and if friendships are built on anything solid, it's gotta be trust with a heaping cup of forgiveness.

"Nae, you're the sister I never had. We're as good as family." I open my arms wide and she wraps around me like a giant teddy bear.

"I won't tell a soul," she says. She hooks her pinky on mine. "I swear." She taps her chin. "Wait—so does this mean if I want you to like magic my hair into a certain style, you could? Or *oooo*, what about like using it to help me get votes with my campaign? Preliminary polling shows Shelby and I are neck and neck. Oh! And—"

"Nae, I can't. I don't think the Magick Board wants us doing magic for people. They don't even want people to *know*. Last thing I need is to get into more trouble."

She shakes her head. "I mean, yeah, of course. I'm sorry, Key. My bad."

We pound fists. She gets it. My chest is lighter, my head less woozy. Even the air is somehow sweeter.

"So what are you going to do about the antidote for the rest of Rockford? What if they do something drastic?"

And just like that, warm feelings gone. "I need a plan to

fix this *before* the mayor finds out about us and the Magick Board decides we all need to be gotten rid of."

She gasps. "He wouldn't!"

"Nae, if the non-Magick world knew we existed, everyone would expect magical fixes to everything. And *bad* people might want to control us, too. It would get ugly, dangerous."

"I mean, yeah, I knew for two seconds and I had a list of things I wanted you to whip up for me. Ha."

"See?"

"So what do we do?"

"We?"

"Of course we! I'm your best friend, dork. Whatever mess you're in, we're in it together. So what are *we* doing? How do we save Park Row Magick Academy? It's so cool that you're this mega cooking potions witch, b-t-dubs."

"Oh my goodness, Nae, that's it! We bake!"

CHAPTER 29

₊✳︎₊✳︎✳︎₊✳︎₊✳︎

With a plan in place, the rest of the week sped by and it's amazing I could focus on school at all. Momma's off to work and Memaw's tending her gardenias in the back. Ten minutes of math done. A regular Saturday morning, except today's the final round and Ashley's at one end of my kitchen, Nae's at the other. And Russ is sitting at the table, glancing back and forth between both of them.

I can read Nae's mind based on her pursed lips and side-eyes. *This isn't going to go well.*

But they're both my good friends. No reason we can't all be friends.

Nae shifts on her feet, digging into an itchy spot on her scalp. Ashley's reading something on her phone.

Okay, seriously? This is ridiculous. PRMA is supposed

to be closing today! But not if I can help it. The final round of judging for the finalists—which somehow includes me—is *tonight. We don't have time for this.*

"Nae, this is Ashley. She's a witch too and we've become pretty tight. She's cool."

Nae does nothing for a good minute. Then she waves a few fingers.

Ash studies her shoes and fiddles with her nails.

"Ash, this is Naomi," I say. "She's been my best friend since forever."

Ash extends a shaky hand but manages to give decent eye contact. "Nice to meet you."

Nae studies her hand a moment. The *last* thing I need right now is more friend drama.

"Yeah, good to meet you, too," Nae says, shaking Ash's hand.

I let out a huge breath.

"Okay, my turn," Russ says, turning to Nae. "I was a complete jerk to you. And I'm sorry. I honestly would have been stoked to be at your party just to see Shelby bust her butt."

Nae's attitude cracks into a giggle.

"Seriously, I'm still gonna make it up to you somehow. But please know I'm sorry."

She purses her lips and eyes him up and down. I hang on Nae's words. "Fine. Not friends, but apology accepted."

"I'll take it," he says, shoulders slumping in relief.

And he's not the only one. "Well, the air is clear and everybody knows everybody now. We have a lot of work to prep for this competition. With me being a finalist and Tommy confirming everyone will be there, this is our best shot at getting this antidote out. *And* hopefully still winning first place to save PRMA."

"Yeah, it's like this huge thing," Nae says. "My parents even took off work to go. All of Rockford city highlife are supposed to be there or something."

"Yeah," Russ adds. "I mean, all those people donated to the prize money so I bet they wanna see who wins. And Tommy told me his dad said all the same guests who got to taste the first-round entries have tickets for the finale, except for Umbrella Lady."

"Yeah, I heard she's locked up in her house," Ash says. "Hasn't come out."

"Man, I feel so bad about that," I say, "but aside from her, that's *great* news, Russ! We need everyone that tasted my cupcakes present."

"And Tommy *assured* you they will all be there?" Ash asks.

"Positive, he said. So we should be golden," Russ says, and the others agree.

Excitement jolts through me like electricity. *Maybe I can actually pull this off.*

In minutes the kitchen is a disaster of butter, flour, and

powdered sugar. A pair of eggshells fall from my hands and disappear into thin air before even touching the ground.

"Got your back," Russ says.

"Thanks."

Russ is whipping his wand in every direction, cleaning as we go. Over my shoulder a broom and mop swish back and forth thanks to a charm Russ brought. Nae's whipping up frosting. Russ moves to the sink full of sudsy water, slashing his wand left and right. With each swish, dirty dishes lift, dunk in the water, and rise, dripping and sparkly clean.

Ash is running her hand along the doorframe, knocking every few spots. Who knows what she's up to. The mixture in my bowl is way too dry.

"A little more butter," I say. Nae hands it over and moves on to greasing a cookie sheet. Crumbled pieces of yellow cake are in bits on the table and the air is sweet like vanilla.

Ding! The next cake layer is ready.

"I got it," Nae shouts, heat escaping from the oven when she opens it.

A buttery, nutty scent fills the air, curling my toes. "Thanks, Nae."

Wand in hand, I'm hunched over Momma's largest gumbo pot, a lavender substance sloshing in the bottom. My spell book's hovering above it, page open.

Slug skin paste. I check the substitution chart and cream together some Kool-Aid powder and cocoa butter, then plop it in. The gritty potion thickens almost instantly and is smoother than butter. These substitute ingredients really do work so much better.

"Thank you, brilliant witchy ancestors," I say, and keep winding my wand. Ash wanders out of the kitchen, wand in hand, whispering something, and I almost forget what I'm doing.

"So what kind of cake are you entering for the final round?" Nae sets the cake pan on the oven top and the last layer goes in. "Looks good." She tosses a chunk of cake crumble in her mouth before winding her spoon around the mixing bowl again. "Ooo, it *is* good!"

"It's Memaw's 1-2-3-4 cake. She makes it every Easter with a lemon buttercream." I glimpse for Ash, careful to keep my eye on my potion. No sign of her, but I can hear mumbling or something. What's she doing? "Ash?"

No response. Just louder whispers. Russ and I share a quizzical look as he ducks into the living room to find her.

My potion needs to sit for a few minutes, so I set my bowl aside. "How's it coming, Nae?" Her bowl is still a crumbly mixture of sugar and butter.

"You sure it's supposed to be stiff? It's not stiff."

"Keep beating it."

She mixes faster. "What about the sugar?"

"Add it little by little. Don't dump it all in there at once."

"Your memaw teach you all this?" Nae asks.

"Sure did." I smile.

"Uhm, Kyana, you might wanna take a look at this," Russ yells from the living room.

Something *thunk*s the carpet. Nae and I rush in and she gasps.

I gasp, too.

Memaw's burgundy recliner stretches out, yawning.

"I did it!" Ash is jumping up and down.

"These friends of yours, Miss Ashley?" the recliner asks, pillow covers batting like lashes.

"Yes. This is Kyana. This is her house, actually. So you'll be living with her. Don't worry, she's cool."

"I . . . you?" I don't have words. Russ and Nae are equally in shock. Memaw's recliner is tethered to an Available?

"Kyana, this is Shirley. She loves pillows, especially shaggy ones, her favorite color is periwinkle, she enjoys long afternoon naps, and loves company, long chats, that kind of stuff. Not a fan of dogs, though, right?"

"That's right. Well, unless it's hypoallergenic. Terrible allergies, you understand."

"Right," I say. "Allergies . . . Ash?"

"Don't be mad," she says. "I just had an idea what with all the stuff your grandmother's been forgetting. I figured having Shirley around could help."

I didn't think of that, to be honest.

Nae is still gaping in utter disbelief.

"I got the idea, but wanted to see if I could actually do it before saying anything. I couldn't ever get the tethering charm right until now!" Ash's eyes are alight with such pride. She's been working on perfecting that tethering charm for a long time.

I wonder what on earth Momma's gonna say. I sigh.

"Something wrong?" the recliner asks. "I'm quite comfy. And a good storyteller if you're into that." Her voice is so soothing, I believe it.

"No, no, sorry. I'm just taking it all in. Ash, I'm so proud of you. Thanks for being so thoughtful. Let's hope Momma's not weirded out by it. But I think it could be really dope for Memaw. And you know she loves watching her stories and gossiping about them with someone."

Ding!

"Oo, *Young and the Restless*, or which one?" The pillows on the recliner fluff out with excitement. "This Memaw person sounds like a good ole time. And I think something in the oven might be ready? I heard a ding."

I check my watch and she's right.

"Ah, see? Helpful already." The recliner twists into a smile.

Back in the kitchen, the cake is pulling away from the edges of the pan and my potion's about ready for the last few ingredients. Russ returns to spotting my messes.

Wolf spider extract.

I drip two gray drops of wig glue in and the substance thickens, bubbling. Smudged grease stains on the page make the next part of the potion instructions hard to read. I squint.

Add two palmfuls of crushed blue morpho butterfly wings. Fold in slowly.

I turn a jar upside down and papery cerulean specks shimmer like crystals in my hand.

"So what's the deal with the potion antidote?" Russ asks, drying his hands. "Is that going in the cake?"

"And how are we gonna make sure everyone actually tastes the cake?" Ash asks, apparently done tethering Availables to furniture in my living room. "That's the plan, isn't it? To make sure every single person there gets the antidote?"

"Yes and no," I say. Two amused stares swivel my way. The cookie faux-fundraiser was a no-brainer. No kid's going to turn down dessert at school. But adults are weird. They'll go places sometimes and talk. Food'll never even touch their lips. Especially if they're dressed in one of those fancy dresses. Nope, can't count on everyone tasting my cake this time.

"I can't be sure everyone is going to taste the cake," I say. "Plus it doesn't have to be eaten—I just need everyone to touch it, somehow."

"*Ew!*" Nae and Ash say at the same time.

"You sure they're going to cooperate?" I whisper to Russ.

"Positive." He winks.

"Sooooo, you gonna ask everyone to finger-paint with that purple potion or . . . ?" Ash asks.

"Oh my goodness, it's working!" Nae squeals over a mixing bowl of satiny frosting. "That's good-looking buttercream if I do say so myself."

"I better be going," Russ says. "Gotta get everything ready for tonight." He bids us goodbye and hands me a gift bag on his way out. "For your grandmother. Just another way to apologize for how crappy of a person I was to you for so long."

"Ouch, that's hot," Ash says, pulling my attention away before I can respond. She flicks her wand and two tiers of cake from the oven set down, one on top of the other.

Inside the bag Russ gave me is a short bob wig with feathered edges. The tag is fancy with gold letters.

SANCTIFIED EDGES
{PREMIER WIG LINE}

"The cake looks so good, Kyana," Ash says.

"It really does," Nae echoes.

I set the bag aside and join them at the table to ogle my cake creation. "It's finally taking shape!"

"It's sort of an odd shape, huh?" Nae sets down the final piping-hot layer on top, fresh out the oven. The idea to do a multi-tiered cake came to me when I was thinking about Park Row.

"Yeah, kind of. Cube shaped. Like a building." I wink and with a quick swish of my wand, the steam evaporates. The cakes are completely cool to the touch.

"Perfect, ready to ice." I work my wrist in an S motion with a flat-edged angled spatula. The frosting goes on messy at first. The crumb coat, as Memaw calls it. Then I add another layer, back and forth, back and forth, until the cake is covered in a delicious buttercream layer with a pearly white sheen.

"Hand me that box of fondant pieces, please?" I ask. Nae hands me a box of shimmery figurines I spent all night making. Several are in the shape of tables and chairs. A couple fondant figures are little people with curly hair. Others are brown and shaped like bookshelves.

First, I dig out a fistful of cake in the top layer so it's like a hollow room with walls made of cake. With steady hands, I place rectangular pieces inside the cake room like tiny walls inside the cake building. My hands are clammy but steady as I put each in place. Inside each room in my cake model, I add the desk- and chair-shaped pieces.

Cold sweat from my forehead is slick on the back of my hand. I wipe it on my pants before placing the last few hardened fondant bits to fill out the space. The entire model is taking shape as my friends close in around me, staring but silent.

This could all be for nothing, but it's the best shot I got. Everyone was so impressed a kid my age could *bake*.

I'm going to show them a kid my age can *dream*—and dream BIG.

When the last piece is in place, I step back and stare at our creation. A cake-sized model of a community learning center made with sugar, butter, and lots of love stares back.

"It really looks great, Key! You think they'll get it?"

"I hope so." I brush my crusty hands on my apron. "I'm hoping that showing them *why* I want this money—well, *mostly* why—will matter. That fifty thousand dollars can build a new learning center not just for magical folks, but all of Park Row. During the week it can be used by the kids that live around here. And on the weekends and after hours when it's 'closed,' we can use it for magic lessons. It's the best of both worlds—a win for everyone."

"I really hope it works," Ash says.

"Me too."

CHAPTER 30

*∗**✳**∗*

We finished with an hour to spare to take a quick bath and book it to City Hall. I thought the first event was fancy with chefs in their button-down white coats. But this evening, half of Rockford is here in glittery gowns and black-tie tuxedos. The final competition is inside City Hall, in a section designated for each finalist, with a dim golden spotlight illuminating each finalist's entry.

My name hangs in bold print on a banner above my area, which is set with a small table covered in a floor-length purple iridescent table linen, thanks to Nae. Swarms of people having hushed conversations with tiny plates in hand sweep back and forth. Occasionally someone glances over at my cake.

The other finalists stand near their tables as well. One is

an older gentleman with a potbelly and a thick Italian accent. His cake is tiered, but rounded. The bottom tier is shaped like a fountain and the layer above it is shaped like bird wings. The topmost tier is an all-edible swan head coming out the center, its eyes dazzling like gems.

Seriously? *That's* my competition?

The trifold they gave us when we showed up sticks to my clammy hands.

Favio Russo, Pastry Chef at Rockford Domain, a swanky downtown strip of patisseries by day turned bars at night.

I'm way out of my league here.

The other contestant looks familiar, two pigtailed red braids tied up in a cross bun. I recognize her from the tent.

Penelope Froberg, Graduate of the Culinary Institute of America and sous chef to restaurateur Hinata Takahashi.

Both chefs. I'm up against two classically trained chefs. I look for her fiery red hair, but her station is swallowed by a crowd of fancy hairstyles and silky dresses.

My bio says: *Kyana Turner, sixth grader at Thompson Middle School.*

What am I even doing here?

"Hey, good luck!" Russ says, popping up out of nowhere. "Nae and I have everything in place."

"Thanks." Russ has really come through. Turned out to be a real friend. "Listen, I wanted to just say I'm sorry."

"Key, you don't owe—"

"No, please. You were a piece of work, yes. But I've also

learned a lot since finding out I'm a witch. Mainly that I shouldn't be so quick to judge myself, but I also shouldn't be quick to judge others, either." I'm still getting used to him not being all blinged-out and looking like he stepped out of a music video. But he's got just as much swag, more even, this way. He oozes confidence. This is a Russ I can hang with. I offer a dap. "Friends?"

"Friends!" he says, and we dap it up.

"Eight-ten," he says, tapping his watch, then scoots off to find Nae. I give him a thumbs-up.

Across the room I spot Momma, chattering away and laughing with Nae's parents. She's in a ruby-red dress that stops at her ankles. I love the way it looks on her radiant, earthy skin. Her hair's up in a simple bun, a brooch tucked underneath, twinkling in the speckled ceiling light. Pearls dangle from her neck. I didn't even know Momma had pearls.

Memaw's at her side munching on something. The hat on her head is piled almost as high as Favio's swan cake. Memaw plopped that wig from Russ on her head and in seconds had a whole new getup complete with a matching church hat and gloves. Sanctified Edges, turns out, is a premier part of that Wicked Edges wig line Mo told us about. Between that and Memaw's new bestie Shirley, she's all smiles, out here acting like a million bucks. (Momma *did* think it was really strange when she met Shirley for the first time, but it made Memaw so happy that she agreed to go along with it.)

Mayor Applegate stops by them, shaking their hands. He

looks so much shorter than he does on TV. I haven't talked to Mo in days. I wonder what happened with Dr. Dixon, the Chair of the Magick Board who was arrested? The thought makes me queasy.

The mayor works his way around the crowd surrounding Penelope's station. The crowd clears and I can finally see her table. My jaw drops. Her cake looks like it's made from actual crystals. It's so blingy, Cardi B would be jealous. It's not tiered, but it's tall. *Really* tall. On its top is a golden tiara.

Is that edible?

That can't be edible!

It's probably edible.

"Pick your jaw up off the floor." Mo's beaming ear to ear, smile so bright it's like someone's turned on a light. Her pale pink lip color matches her gown perfectly, setting off her velvety, sable skin. Her hair's in an updo and a tall man with ombre locs is on her arm.

"Kyana, this is Max. Max Wriggly."

"Nice to meet you," he says. "I hear you're quite the witch." He offers his hand and I shake it firmly the way Momma says you're supposed to do.

Wriggly? I know that name. "You're the wizard—" I shout, before stuffing my words down my throat. "Sorry," I whisper. "You're the guy who went to school with Mo, made that invisible barrier?"

"That would be me."

"That's really cool. I still haven't quite figured out my community project."

"Judging by what I'm seeing today, I'm sure you'll think of something," he says with a smile, before excusing himself to chat with some man wearing a peacock for a hat.

"I'm so nervous!"

Mo hugs me, smoothing the edges of my hair. "Don't be. You made it to the top three. That's a *huge* accomplishment, Kyana. If nothing else comes of this today, you're already a—"

Now *her* jaw's dangling wide open.

She gawks at my cake table, hands over her mouth. "You . . . it's . . . Kyana, what *is* this?"

"It's what I want to do with the money if I win. It would be a learning center for all of Park Row to use after school during the week. And then the witches and wizards could use it when it's 'closed.'" I add air quotes to the last part. "Isn't that perfect?"

Mo's chest rises slow and falls even slower. "Kyana . . . this . . . this is . . . I don't even know what to say." She rests a hand on my shoulder. "This is a *dream*. A beautiful, kind-hearted, generous, compassionate *dream*. But, sweetheart . . ." Her smile dissolves.

"But what?"

"It's not looking good." She points a polished nail at someone in the distance and I immediately recognize the fuzzy cloud of hair, square-rimmed glasses, and deep-set eyes under wild brows. It's Dr. Dixon, the Chair of the Magick Board. The one I saw being arrested on TV. And for some reason he looks madder now than he did then.

I try to swallow the lump in my throat but it won't go down. "He's here?" I ask.

"Yeah, they couldn't find any evidence of foul play so they released him without charges. And well . . . he's not happy . . ."

"Is he here for me?"

"I don't know why he's here, but . . . I shouldn't be telling you this." Mo glances around, then whispers. "With how much news this has gotten I imagine he's planning to take it straight to the Grand Council of Magicians. And they're known to take drastic measures . . ."

How drastic? I wanna say but the words stick in my throat.

"Kyana, if the higher-ups get wind of this, it will be bad. They would sanitize the lot of us. Rid Rockford completely of magic." Disappointment glistens in her eyes.

What?! Every magical person in Rockford's gonna be stripped of their gifts because of one mistake?! How's that fair? How's that okay?

"No!" My voice is louder than I mean it to be. "No. I—!"

She brushes a rogue tendril of hair from my face. "Your

heart is so big. Never change that about yourself. If you win here today, Kyana, take that money and do something nice for your family. You could have a different life."

"I like my life," I say. "Just the way it is."

She smiles. "With that kind of money, and that house y'all got, you could move away. You could do whatever you want. Whatever your family wants."

"*This* is what I want, Ms. Mo." I straighten a sugary figurine falling over. "Park Row is my home. Everyone in it, magic or not. This would be for us, for all of us."

"I admire that in you, dear. Just—as far as magic goes, I'm afraid that ship has sailed. Those who can afford to up and relocate on short notice will, to keep their magic, but . . ."

"This isn't right. I *don't* accept that." My lip trembles. "I *won't*. I'm a member of this community and I have a say."

"Kyana . . ."

A booming laugh echoes across the room. I turn my head, and there he is. I jet in that direction with Mo on my heels saying a bunch of stuff I'm not trying to hear. *He can't do this. Well, he can. But I won't let him.*

"Excuse me," I say, slipping between two slender white women with even skinnier glasses in hand. They shuffle aside without even a glance my way.

He isn't going to take away what makes us special.

Closer now, Dr. Dixon is more quirky than polished and

posh like the rest of 'em but he's definitely the most stern looking.

I tap his shoulder.

He passes a glass with copper liquid to a woman on his arm. "Well, you must be Kyana." His smile is plastic. "The youngest contestant." He pats my shoulder and I study his greenish-blue eyes. The eyes of the man that would take away everything that makes us special with the swipe of his pen.

"I haven't made my way over to your table yet," he says. "But I can't wait to see what you've put together."

Does he know what this means to us? Does he even care?

"This is a big thing you've done for someone your age." He keeps filling the space with words. "You should be proud, for being so *brave and bold*."

It's now or never, Kyana. I stand up straight. "Dr. Dixon, can I speak to you? In private, please."

His smile cracks and a flicker of irritation shows itself, then disappears. "Of course, dear."

Mo said she never told anyone I bewitched the cupcakes. There were a lot of contestants that day. And he showed up after it was all said and done. But something tells me he knows it's me. And if he doesn't . . . he's about to.

I spot Mo over his shoulder as we make our way to the doors. She's hustling toward us, lips in a straight line. She's pissed. Oh, well. Memaw said fight for what I want. I lead the way around the chatters, past the other contestants, between armchairs full of boisterous women, falling over themselves laughing, gems hugging their knuckles.

"Let's step out here if you don't mind. So no one overhears."

The creases on his face deepen. Cool night air blasts me in the face when the door opens.

"Kyana." Mo's voice is stern as she slips outside to join us. "Sir. Good to see you again."

When he spots Mo his smile dissolves completely. He clears his throat and glances over both shoulders. "Good evening."

Wind whips through the trees and something's rummaging in a cluster of bushes nearby.

"What's this about?" He looks down at me and I've never felt so small.

Do it! Talk. Now's your time. "I heard you are planning to take what's happened since the baking competition with . . ." I whisper, ". . . *magic* to the Grand Council."

He shoots Mo a stern look. "So you're in the habit of sharing what happens at government meetings with children, I see?"

Mo plants a hand firm on her hip, fingers waving. "Y'all might think it's fine to do things in secret and keep people in the dark. But that's not how our community's run. We're open and honest with each other. Learn a thing or two. And you need to watch your tone."

He reddens, turning back to me. "You don't know what we're dealing with, kid. This has gone too far. I tried to keep this contained but we're on the verge of exposure. It's out of my hands."

The rummaging in the bush turns to hissing and a band of ferrets rushes toward us. Mo's eyes bulge out of her head as the lanky furballs surround us. A white one climbs on Dr. Dixon's shoulder, hissing and shaking his paw at me. The Chair's brows raise as if he understands whatever this critter is saying.

"It was you," I say. "I knew it! You've been spying on me with those ferrets! You're a Link."

"You're certainly bright," he says. "Yes, Links was my specialty and with them already in charge of hazardous material disposal, it wasn't a stretch to have them look into who was behind all this. I did what I had to do to find out the truth. Do you have *any* idea how much trouble you've caused?"

I study my feet. *Now's not the time to cower. Just tell the truth.* "I do. And that wasn't ever my intention. I was trying to keep magic a secret, like we're supposed to, and turns out that's not easy to do. It was an honest mistake and it's behind me."

That feels good to say. My mistakes are behind me.

He puffs his chest out. "Behind *you*, maybe."

"*Please* just listen," I interrupt. "Let me finish! I have a plan—in place—to fix this. To make sure everyone leaves here with the antidote."

"The level of magic that would require is . . . You'd need a custom antidote," he scoffs, as if my suggestion is utterly ridiculous, "by a *highly* astute Potions witch. Every single person present would need to touch it."

"And I fit that bill."

"You can't be serious." Dr. Dixon laughs to himself, more deranged than entertained, and even his ferret's arms are folded. "You're beyond yourself with ambition. It would almost be cute if it wasn't so foolish. If you could fix this yourself you'd have done it by now." He checks his watch. "And besides, the email is scheduled to be sent first thing tomorrow morning. You're too late, kid. I'm just here to make sure nothing else happens in the meantime."

"IT'S AN EMAIL! *UNSCHEDULE* IT!" I fight back the tears. "You *don't* want to do this. Please!"

"This one's quite sure of herself, isn't she?" he says to Mo. "I've thought long and hard about this, Kyana. This is serious."

"Exactly. You've dedicated your entire life's work to serving the magical Rockford community. Creating a space where we can hone our craft and grow. You've been Chair, Mo said, since before she was born. I *know* you care magic exists here. I know you don't want to leave this place and just go on living. I know you wouldn't wish that on anyone."

He lifts his chin at that part.

"I think you're just not sure how to fix this. And I cast this spell. *I* messed this up, which means *I* have the—"

"The ability to make an antidote. Yes, of course. But your witch track record isn't terribly clean. You're not even fully trained!" He rakes fingers through his hair. "This is preposterous!"

"Sir, I'm a Balestrieut."

That stills him.

"I can *do* this. Park Row needs this. My family needs this. And I need this. Let me fix it. I can. I'm *sure*."

He looks away.

"I'm not asking for days or weeks or months. Just give me the rest of tonight. If I succeed and the antidote is distributed tonight so that magic is completely contained, let the witches and wizards in Rockford stay here under the radar, like before. Delete that email."

He gazes in at the swanky cocktail party, where people shuffle around the glitzy pastry creations by my competitors. My cake sits alone.

"You have until the end of the night," he says. "If you fail, Ms. Turner, all bets are off. Magic and Rockford are done." He storms inside.

Now, I gotta win.

CHAPTER 31

∗∗✳∗∗

The sky is as dark as the hope I have I'll actually pull through this competition.

Servers are making their way through the crowd with scorecards in hand and miniature pencils. Any minute the emcee will interrupt the tunes flowing and it'll be time to fill them out and turn them in.

And *no one's* even tasted my cake.

The crowd's devoured pieces of the other contestants' cakes, but my table is still surrounded by rows and rows of tiny cake servings, all untouched. The top layer is still intact, the perfect model of Park Row. Only the bottom corner has been carved. But for what? No one's biting—literally.

My cake's pretty, to me. It's not a fancy bird or anything. It's *really* yummy and Memaw says that's what matters when you're making food for people.

"Don't nobody wanna eat no bland unseasoned food," she'd say all the time. "Put you a little spice in there, girl. Make it taste good. If you baking, extra sugar."

My cake tastes good. I know that for sure.

"Cooking is love, baby," Memaw said. "It's food for the soul."

And I wanted to be able to do that. Give that to people. Do something to make people feel some joy. A taste of happy. That's why I started learning to cook.

The first time I baked for Momma, I made red velvet cupcakes. It was Mother's Day and she'd just finished her third shift, and I carried one in to where she was propping her feet up. She told me words I'll never forget, words that stick with me each time I step into the kitchen: "You've outdone yourself, baby," she said after she took her first bite. "You and this cupcake are the *best* part of my whole day."

If food can make people feel *that* good, I wanna make sure I keep doing it.

That's it! That's why no one's fawning over my cake. *OMG, how could I be so dense?*

My cake is beautiful to me because it's a model of Park Row. But no one knows the story behind it, why it's shaped this way. And no one knows what it *tastes* like. I know my cake is bomb. I just need to get people eating it.

And if they won't come to us, let's go to them.

With Ash's, Momma's, and Memaw's help balancing several

plates on our arms, we shuffle through the crowd, passing out servings while the other contestants stick at their tables.

"Hello, sir," Ash says. "Would you try a slice of this cake made by my best friend? The one over there?"

From the corner of my eye, I spot the emcee moving through the crowd toward a mic stand on the far corner. Time's winding down.

"Momma, you and Memaw go over that way. And I'll go this way."

She nods, bustling off in her gown. I hurry past Ash and offer slices to everyone I see.

"Excuse me, hi. I'm one of the contestants. Please try a piece of my cake. It's a recipe that's been passed down for generations in my family. I guarantee it's the *best* cake you've ever had."

A gentleman in a tuxedo titters. "Well, how could I pass up that sales pitch? How old are you?"

"Twelve," I say.

He peers around me. "And you made the cake by yourself?"

"Sure did."

He takes a bite and his eyes double in size. "What's your name?"

"Kyana Lacreshia Turner."

"You weren't kidding. This is the best cake I've *ever* tasted. And don't tell my wife I said that. *Ha!* Come with me."

He leads me to the same corner as the emcee. Apparently they know each other, because the emcee greets him with a handshake.

"Mr. Belwoimer," the emcee says. "Good to see you, sir. Thanks again for coming all the way down to little ole Rockford to see this competition."

Who is this guy?

"Of course. Wouldn't have missed it for the world. Mind if I . . ." He points to the mic the emcee was about to grab and suddenly I can't breathe. I haven't had enough time to pass out all the samples. Momma and Memaw are moving around the room as fast as they can, but still no scorecards yet. We're not ready. Mr. Belwoimer brings the mic to his lips.

What's he doing?

"Ladies and gentlemen, honored guests. Thank you for coming out this evening and supporting the city of Rockford. These three finalists have *all* put together impressive presentations and, while the judging will begin very soon, I'd love your attention for a moment to tell you about someone I just met.

"Tell us your name, how old you are, where you go to school?" He holds the mic to my mouth.

Breathe. "Kyana." My voice bounces off the walls and my pulse rattles. "I'm a sixth grader at Thompson Middle in Park Row."

Every eye in the room burns my skin. Not a single person moves. The band isn't playing anymore and my panting is the only thing I hear.

He pulls the microphone back. "Now, I tasted Kyana's cake," he says, "and . . ." He looks around, loosening his tie with a smirk. "Where's Barbara? She's gonna get me for this one. This is the *best piece of cake* I have *ever* tasted. Anywhere. Bar none."

Did he just . . . I . . . OMG!

"If you haven't had a piece, do yourself a favor and get to that table before this cake is all gone. Kyana, is there anything else you want to tell us about your cake?"

The why! They'll care about the why.

"My cake isn't in some fancy shape with shiny icing or anything. But it's still special—to me at least. See, I'm from Park Row, on the other side of town."

I catch the eye of the Chair of the Magick Board.

I speak louder over the chatter. "A lot of kids where I'm from are looking for things to do after school. We don't have any kind of places we can go to and try out our skills. Like my best friend, Nae, she's good at painting. She does wild designs on our nails. I know she could be *really* good if she could practice more, like at an art center or something. But the closest one is across town. And I—" *I'm a witch*, I wanna say. "I like to cook and bake. I'm pretty good at it. I mean, I placed top three here. It would be cool to meet up with other kids and show them some of the things I learned to do in the kitchen from my grandmother. My other friend likes making robots and stuff with all sorts of scrap materials. There's a lot of kids where I'm from that would probably like a place to hang out after school. Like a learning center. So, I don't know, that may sound basic, but that's what my cake is—a model of a learning center. And if I win, I'm going to use the prize money to build it."

There isn't a sound in the building.

Other than my heartbeat, that is.

Mr. Belwoimer's gawking at me. *Is that a good thing?* Then the room bursts into applause. It goes on and on and *on* for what seems like forever. Even the other contestants are clapping.

"If you win, Kyana," Mr. Belwoimer says as the crowd pipes down, "I'll match that fifty thousand dollars."

"No way!"

Momma's in the front row of the crowd bawling her eyes out. Memaw too. No sign of Russ or Nae, which is a good thing. Means they're doing what we agreed to do. Getting that antidote out. My insides wriggle.

"I'll match it too." A woman from the crowd shouts. I look but can't find the face. *$150,000? I could win $150,000 for Park Row? WHAT?!*

I don't have words. I can't believe this!

"Well, with that, everyone make your way to Kyana's station to taste her cake. Make sure you get a scorecard."

He gestures and servers continue among the crowd, passing out more forms. "We'll be tallying them and announcing the winner shortly." He turns to me. "I need to talk to some people," Mr. Belwoimer says. "Whether you win or not, grab your family and come find me after this is all over. That sound okay?"

"Yes, sir."

The next half hour flies by. I'm asked a million questions. So many my mouth is dry as a desert. I hear hushed chitter-chatter at one point as a couple swishes past. Something about the swan cake being pretty but not tasting like much. That made my heart flutter. But no matter how excited I am I can't keep my eyes off the Chair of the Magick Board. He's standing against the wall, arms folded, as the tallies are counted.

I don't know how this is going to go, but I've done my best and I learned a lot. If I'd stopped baking the first time I burned something, I'd never have made it this far. And if I'd stopped using magic because I messed up a few times, I'd never know that I'm a *great* witch.

I am *not* my mistakes.

But I *am stronger* because of them.

Glasses clink and my heart stops when the emcee takes the microphone. *It's time.* I spot Nae's face in the crowd and she gives me a big thumbs-up. My stomach flutters. They're in position. I check my watch.

8:00 p.m. Ten minutes.

Oh my god, people are going to flip out. They better hurry up and announce these winners because things are about to go berserk in ten short minutes.

As if the emcee could read my mind, he says, "The moment we've all been waiting for is finally here. The City of Rockford's Harvest Fest Baking Competition tallies are done."

Is someone beating a drum? Oh no. That's my heart.

8:02 p.m. Eight minutes.

Momma moves next to me, Memaw on the other side. Ms. Mo's there too and Ash is in arm's reach. Nae wiggles her way through people and wraps her hands in mine. Eric waves from the audience.

"In third place, the Italian baking sensation, Mr. Favio Russo!"

He comes forward, the crowd rampant with applause, and shakes the emcee's hand. "Our third-place winner gets a feature piece on their culinary prowess in the city paper." He hands him an envelope and they shake hands.

Nae squeezes my hand.

"Whatever happens you're already a winner," Mo whispers.

8:07 p.m.

"I'm so proud of you, baby!" Momma's hand is warm on my back. Memaw winks.

I went after what I wanted. I didn't quit.

And that's enough for me. Whatever happens.

"In second place . . ."

Breathe.

8:09 p.m.

"Miss Penelope Froberg, graduate of the Culinary Institute of America. Congratulations, you've won a summer intensive at Le Cordon Bleu."

I don't hear the rest. It's all screaming. Momma's jumping.

I won. I can't believe it. I won!

I'm squished between a crowd of family and friends hugging me. It's unreal, the best feeling in the world.

And then . . . 8:10 p.m. . . .

"*Meow.*"

"*Vrriiiip.*" A ripping sound splits the air.

"What the—?" someone shouts. "What on earth have you been eating?"

"Oh good heavens, that's stinky."

Another rip.

And another.

Until everything's a pink cloud.

"Who let that mangy—?"

"Ewww, Ralph, get it off me! Get it off me!"

"*Ah!* There's hundreds of them!"

Groits scatter, trying to get away from people, and people scatter, pinching their noses, trying to get away from them.

I blink and we're engulfed in a pink cloud and the squeals turn into coughing. My nostrils sting with the scent of rotten eggs.

"That special diet worked," Russ says. "Just a minor complication."

"Yeah, isn't their gas supposed to smell like roses?" Eric asks, tucking his nose in his shirt.

The world around us is chaos. Everyone's freaked out by the herd of cats Russ and Nae snuck in, but I don't care.

I won!

I can't believe it.

Nae and Ash barrel into me. We're giddy and grinning. My ribs hurt from laughing so hard. Our plan worked *and* I won! This is the best day of my life.

Mo comes over, fanning under her nose. "Guys, what is going on? Are those groits?"

"Yep."

"And this . . . smell is . . ."

I wink. "The antidote."

She gasps, then bursts out laughing.

"Ms. Mo, you think saving Park Row can count as my community project?"

She shoves down a giggle. "Oh, yes, Kyana, I think you've outdone yourself with this one!"

TWO MONTHS LATER

✳

Winter Break is always exciting.

Lights everywhere and it's finally not as hot. There's no school for like three weeks. And it's the only time all year Momma takes off. But this break's more exciting than any other. For starters, I finished the semester with a B+ in math, which, considering how I toted around an F for so long, I'm pretty proud of.

Ashley hops out of her mom's car in front of my house just as Nae comes skipping down the sidewalk with full hands.

"Ash, hey!" Nae says, and they hug.

"Well, *hey*, Miss Class President," I say. Nae beat Shelby by a landslide. It helped that Russ signed on as her campaign manager as a way of making up for the jerk he'd been. And he helped Nae *charm* the whole grade—without magic—with her commitment to cheaper vending machines and casual Fridays.

"Don't dally too long with your friends," Momma says, a moving box in her hand. "Get on in here and help."

It was a whirlwind finishing the semester as the winner of the competition. Once it was all said and done, with donations from people who wanted to match the prize money funds, I ended up with $437,009.83.

Momma also put our house up for sale and, like she said, these banker people paid us a lot of money for it. I asked her how much, but she told me that was rude.

"Enough to buy a new house, without a loan," she said.

I was sad at first, thinking it meant we had to leave Park Row. But Momma said our community is *ours* and we're staying. The house three doors down from Nae went up for sale just as Momma's money came in. It's like all of this was meant to happen.

"One more box," Nae yells, her skip now a full run.

Ash and I slap hands and elbows. It's a little thing we came up with like a secret handshake. Me, Nae, and her know it. No one else.

"You guys are so nice to help us move in," Momma says.

"You kidding me?" Nae says. "My best friend lives *on my street*! I'm never leaving your house."

We laugh.

"We'll be moving boxes all week, with the center going up soon." She's not kidding.

Ground breaks on the Park Row Learning Center this summer. They said it'll take eight months to complete. So by the time we finally get moved in and settled in this new house, it'll be time to start setting up our new neighborhood center.

Nae's dad agreed to host STEM activities in the evenings one night a week. The art teacher from Thompson got a few artists together and they'll be rotating afterschool classes, too. There's even going to be a kitchen in the space for culinary arts, a karate room, a garage area for graffiti art classes, and a whole host of other activities, all sponsored and run by volunteers. It'll be open every day after school and on the weekends for PRMA.

Ash heaves a box from Momma's trunk and closes it. "Think I got the last one," she says.

We head up the steps to our new home. It's a two-story house with yellow siding and a wide wraparound porch. There's a giant tree in the front yard with lots of shade for summer.

The walk up to the front door is lined with rosebushes and there's Memaw, hunched over pulling up some fresh parsnips from the garden. "Y'all be careful with my recliner now," she yells.

Her and Shirley are *still* BFFs. Doctor's had to change up her medicine again, but she's doing good. I spend every moment I can with her. I've been taking lots of pictures, too. We started scrapbooking on the weekend. In my book I note dates and journal about the things we've done together. We put in recipes, too. She has so many she doesn't ever write down. I'm going to make sure I get 'em all documented.

Momma swings the front door open. The lines in her face are softer and she smiles more. I finally told her about the conversation with the Chair of the Magick Board and she about had a heart attack. Turns out he isn't a complete jerk. He just didn't know what else to do. He honored his word; with the problem fixed, there was no need to go to the Grand Council. Email *deleted*. Our community can continue to exist in secret and at peace. I was worried he'd still want to at least sanitize *me* for what I did, but he was impressed with the antidote. He said he sees a lot of potential in me.

"Girls, y'all move slower than molasses," Momma yells, waving for us to come on. "Get on in here. The cookies Memaw made are fresh out the oven, still warm!"

Memaw gets up, a basket of roses on her arm, and joins us as we head inside.

"I can't remember the last time you baked, Memaw!" I grab my phone. "That's usually my thing." Gotta get a picture and add this to the scrapbook.

"Girl, I got mo' recipes up my sleeves than hairs on your head." We laugh. "It's in my blood."

She's right, we Potions witches love being in the kitchen.

1-2-3-4 CAKE

INGREDIENTS

1 Cup Butter +1/3 cup shortening

2 Cups Sugar +1/3 cup

3 Cups Flour +1/3 cup

3 Teaspoons Baking Powder
                    +1/2 teaspoon

¼ Teaspoon Salt

4 Eggs

1 Cup Milk +1/3 cup

1 Teaspoon Vanilla

DIRECTIONS

* Preheat the oven to 350 degrees.
* Cream butter in a mixer, gradually add sugar, beating until light and fluffy.
* Add baking powder and salt to flour.
* Add eggs one at a time to creamed mixture. Beat well after each addition.
* Add flour mixture alternately with milk and flavoring. Beat until smooth.
* Pour batter into 3 greased and floured 9-inch cake layer pans.
* Bake at 350 degrees for 25–30 mins. You'll know it's done when the cake is pulling away from the edge of the pan.

NOTE: For lemon cake, substitute lemon extract for vanilla extract.

CHOCOLATE CAKE BROWNIES

CAKE INGREDIENTS

2 Cups White Sugar

2 Cups Flour

½ Cup (1 stick) Butter
   or Margarine

½ Cup Shortening +2 tablespoons

1 Cup Water

3 Tablespoons Cocoa

½ Cup Buttermilk

1 Teaspoon Baking Soda

1 Teaspoon Vanilla Extract

2 Eggs   and 1 teaspoon
              cinnamon

FROSTING INGREDIENTS

½ Cup (1 stick) Butter
   or Margarine

6 Tablespoons Milk

3 Tablespoons Cocoa

1 Pound Powdered Sugar

1 Teaspoon Vanilla Extract

1 Cup Chopped Nuts

CAKE DIRECTIONS

* ✳ Preheat the oven to 400 degrees.

* ✳ Measure white sugar and flour into a 2-quart mixing bowl.

* ✳ Melt butter/margarine in a pan on the stove.

* ✳ Add shortening, water, and cocoa to the pan. Bring to a boil.

* ✳ Pour boiling mixture over the sugar and flour mixture
  and stir until moistened.

* ✳ Add remaining ingredients and mix well, removing all lumps.

* ✳ Bake in a jelly roll pan (15½" x 10½" x 1") for 20 minutes
  or until cake starts pulling away from edge of the pan.

  or 13 x 9 pan 45 min

ICING DIRECTIONS

* ✳ Once the cake is cooled down to room temperature,
  melt butter or margarine in same pan used for the cake batter.

* ✳ Add milk and cocoa; heat thoroughly.

* ✳ Add remaining ingredients.

* ✳ Mix well to remove most lumps. Spread mixture over top
  of cake.

TEA CAKE COOKIES

INGREDIENTS

1 Cup Butter *softened*

¼ Cup Shortening

1 ⅔ Cups Sugar

2 Eggs

4 Cups Flour

2 Tablespoons Vanilla Extract

2½ Teaspoons Baking Powder

1½ Teaspoons Nutmeg

DIRECTIONS

* Preheat the oven to 350 degrees.
* Beat butter, shortening, and sugar together; mix well.
* Add eggs to mixture; mix well after each addition.
* In a separate container, mix flour, vanilla, baking powder, and nutmeg together.
* Gradually add flour mixture to butter mixture, pausing to stir well as you add.
* Chill dough for 1–1½ hours.
* Once chilled, roll dough into 1.5-inch balls (about the size of a golf ball).
* Flatten balls *slightly* with fingers.
* Bake on a greased cookie sheet or parchment-lined sheet for 20–25 minutes.

(Makes approx. 2 dozen)

Don't let them brown!

ACKNOWLEDGMENTS

⁎✳*⁎*

This book is the summation of so many emotions. The idea came to me in a rush in 2019 and over nine days I let it spill out on the page, documenting my speed-drafting on YouTube for my followers to see. I was in a writing slump at the time. I had also just finished my first novel—*Wings of Ebony*—and was convinced that was the only story I'd ever be able to write. So I set out to prove myself wrong, and that with a bit of persistence, much like Kyana, I too could do what, at the time, felt impossible.

So, I poured so much of my own insecurities into Kyana, Russ, and Ash. At the time, I lived hundreds of miles away from my family, my own "Memaw," my own always-working momma, and my younger sisters. I missed them all so much. So I drummed up the scents and smells of home in my memory and turned those into deliciously descriptive words. I furiously transcribed daydreams of being back in the kitchen with my grandma into the plot, magic, and characters.

Then, during revisions in late 2019, my entire world shifted on its axis. My real-life Memaw, the source of all those great tips Kyana learns, the author of these delicious recipes in the back of this book, was diagnosed with leukemia. I grieved and wrote and wrote and grieved. I poured more of Memaw into these pages with each revision, steeping myself in memories, writing moments in fiction I wished could be real again. Then 2020 arrived with a fury and the picture of the world began to distort further. Grandma was still holding on, but the doctors weren't sure for how long. The world was quarantining. What did all of this mean? What would the world look like six months later? Two years later? Who would be in it?

Suddenly it hit me—my questions could not be answered. No one could know what was to come. I could only know the now. The joy in my hands. The people I could call up right then. I FaceTimed my grandma that day, and we just held the phone. She was too winded to talk for most of it. So, I'd just sit and look and listen to her breathe. I then lost myself in Kyana's world all over again, reading and rereading, waiting for the next pass of revisions. I folded my questions over what would come in a pandemic world into humorous magical creatures and wacky world-building. I made up a talking stove because the idea made me giggle, hilarious BFF banter, a security squad of ferrets, which kept me laughing at their ridiculousness. I wrote a story that gave my soul what it so desperately needed—sweet, unrestrained laughter. JOY.

And after much drafting and a few months of revising with my agent, Kyana's story was ready to start its journey into the world, and the wonderful team at Bloomsbury enthusiastically agreed!

I couldn't have done any of this alone, and the list of people to thank is truly endless. It feels like a decade has passed since 2020 alone, so I sincerely apologize if I've missed a name of someone who's been on this journey with Kyana and me.

First, thanks to God, who gave me this gift of words. To my husband, who is forever the cheerleader. And whose own sacrifice of his work and personal goals allows me to pursue this writing dream. Huge thank-you to my kids, who inspired these characters so much. Who so patiently, over and over again, put their wants on hold so Mommy could "get some more words down." To Mariah, my shy little bird, you will soar. Dare to claim the sky, darling one. Ash reminds me of you so much. To Daniel, my supadupa fly middle kid. Your confidence is its own set of wings, son. Fly to the moon and back. This world is yours. Russ's confidence and coolness remind me so much of you! And to little Sarah, who knows what she wants unapologetically. You shine like Kyana. I love that you're not afraid to take up space. Never lose that, sweet one.

To my grandma, who inspired this book, whose persona has infused its pages with tenderness and sweetness. You're still holding on as I write these words. You've stubbornly defied the doctor's time clock! I'm so grateful to be in the same city now. It is my greatest hope you'll be able to hold this book in your hands once it's in print, and really behold a big part of your life's work: giving all you had to raise me. To see that all you poured into me is being reflected back to the world.

To Grandpa, my ace, who keeps Grandma taken care of and keeps me lifted. You are my rock. Have been my rock. Will always be my rock. To Mommy, Paigey, and Yunei, who are my go-to girls! I reach for the stars, so you can dare to dream bigger and beyond. To Unc and Syd, Micah, Roslyn, Rocqell, Aunty Regina, Uncle Roy. All of you who were the village to make sure my dreams found solid ground to stand on. To Jennifer and Diarra, who keep me rooted—love you, my sisters! To Kim W., Marian F., Amy D., and Alyssa Shaw, thank you for always encouraging me to keep writing and for being proud of me. And to my Book Mom, Nic Stone, who keeps me grounded, hopeful, and realistic. Love you endlessly!

To Sarah Shumway and Claire Stetzer, who gave so much time and energy and love to this story from the very beginning. To Lily, Faye, Erica, Beth, and the entire team at Bloomsbury, both those I've had the privilege of being able to meet and those I have not—this book could not exist without your diligence.

Thank you! To Natalie, who knew from the moment she met Kyana she would make it to shelves. For believing, fighting, hoping right alongside me. To Jodi, my ever-amazing agent. I could not have shepherded this book into the world without you! Your energy and relentless passion for my stories and my career are such a gift. You've changed my life. Thank you!

To my writing loves, who let Kyana into their heart: Jessica Froberg, Mary Roach, Del, Ana Franco, Naz Kutub, Jessica Lewis, Jessica Shaut, Sarah Janian, Jas Hammonds, and Emily Golden. Thank you for every read, bit of feedback, and fierce love of this story. To my Twitter family, who kept me going when writing this book was hard. To Kelis, Kris, Lisa, Steph, my entire Queen Squad crew, every critique partner, beta reader, friend in DMs with encouraging words. For every like, tweet, story-share, every blogger, bookstagrammer, educator, bookseller, and librarian who put this book in a reader's hands. I am so grateful for all of you!

This book is the hug I needed, a canonized memory if there is such a thing. A reminder that we can spend our lives chasing what we wished we had or clinging fiercely, fighting to protect, remembering to cherish, the things we do have. I coped and healed and loved on myself through Kyana's story. And it's my hope that these pages do the same for you!